CW00848225

The Affair of t
Christmas Card Killer

The Affair of the Christmas Card Killer

The First Lord Kit Aston Mystery

JACK MURRAY

Books by Jack Murray

Kit Aston Series
The Affair of the Christmas Card Killer
The Chess Board Murders
The Phantom
The Frisco Falcon
The Medium Murders
The Bluebeard Club
The French Diplomat Affair (novella)
Haymaker's Last Fight (novelette)

Agatha Aston Series
Black-Eyed Nick
The Witchfinder General Murders
The Christmas Murder Mystery (Dec 2022)

Nick Jellicoe Series
A Time to Kill
The Bus Stop
Trio

ISBN: 9798514473502
Imprint: Independently published

For Monica, Lavinia, Anne, and Baby Edward

Prologue

6th December 1917: Cambrai, France

'You're on watch now,' said the soldier returning to the shelter. He gave a gentle shake to the man lying in a bunk then threw his coat and equipment onto the wooden floor. Stepping back, he gave his replacement room to climb down from the bed.

The other soldier sat up and rubbed his eyes. He was a young man, too. Barely in his twenties. It seemed only minutes since he'd slumped onto the bed. Hopping off the bunk, the young soldier grabbed hold of a rocket pistol and some flares. His hands were stiff with cold. He could barely feel his feet. In one rapid movement his raincoat was on with the equipment slipped over it. The other soldier handed him a cup of scalding hot tea.

'Here, you'll need this.'

'Thanks'

In less than a minute he was stumbling out of the shelter cut into the side of the trench and then the chill hit him. It stung his face but also helped him wake. He jumped up onto the fire-step to take over as sentry. It was still dark. There was a lingering hint of the sweet, spicy smell of gas in the air clashing with the malodorous stench of the latrines. Or was it death? The smell no longer sickened him. He had long since become desensitized to this if not the horror around him.

Immediately in front of the trench were the wooden pickets supporting the barbed wire. Looking ahead, beyond the barbed wire, he could see the barren landscape pitted with holes made by shells. This was No Man's Land. Perhaps a few hundred yards in front of the British line sat the Germans. The thought of them out there made him duck his head a little.

The trench was quiet. Sentries were posted every ten yards. Periodically, the trench was lit from a flare sent up by the Germans. They were obviously as bored as he was. No stars were showing through the thick blanket of cloud until the latest flare turned the sky a bright white. He leaned against the trench wall to avoid getting caught by the perfunctory rifle-fire that often accompanied the flare.

While the ground in front was visible, he used the opportunity to look through the periscope to scan the horizon. It was pockmarked with shell holes and tank tracks. In the far distance he could see the sandbags indicating the German position. No sign of Fritz. More sense.

As the flare died, he thought he saw something a hundred or so yards in front. The fading flare left darkness and him cursing. Turning to the sentry on his right, he waved to attract his attention. It took a minute of furious gesticulating before the other sentry nodded back. The soldier pointed to the open ground.

'I thought I saw someone out there,' he said in a loud whisper.

The other sentry shrugged and shook his head. As a rule, all soldiers avoided stepping out into No Man's Land unless ordered. He decided that it was his imagination and tried to think no more about it. Ten minutes later he heard it. This time there could be no doubt. A groan. Someone was out there. He jumped down from the fire-step and almost collided with a battalion officer who was doing an inspection on this stretch of trench. The officer towered over the young soldier. He looked down.

'Careful,' he said, more in jest than anger. 'Is there a problem?'

'Sorry sir, I think there's someone out there,' answered the soldier before remembering to add a salute.

'Aside from the German 3rd Army?' responded the officer sardonically.

'Yes sir. I heard a noise, definitely a man. Might have caught one. One hundred yards almost directly ahead. I thought I saw something when the last flare went up; now I'm sure.'

'Well show me. It could be a trick, but it might be someone from a patrol that went out earlier. We haven't heard anything from them, and they left two hours ago. The Boche have been a bit frisky tonight. I don't know what's wrong with them. Let's hope he wasn't caught up in something.'

The officer climbed up onto the fire-step and took out his binoculars.

'Tell you what. Let's stir Fritz up a bit. Maybe he'll send a flare over. May as well use up his flares rather than ours. We're running low.'

He took out his revolver and fired twice into the darkness. Within a minute the Germans helpfully sent up a flare to see what was happening. The officer and the soldier stood side by side on the step. The soldier used the periscope and scanned the area where he had looked earlier.

'There,' he said pointing. 'Do you see over between the tank track and the crater, two o'clock? He looks like he's in a crater, but you can just see his arm caught in the wire.'

'Yes, I see it,' replied the officer squinting through his binoculars. 'Could very well be one of ours. Not sure I can see him moving, though.' The flare died again preventing confirmation.

'Do you fancy taking a closer look? The cloud cover's good.'

It was not a question, and the soldier knew it. The officer looked down at the man before him. Clearly a Londoner, he was short, probably around five feet six or seven and, like so many in the trenches, malnourished. However, looking onto his eyes he saw a mixture of the terror and determination that characterized so many of the men he had under his command. The soldier nodded back to the officer.

'It'll be too risky to send more than one man,' added the officer apologetically.

'I know, sir.'

'Good man. Get ready, I'll stand watch.'

A few minutes later, heart beating rapidly, the soldier was crawling through the pickets towards his object. The ground was frozen hard with just a hint of a frost on the top. Looking ahead, he mapped out a route that would take him from crater to crater. Unfortunately, there was also a little too much open ground to be negotiated for his liking.

Progress was slow. He went ten yards at a time then stopped to rest and take stock for a few minutes. Each movement was accompanied by a prayer. More than once he felt the remains of old barbed wire rip into his clothing and sting his skin. The journey of one hundred yards was accomplished in just over an hour. He'd made it.

The body lay crumpled in a depression. Barbed wire hung lazily off a post by the soldier's side. The unconscious soldier's arm was partially caught in it. He looked a mess. Incredibly though, the young soldier could feel a pulse. He whispered in the soldier's ear.

'Don't worry, we'll have you back soon.'

Obviously, the soldier was done for, he thought. What harm would a lie do now anyway?

4

Slowly, he extricated the soldier's arm from the hooks on the wire. No other part of the body seemed to be so entangled. Slipping a wooden board underneath the soldier, he wrapped the rope attached to the board around himself so that he could pull the soldier over the frosty ground. With one final glance towards the enemy line, he made ready to move the prone soldier.

By now it was after four in the morning and bitterly cold. Thankfully, it had not rained in the last few days. Muddy ground would have made a perilous journey impossible. He pulled the body out from the depression causing a muffled groan. This was not good. It was one thing to know the man was still alive, but the last thing he needed was noise to attract the attention of the Germans.

They progressed slowly across No Man's Land stopping regularly to rest. The young soldier was exhausted. The crossing was taking a mental, physical, and emotional toll. He knew it was only matter of time before the noise they were making would result in an exploratory flare.

Minutes later, he was proved right. A flare went up. He scrambled into a small crater. German voices were audible. He waited for the inevitable gun fire. The flare died and then there was silence. Maybe his luck was holding.

This hope was dispelled seconds later. Another flare went up. By this point he had yanked the injured soldier into the small crater alongside him. He rested there for over ten minutes until he was sure the Germans had lost interest.

At the British trench, the officer looked on grimly. The word had spread along the line. An audience had assembled to view the grim proceedings. He turned to the men alongside him.

'Be ready to let Fritz have it, men. Are there any medics here yet?' One man nodded in confirmation. The officer fixed his eyes on No Man's Land. His heart was racing.

Thirty yards to go: another flare went up. The soldier looked up and groaned inwardly. This time he was in a completely exposed position above ground and between craters. There was no opportunity to hide. If anything, this was the worst part. The barbed wire and the stumps were directly in front of the trench. They would make it very difficult to move quickly along the ground.

He had a choice to make.

-

Seventy yards further back, another officer was gazing at the scene. Hauptmann Max Kahn held the binoculars to his eyes and scanned the British front line slowly. Finally, he found what he was looking for.

'Yes, I think I see them now. Well done.'

His companion was Thomas Vogts, a sniper. In fact, Vogts was a highly effective sharpshooter. He'd lost count of the kills he'd made over the last two years since his unique talent had become apparent to his fellow soldiers.

'Let's see what they do,' said Kahn.

'Shouldn't we tell Artillery?'

'To shell two Tommy? I think they might justifiably ask what your job is meant to be. Stick to your orders. We're not here to finish off a Tommy who will probably die anyway. Don't move your gun keep it trained on our target. Can you see him yet?'

Vogts looked up at Kahn, and then fixed binoculars to his eyes to hide his anger. His gaze was not on the two soldiers in No Man's Land, but thirty metres to their left on a shallow outcrop from the main British trench. Lying there were two British soldiers on a similar mission to himself and Kahn. His rifle and its telescopic sight were trained on this dugout.

'No sign but they're there. I can see cigarette lights.

'Do you think it's him?' asked Kahn.

'Don't know. It's still too dark to see his face. He's been here nearly two weeks now. They'll move him soon.'

6

-

Further ahead, the young soldier had reached a decision. The other soldier was a goner. He was sure of this. The longer he stayed in No Man's Land, the greater the chance of being spotted. This was especially the case so close to the front line. If he was able to put the injured soldier on his back, then he could cover the last thirty yards more quickly and avoid the barbed wire entangling them. Decision made, he lowered himself onto his knees and hoisted the soldier up. He stayed in the crater for half a minute taking deep breaths and then the final push.

The British officer immediately saw the soldier's intention. He nodded to the soldiers beside him to be ready.

'Come on my boy; you can do this.' He prayed fervently the Germans would not choose that moment to send up a flare. Just then, the sky lit up. It seemed impossible for the young soldier to remain unseen. The officer held his breath.

-

'I have a clear shot,' said Vogts.

'Of our man?' said Kahn regarding Vogts.

'No, the two Tommies up ahead.'

'I told you to ignore them. I want the British snipers. Keep looking, in their direction,' said Kahn angrily.

The officer glanced at Vogts. How he detested this man. Vogts had developed a murderous talent in order to avoid being involved in a direct frontal attack. A man who skulked in craters and killed, murdered even, wounded soldiers, or worse, the Doctors attending them. Kahn had heard the stories. Vogts was playing a deadly game of numbers. The more he killed, the less likely it would be for him to be sent over the top. He knew it would be a straightforward shot for such a man.

'Sir?'

'No.'

'Sir? It would only take a second.' This time more insistently. Kahn glanced down at Vogts with a raised eyebrow.

'It's an easy shot,' pleaded Vogts.

'I realize this, keep your eyes on the other position,' replied Kahn. He looked at the two figures, one carrying the other on his back, staggering drunkenly towards their trench.

-

'Why aren't they firing?' asked the British officer, as much to himself. As he said this the flare died. By now it was taking a great effort from the men in the trench to avoid cheering on their fellow soldier. The officer held up his hand to prevent any supportive cheers. They were fifteen yards away. Surely, they would make it.

By now even the young soldier was hoping a miracle would really happen. There were ten yards to go; his route blocked only by barbed wire, maybe two feet high. Keep going he thought; keep going.

-

Why aren't we firing thought Vogts? What was this dilettante Jew thinking? Honour? Had he not noticed the carnage of the last four years? Honour lay dead and rotting in the mud of Passchendaele, of Verdun. Of a hundred other fields where his class had sent people like him to die. His duty demanded one thing and one thing only. Kill the enemy. They would have done the same to him. He glared up at Kahn. How alike were he and that Colonel Adler, who had left them an hour previously. They belonged to a class whose time would soon be over.

Leave them thought Kahn. It was almost Christmas. What bravery. One of the soldiers would probably die anyway. He sensed Vogts glaring up at him. Kahn shook his head and began to step down from the viewing step when…

-

8

Less than a few yards from the British trench an explosion rocked the darkness. The officer instinctively shielded his head from falling mud and rock. Regaining control immediately he shouted down to the medics in the trench. 'Quickly! Get them in.' Instantly, he and two men leapt out of the trench and grabbed hold of the two soldiers who had collapsed following the explosion.

The young soldier looked up at the officer and the medics. He could hear little, other than muffled orders. 'Did I make it?' He thought he heard the sound of gunfire before all went black.

-

Beside him, Vogts had loosed off several shots. Kahn stared down at him. 'Did you see their sniper?'

'Yes, he fired a shot,' replied Vogts.

'Did you get him?' said Kahn hopefully.

'Maybe the other one. The watcher; not the sniper. Why? What happened?'

Kahn didn't answer immediately but continued to study the activity in the British trench. He looked at Vogts and stepped down to peer through the telescopic sight on the rifle. It was still trained on the British snipers.

Vogts felt the hatred rise in him again, the unspoken lack of trust. Finally, Kahn answered.

'I don't know. I really don't know, Vogts. Do we have other snipers in this area?'

He asked the last question more of himself than Vogts.

Chapter 1

Christmas Eve 1919: Cavendish Hall, Lincolnshire

Arthur Cavendish walked to the window of his library and gazed out onto the expansive driveway at Cavendish Hall. It was Christmas Eve. His guests would be arriving soon. The sky had a yellowish glow which he recognized meant snow. As soon as he thought this, he detected the first flakes swirling gently in the air. The fountain at the front had been switched off; the surrounding pond was already beginning to freeze over. He walked away from the window and went out of the library. Curtis, his butler, was walking towards him with ecclesiastical dignity.

Curtis was a man in his mid-fifties. He had worked in service all his life. His dark hair was greying to match his complexion. There was a look of sorrow on his face that was partly professional but also a comment on his life.

'I believe the train is due around ten. I've sent Devlin to the station. Will there be anything else my lord?' asked Curtis in response to the question he knew was coming.

'No thank you. Oh, one thing. Where are the girls?'

'I believe they went out riding about an hour ago.'

'Rather them than me. A little bit cold,' said Cavendish with a smile.

Cavendish nodded to Curtis and returned to the warmth of the library to wait. He sat down in his leather armchair. The morning's paper lay unread on the table beside him. He looked out of the window once more at the fountain. He thought it an eyesore, like much of Cavendish Hall.

Cavendish Hall was built in the Tudor period. It was a reward to Edward Cavendish for his loyalty to Henry VIII following the aftermath of his split with Rome. The choice to side with the King was an easy one and it caused not one moment of regret. It did, in fact, bring many economic benefits especially following the Dissolution of the Monasteries. The impoverishment of the Catholic Church had become the basis of the Cavendish fortune for the next four centuries.

Over the years, successive Viscounts had added personal touches to the original Hall. It was now a remarkably incongruous combination of Tudor, Baroque and Georgian styles. Half-timbered and gable roofs fought gamely against the highly elaborate, Baroque extension built by Lord Henry Cavendish. With remarkable enthusiasm, he had insisted on gargoyle features decorating every possible corner. It was difficult to say which was more frightful, the faces of the gargoyles or the resulting impact on Cavendish Hall.

Henry Cavendish's grandson, William, spent a long honeymoon on the Grand Tour. This honeymoon resulted not only in an heir but also a lifelong appreciation of the Palladian style. He made wholesale changes to the front of the Hall reducing the number of gargoyles but introducing, instead, columns with acanthus leaf capitals around the entrance.

The final inharmonious addition came from the garden designer Joseph Brown. Very distantly related to Capability Brown, he used this connection to great effect in Lincolnshire and Yorkshire. Following a week spent in Versailles in which he took copious notes and made countless drawings of the

11

design of the various gardens at the Palace, he set himself up as a garden designer. These notes formed the basis of a moderately lucrative career creating variations on a Versailles theme throughout the county. His work was popular and found favour with William.

The resulting commission proved to be expensive and contributed to the dwindling of the Cavendish fortune. Trees were imported from around the country and planted to create a small woodland area. Statues were also purchased and placed around fountains. The cost of maintaining the gardens ensured no future modifications were attempted.

Lord Arthur Cavendish's father had recognized that the ongoing development of the Hall should stop lest it cripple the finances of the family forever. The exigencies of the family's financial position were clear to young Arthur when he inherited the title on his father's death in 1882. He maintained a more frugal approach to the upkeep of the Hall. This was partly pragmatism; the family was not wealthy enough to improve the ill-considered work of his predecessors. It was also a recognition of Arthur's military career which took him far and wide protecting and expanding Britain's sphere of influence around the world.

Cavendish had been sent to Sandhurst at the age of eighteen. He took easily to army life. Most of his ancestors had served in the Blues and Royals, a branch of the Household Cavalry. He joined the Royal Dragoons.

Not unreasonably, he considered himself officer material. While his family was not among the great families in the country, he felt it his destiny to lead. A combination of ability and the good fortune to be alive at a particularly quarrelsome period, even by the acquisitive standards of Britain, meant he gained valuable experience and very quickly moved upwards through the ranks.

He used his time productively before military service became truly active. At his father's insistence, he found himself a suitable wife with whom he could ensure the future lineage of the Cavendish family.

Mission was duly accomplished within a year, and he wedded Lady Katherine Hayward. Her beauty was, sadly, not matched by her fortune. However, the match was a successful one in most every respect. She understood the reality of military life and was more than happy to raise a family while her husband fought for Queen and country in India, Afghanistan and later in South Africa.

He studied the portrait of her by Sargent in the library. Cavendish's father was as entranced by Lady Hayward as he had been. He played the role of grandfather and even father to the two children from the marriage. Cavendish looked at their portraits, by Lavery. They showed two young men in uniform. His boys, just before they left to join him in South Africa. He was so proud when they had all served together at the same time, in the same place.

The first child, John, arrived in 1874, followed by Robert in 1878. Both would become Dragoons like their father. Both would die within a year of one another. By then, Katherine had also passed away following a burst appendix, the same day Princip assassinated Franz Ferdinand.

The Great War began with Cavendish becoming a widower. He decided not to retire but to continue his service. It seemed the best way to stay close to his boys. As he thought of them a wave of grief enveloped him and tears stung his eyes. By staying on he had been able to retain regular contact with his sons and yet, when the time came, he couldn't save them. Nothing could have. The waste of their lives seemed horribly inevitable from the earliest days of the War when Cavendish realized how woefully under prepared his country was for the fight.

The clock struck ten. The sound echoed in the room and interrupted his thoughts. It reminded him that his guests would soon be here. He heard young female voices in the hallway.

13

His granddaughters had clearly returned from riding. Their voices brought a swell of comfort. He heard them ask Curtis where he was. Life began to return to him as he anticipated their arrival in the library. The door opened and his youngest granddaughter, Mary, entered.

'I hope you're not moping in here, grandpapa.'

His eldest granddaughter, Esther, followed her sister. She looked at her sister and said, 'He's not moping, is he?'

'With you two around, I scarcely have the opportunity to mope, as you would say,' replied Cavendish grinning. The two girls were always such a tonic for an old trooper.

They both kissed him on the back of his head. Mary observed the unread newspaper and glanced at Esther. 'What news is there?' she asked.

'I haven't had a chance to read yet. Two young scamps interrupted me,' complained Cavendish affably.

Mary put her arms around his neck and hugged him. 'Let me guess then, Paris Peace Conference erupts in disagreement. Britain walks out. Mr Keynes denounces France and….'

'Lillian Gish declares Broken Blossoms to be her best film yet; praising her director Mr Griffiths…' added Esther airily.

Esther and Mary both giggled as their grandfather shook his head, albeit with a smile. 'You know, it's not too late to send you both to the workhouse. A spell up some chimney would soon see more discipline and respect for your commanding officer.'

'You're positively Victorian, sir,' laughed Mary. Changing the subject, she asked, 'When do our guests arrive?'

'Devlin is at the station already. They're due in at ten from London,' reported Cavendish.

'All of them?'

'No, your aunt is coming with young master Henry by car.'

'Seventeen hardly qualifies as either young or master, these days,' said Esther. 'He's only five years younger than me.'

'I agree with grandpapa,' said Mary. 'He's still a child. A horrible one at that. I don't know what happened to him. Ahh, I think I do. How is our sweet Aunt Emily?'

Cavendish glared at Mary. 'Don't, young lady. No matter how provoked you feel by Emily or Henry, I will not have that tone. Do you understand?'

Mary executed a perfect military salute, before breaking into a grin and giving her grandfather another hug saying, 'I shall be sweetness personified.' Then she pointed dramatically at Esther, 'And as for you, young lady, I will have none of your ill temper and gutter language. Don't think I'm not aware…'

Esther laughed, her grandfather, too.

'I shall keep Mary under control, grandpapa,' said Esther.

Both girls left a few minutes later to make ready for the arrival of the guests, leaving Cavendish alone again with his thoughts. He wondered how this Christmas holiday would unfold. The two girls had certainly lifted his spirits, as they usually did, but a feeling of gloom remained. He was not sure if it was the time of year and the loss he felt for Katherine, the boys or something else.

The future of the girls was also a major preoccupation. He wondered if this Christmas holiday might provide some resolution. Then there was the issue of Robert's wife, Emily. They had never bonded in the way he had been close to John's wife, Rebecca. She and the two girls had comforted him since the loss of his boys, in a way Emily had not. Sadly, Rebecca had succumbed to Spanish flu the previous year.

He resolved to try again and build something stronger with his daughter-in-law and grandson. More pertinently, young Henry would inherit the title when he died, as well as Cavendish Hall. He sometimes wondered if Emily hoped this event happened sooner rather than later. Immediately he regretted thinking such a foul thought. Cavendish looked out the window again to see if there was any sign of his guests.

His guests: this was the next worry to consider. How would Esther and Mary respond to what was clearly a transparent attempt by him to marry them off? He felt confident that one of his guests would be very welcome. He thought of Esther again. As the eldest daughter and now, of age, it was natural that she should be considering her future husband. Lord Christopher 'Kit' Aston was eminently qualified in Cavendish's view.

Cavendish had first met Kit in France. He was a Captain in the same Dragoons where Cavendish was a Colonel. From their first meeting he had been impressed by this young man. If he had chosen to make the army a career, his intelligence and character would have marked him out for the highest of ranks. His bravery had already been rewarded with many medals and his men adored him for the principal reason that they believed him 'lucky'.

His one concern involved Kit's activities towards the end of the War. He had left the Dragoons, and for a period little was heard of him. There were some whispers he was working in Intelligence. Cavendish had heard from a friend this was indeed the case. After the War there was a famous case in the papers in which Aston had solved the murder of a French Diplomat. The newspapers suggested Kit was now engaged as a private consulting detective, like a Sherlock Holmes. Following the case, Kit seemed to disappear, probably to avoid the public attention. There was a suggestion he'd gone to India.

That he had agreed so readily to be a guest over Christmas, gave Cavendish grounds for hope. He knew Kit would be aware of his granddaughters, particularly Esther. What young man of means would not be aware of Lady Esther Cavendish? She was considered one of the most beautiful young women of the day. He had turned down several invitations for their family to be a guest with other potential matches. None compared, in his mind, to Kit in terms of rank or character

16

and he hoped fervently this project would bring success and happiness to both.

His thoughts turned to the younger sister, Mary. He wondered how she would react to Kit or to the idea of Esther and Kit. The sisters were very close. Would there be jealousy? It made him wonder why he discounted so easily the idea of Mary with Kit. There seemed little sign of her adventurous spirit calming. For this reason, he could not see her wanting to be trapped by marriage; at least not yet.

Of the other young man, Cavendish knew less. Eric Strangerson, like Kit, had been a scholar at Cambridge. He appeared to be an adventurous sort as he had left Britain to be involved in various scientific expeditions. Strangerson had accompanied Shackleton in his quest to reach the South Pole in 1909. Following this, he had gone to South America to be involved with an American called Bingham who had made some discoveries in Peru.

These adventures might make him more suitable for Mary. She would be of age later in the year. Perhaps a match with Strangerson would be just the thing for her. He would not try to exert control instead he might provide an outlet for her energy.

Strangerson had served under Robert with the 5th Dragoons. Cavendish scrutinized the letter Strangerson had sent him a few months ago. He picked it up and read once again the line that had prompted him to invite Strangerson to Cavendish Hall for Christmas.

It read: '*I was with Captain Cavendish at the last. As usual, he was leading from the front. This is the type of person he was. I saw he had been hit and I ran over to him, but he died instantly. There was no pain...*'

Cavendish put the letter down as the writing became blurred. His boy: such a brave boy, such slaughter. He looked around the room. The library contained extensive writing on the subject of war. There were clues contained in these volumes on the nature of modern warfare. The various conflicts where the British Army had been involved like South Africa or Crimea had not prepared the country for the Great War. Why had the lessons of the American Civil War not been learned? Cavendish saw very early on how this conflict would progress. The parallel with the Civil War's trench-style attrition was painfully obvious.

Outside the first of his guests had arrived. He looked out of the window and saw Lord Kit Aston stepping gingerly from the back of the car followed by Eric Strangerson. Another, oddly familiar, man climbed out, this time from the front of the car where he had been sitting with the driver, Devlin. Cavendish assumed this was Aston's man.

Cavendish rose and went into the hallway. The front door was already open, he stepped through to greet his guests. Walking forward he held his hand out to a tall, slender man, in his late twenties.

'Kit, so good to see you again.'

'And you too, sir.' They shook hands, both smiling warmly.

Eric Strangerson stepped forward, also smiling, and held out his hand. 'Lord Cavendish, a great pleasure to meet you sir.'

'Come inside, you'll find it warmer,' said Cavendish. 'I fear we're in for a heavy snow soon.'

Cavendish allowed both men to go ahead of him, and they entered into the hall. Before them was a large Christmas tree. It was decorated tastefully to suggest rather than exclaim the time of year. The small staff all presented themselves in the hallway. Curtis the butler, Miss Buchan the housekeeper, Polly the maid and Elsie the cook. The three ladies curtsied to the guests and Cavendish made the introductions. As he finished the introductions he turned and saw Harry Miller enter with Kit Aston's baggage. He regarded him for a moment as if in recognition then, turning to the men, he said, 'If you wish, Curtis can show you to your rooms. Then he can take your man to his room.'

18

'Thank you, sir,' said Kit.

'I say, sir,' said Strangerson, 'Did you put the tree up yourself?'

Cavendish laughed and claimed credit only for the placing of one or two ornaments. He found himself taking a liking to Strangerson, who seemed to be full of good humour. Although perhaps not someone you would say was handsome, he seemed to be a good sort: there was a humorous streak to his character allied to more substantial qualities that had seen him serve bravely for his country. In addition, he was an academic, but he appeared, on first impression, to wear this lightly.

He wondered, one more, how Strangerson would be perceived by Mary. Unlike Strangerson, who was of average height and a little too fond of his food, Lord Kit Aston could only but impress his granddaughters. They would know of his record in the War, his background as a Cambridge scholar and, most importantly, that he would be a Viscount. Without knowing why, he thought of Esther and Kit together. In every respect, Kit should be of interest to Esther. He hoped she would return such interest.

Returning to the library, he felt the wave of sadness overcome him. Seeing Kit reminded him of those who had gone. When he looked at the young lord, it was difficult not to think of his boys. His bearing, his confidence and undoubted good looks made him an attractive person to be with. There was also a good humour in his manner but mixed with the right amount of respect. Yes, he hoped Esther and this young man would like one another.

Chapter 2

Kit Aston sat on the bed and surveyed his room. It was furnished simply but elegantly: one wardrobe, a writing desk, and a small chaise longue. The view onto the gardens created by Brown was stunning. The green wallpaper was not to his taste but overall he liked what he saw. It felt comfortable. He looked up at his manservant, Miller.

'What do you think, Harry?'

'Odd looking place, sir. Lord Cavendish seems a good sort though.'

'I don't suppose you saw the look he gave you?'

'Yes, I noticed, sir. I wasn't sure what to make of it.'

'Trifle odd, I thought. It looked as if he knew you from somewhere.'

'I'm not sure how, sir,' replied Miller. 'Remember, we were in different regiments.'

'That's what I thought. Are you sure you didn't pay the Hall a nocturnal visit before the War?' laughed Kit.

Miller shot him a look but continued to unpack Kit's clothes without saying anything. Kit contemplated Miller. He had not known the short Londoner for long. They had met late on during the War. However, at the first opportunity following the end of hostilities, he had no hesitation in asking him to be his manservant. Miller accepted immediately.

Since then, both had many occasions to thank Kit's decision. Miller had proven a particularly useful accomplice during the French Diplomat affair; as brave and resourceful then, as he had been at Cambrai when they first met. From Miller's point of view, life with Kit Aston had certainly proved very interesting.

'What about the boy?' asked Kit.

'Oh, he's still sleeping in his basket, sir. I may have overdone the sleeping draft.'

'That'll put him in a foul mood.'

Miller looked up from the suitcase he was unpacking and raised his eyes. 'Couldn't be any worse than normal.'

Kit laughed, 'You and he will become best chums, I'm sure. Still, it would be good to get him out for a walk sooner rather than later.'

'I think I'd rather take on Fritz again,' said Miller. Kit grinned but did not respond.

When Miller had completed the unpacking, he glanced at Kit. With a nod of his head, Kit indicated he could go to his quarters. As Miller left, Kit said, 'Harry, I couldn't help but notice how attractive Polly was. I trust you'll be a good soldier and refrain from making this young lady fall in love with you. Or worse.'

'You know me, sir'

'Indeed Harry, that's my point.'

Kit stood up and went to the window to gaze over the grounds. The snow was falling a bit more heavily now. Over by the fountain he caught sight of two girls. They were walking together in the gardens; both were laughing. It was difficult to see their faces clearly as both sported cloche hats. He turned away from the window lest he be seen. Glancing back again he was disappointed to see them moving away from the house rather than towards it.

-

Esther and Mary walked towards the Rose garden. Both were wrapped up against the cold. Mary looked up and felt snow fall softly on her face.

'Do you think they're looking at us?' asked Esther.

'No question Essie,' stated Mary with a smile. 'How much longer do you want to do this tour?'

'Another couple of minutes and then we'll go inside. I think by they'll have had enough opportunity…' Esther left the rest unsaid.

'That should be three minutes before the frostbite sets in.'

Esther laughed. They turned around and headed back towards the house. Both avoided glancing at the windows of the guest bedrooms, but Mary couldn't resist asking, 'Can you see anything from the corner of your eye? I'm too exposed.'

'Yes! Mission accomplished. I definitely saw two figures. Good idea to put them there, Mary.'

'You're welcome. How are you feeling?' asked Mary.

'I don't know. Lord Kit seems so impressive. I'm sure I won't know what to say to him,' she said doubtfully.

'You shall, don't be silly.'

'Anyway, what about you? You assume too much Mary. He might prefer you. Then there's Mr Strangerson. What of him, I wonder?'

Indeed, thought Mary. What of Mr Strangerson? Unquestionably he seemed interesting but the quick view of him stolen as they came out of the car had left her unimpressed. Unlike Lord Kit Aston.

Her objective this Christmas was to help Esther. If she could do this it would please her grandfather and Essie. Better still, it would leave her free. She was too young to settle down. Maybe she might become friends with Strangerson who, at least, had travelled and done interesting things. But romance, no.

She thought about her sister again. Mary suspected her sister was keen to be married. In fact, she had never denied this. Esther had shown Mary photographs of Kit Aston in the papers, but she already knew what he looked like. He was undeniably attractive. It seemed almost unfair to Strangerson who could not fail to understand the undercurrents.

The only question was not if Kit would fall for Esther. On this, Mary was convinced. How could he not? Her sister was beautiful, serene, and impossible not to adore. She felt a little less certainty about Esther falling for Kit, however. Either way, she would make sure that he saw her to best advantage. With any luck Strangerson would not prove too much of a hindrance in this plan.

They went back into the house through the kitchen. Elsie was by the cooker stirring a broth. Esther leant over Elsie, 'Mmmmm, this smells delicious.'

'Thank you, Ma'am. I just hope you eat a good lunch. You're always so fussy about food,' scolded Elsie. She glanced over at Mary. 'And that applies to you too, young lady. There's hardly a pick on either of you. If I know anything about men, there's nothing they like more than a lady who they can hold.'

'Well, we want to hear all about your experience with men, don't we Essie?' responded Mary.

'Indeed, do tell,' added Esther, leaning in conspiratorially.

'That's quite enough from the both of you. It may surprise you to know I've had my admirers. Now off with the both of you, I've work to do,' ordered Elsie.

The two girls left the kitchen smiling broadly.

-

Miller glanced at the two sisters as he went into his room. Although Lord Aston had mentioned nothing, he suspected there were moves afoot to launch an attack on his master's bachelorhood. Both girls, even on his quick perusal, were stunning. Esther seemed to move as if on air. He had never seen so much natural grace in a young woman. However, if it was him, Mary would be his choice. There was a liveliness

23

there, he thought. He wondered how his lordship would resist such beauty.

Miller rarely tried to resist a pretty face. He was not tall or striking to look at, but he had a ready wit that he deployed to great effect. From an early age he had found women liked his cheek and he used it with relish.

His room was small but seemed more than comfortable. Sadly, the bed was single. Even if he had wanted to disobey his lordship it would prove very difficult in this room, especially as he could hear two people arguing in a room nearby. It sounded like Curtis and the housekeeper, Miss Buchan, were having a heated discussion. In such a situation there was only one thing a chap such as Harry Miller could do. He listened at the door

'I tell you; I heard every word. He's going to change the will. Wait and see.' This was Curtis. When he had finished, he stood erect and gripped the lapels of his coat in the hope it might lend a degree of respectability to what was, in essence, gossip.

'There's nothing we can do about it. Whatever happens, young master Henry will inherit. He's a hateful child. Like mother, like son,' responded Miss Buchan, lips pursing to maximum disapproval level.

'They'll throw us out. I know it. They hate us,' concluded Curtis with a dramatic sigh.

'What will happen to us then?' This was a rhetorical question but the butler answered anyway.

'That's the point, I'm sure Lord Cavendish said you and I would receive an income for the rest of our lives. I heard it.'

'How much? Did you hear?' probed Miss Buchan.

'I wasn't able to hear that part. I'm sure he knows what she'll do. He'll take care of us, just you see.'

The conversation seemed to end, so Miller backed quietly away from the door. His lordship would find this of interest. Although Kit never sullied himself with eavesdropping, he had

24

absolutely no qualms about using Miller's intelligence gleaned from overheard conversations and general observations.

There was a knock at his door.

'Come in,' said Miller.

The door opened and young Polly, the maid stood, without entering.

'Mr Miller, Mr Curtis has asked me if you would like to join us in the kitchen for a cup of tea and a briefing on luncheon.'

'Harry, please call me Harry. Mr Miller seems very formal.'

Polly seemed very unsure of this familiarity and glanced in the direction of Curtis.

'Ahh I see. Well, Mr Miller it is then, but when the two old codgers are not around, it's Harry.' He followed this with a wink.

Polly smiled and left him. Harry smiled to himself. No reason why his lordship had to know if he tried to have a bit of fun for himself. Anyway, what was the worst that could happen?

-

Curtis sat at the head of the kitchen table. Also sitting at the table was Miss Buchan. Polly and Elsie were busy preparing lunch in the kitchen. Miller arrived in and Curtis graciously motioned for him to join them at the table.

'Tea?' asked Miss Buchan.

'Yes thanks, white no sugar,' replied Miller.

Curtis smiled with pontifical benevolence at Miller. This made Miller groan inwardly. With the whole kitchen now held captive, Curtis rested his gaze on the congregation and proceeded with his sermon.

'I thought it would be a good idea if we discuss how we'll organize ourselves over this festive period.'

Miller remained quiet sensing Curtis was not a man to respond well to interruption or, indeed, humour. There would be plenty of opportunity to create mischief with this pompous idiot before the stay was complete.

'I was wondering,' continued Curtis, 'how long you've been in his lordship's service?'

'I only met him towards the end of the War. When it finished, he contacted me and offered me a position as his manservant. Naturally, I said yes.'

'Ahhh, very interesting,' said Curtis. 'You served in the same regiment?'

'No, our paths crossed for different reasons.' Miller was not inclined to elaborate so Curtis moved the conversation on.

'Have you had much experience of service at country houses?' inquired Curtis.

Miller's pre-war experience of country houses had primarily been confined to safe cracking. He'd enjoyed a moderately lucrative livelihood in crime before the War interrupted his career and diverted him onto another path. His lordship's offer of a job had prompted him to give up burglary although, as he was to find out, the skills developed in the family trade had proved useful on occasion.

'None, I'm afraid,' replied Miller.

'So, you have no experience of serving meals.'

'None, sorry.'

'But how do you manage with his lordship?' asked Curtis.

'He's quite flexible. We also have an extensive staff at his father's estate in Hertfordshire. Although he rarely goes there. So, my role is more as…' at this point he struggled. How could he explain his role with Kit? Being a manservant barely began to cover a range of duties encompassing safe cracking, detective work, rescuing damsels in distress, averting war and all within the last year. He struggled on manfully, '…more as a chauffeur, personal secretary, in fact anything that he needs.'

That does not require me serving luncheon, he thought ruefully.

26

Curtis seemed a little crestfallen. Seeing this Miller took pity and added, 'but I'm happy to learn from you.' He looked up at Polly who had been standing nearby. Yes, he thought, more than happy to help out my dear. He detected a fleeting smile on her face as she moved away again.

This news seemed to perk Curtis up a little.

'Splendid! Thank you, Mr Miller. I hope you don't mind if we retain a certain formality in our association. I would prefer to be called Mr Curtis and naturally a similar formality should apply to Miss Buchan.'

Miss Buchan smiled at Miller. The least Miller could do was smile back. He still was not sure what to make of this lady. She was in her fifties at least. Her face had a pinched countenance that did not so much suggest spinster as declaim it via the offices of the town crier. Despite this, she seemed less self-righteous than Curtis. He realized Curtis had still not finished, and he tried to re-focus on what was being said. It seemed he was expected to dress in Cavendish Hall livery and assist with luncheon and dinner. This was not good news. His lordship would rib him mercilessly about this. Above and beyond, he thought.

Curtis was still chattering as he led Miller to a wardrobe containing the relevant attire. His worst fears were confirmed. It was every bit as bad as he had expected. He resolved there and then that his reward would be in the very shapely form of Miss Polly, whatever his lordship might dictate. Miller took the relevant clothing and went to get changed. Curtis had informed him that a light lunch would be served soon after Lady Emily and master Henry had arrived.

Chapter 3

Somewhat earlier than expected, Lady Emily and her son, Henry, arrived at Cavendish Hall. The news was relayed via Devlin who had first spied them as he was parking the Austin Twenty. Sprinting from the car to the kitchen door, he shouted, 'They're coming!'

In these situations, leadership, calmness, and authority are required. Curtis had never has any of these qualities and was too old to acquire them now.

'Oh my God, they're not expected for another hour. Quick, all of you. We have to get to the hallway,' he said, waving his arms frantically.

'We should let Lord Cavendish know,' suggested Miss Buchan.

'Oh my God, you're right, Lord Cavendish,' cried Curtis looking decidedly sick.

Curtis arose from his seat hurriedly, all parson-like dignity evaporating with every second Lady Emily made her stately progress towards the house. He reached the library just in time to see Lord Cavendish coming out. Out of breath from a combination of panic and poor conditioning, he was just about to relay the news when Cavendish, seeing his obvious discomfort raised his hand and said, 'Yes, I know.'

Curtis nodded and tried to fix his hair in as dignified a manner as was possible in the situation. Meanwhile, Miss Buchan was already on her feet and waving for Polly and Elsie to join her. All four rushed up the stairs into the hallway, brushing past the large Christmas tree that swayed and rustled.

Cavendish had observed the arrival of Lady Emily from the library window. The snow had not yet settled on the road but would do so in another hour. He glanced at his pocket watch and tapped the cover to make sure his watch had not stopped. It had not. They were early. No doubt hoping to catch him and the staff unaware. Then he felt a moment of remorse. He needed to resist his usual instinct towards Emily of being unkind.

Rising from his desk, Cavendish walked out of the library just as the staff squeezed themselves through the door into the hallway. He walked out the front door to greet his new guests. Lady Emily stepped from the car helped by her chauffeur, Godfrey. She smiled towards Cavendish and gracefully brushed away a snowflake that had fallen on her nose. Cavendish went over to her and gently kissed her on the proffered cheek. He glanced at Godfrey and nodded.

'So good to see you again, Emily, my dear,' he said, not without a stab of guilt. His only comfort was that she was probably every bit as dismayed to be with him. 'Just in time as well. This snow is getting worse,' he added, glancing upwards.

'And good to see you Arthur. You're looking so spritely,' replied Lady Emily.

Cavendish suspected this was intended to enrage him. To be fair to Emily, her aim was usually unerring. It had. He smiled back to her.

'Oh, you know, Emily, I make sure to have lots of exercise and fresh air. I intend being around for a long time yet, my dear. A very long time,' he emphasized.

Fifteen all.

And then there was the beastly boy. Cavendish studied him closely. Boy? He seemed like a young man, now. Was it really a year since they had last been together? The extent to which he was growing up became apparent when Henry stepped out of the car. Cavendish found himself having to look up into the young man's blue eyes. He had grown a couple of inches since Cavendish had last seen him. They shook hands civilly but there was a limpness of grip that disappointed Cavendish.

'Good to see you too, young man,' said Cavendish with a smile and warmth he surely did not feel.

The height gave him a presence and a nobility he had previously lacked. The Cavendish nose was a Roman affair, but the blond hair, with just the hint of a curl, was definitely from Emily as were the fine features and clear eyes. He was, in some ways, like a Greek God. However, Cavendish detected in him a detachment, an unknowable depth that, as yet, had not resolved itself as either brilliance or stupidity. He was so unlike Robert at the same age.

His father was always destined to be in the army. A sportsman from before he could walk. He was an intoxicating mixture of devilry and duty. Unlike John, who was more serious and bookish, Robert had revelled in the outdoors, questionable company, and beautiful girls. However, this stopped short of outright self-indulgence. Instead, it made him a leader adored by his men from South Africa to the fields of France. He took risks, ended up in a few scrapes and bravely led from the front. Despite this, he seemed to be indestructible. Until Cambrai.

Henry abhorred sport. Although tall, he had not yet filled out. Where his mother had a complexion of peach, he had an unattractive pallor. Where Robert was self-assured and open, Henry was touchy and sullen. There was no hint of the quick humour and charm that had bewitched Emily and made Robert so cherished by Cavendish, his brother, and his fellow soldiers. Henry tended towards sarcasm rather wit.

Cavendish regretted the lack of time spent with this young man. He realized it was incumbent upon him to make the effort. Clearly, he needed a new school. Somewhere he would be educated from the neck down. A greater emphasis on sport and outdoors would build the character that he found so difficult to detect in his grandson but wanted to see so badly.

He would try this Christmas. If Henry was to inherit his title and the responsibilities that came with it, Cavendish wanted him to have the right leadership qualities. There was time yet, he thought.

Events were to prove otherwise.

'Grandfather,' said Henry nodding. As he did not seem inclined to add to this statement, Cavendish turned and took Emily's arm, leading her into the house.

'Our other guests have arrived.'

'Jolly good, I'm looking forward to meeting this Lord Kit Aston. I've heard so much about him. Very much the coming man, they say.'

'I wouldn't disagree,' nodded Cavendish.

'But who is this Strangerson? I don't remember Robert mentioning him in letters to me. I fear I shall find it difficult to talk about the past,' said Lady Emily. There was a something in her voice. There was no questioning her sincerity.

Cavendish shot her a look as she said this. For a moment he believed her. Had there been just a hint of a catch in her voice? In truth he had never quite trusted the motives of Emily in marrying Robert. However, if Emily's motives were suspect, could he really criticize?

She was also an heiress. Her family owned one of the largest pharmaceutical companies in England. The family's wealth had certainly been a point in her favour as far as he was concerned. Even Robert must have considered this. She was a beauty also. Robert would certainly have been attracted to her, irrespective of her family circumstances. Something in her tone had suggested he may have misjudged her. Or maybe he

31

had imagined it. As with Henry, Cavendish felt this Christmas could be an opportunity to start anew with Emily.

They walked through the Palladian doorway. Once again, the staff had lined up to greet the new guests.

'Lady Emily,' said Curtis, bowing slightly and smiling deferentially at her and Henry. Neither acknowledged him or the other staff.

Cavendish observed this interaction and it irritated him greatly. All of a sudden, the old prejudice returned. This was not how one dealt with staff. She was just a social climbing parvenu and always would be. Immediately he felt ashamed for thinking this. It was too easy to let sympathy for Emily evaporate. It was unacceptable to sit by and not address the problem directly. They had all suffered so much in the last few years. It was time to come together. However, Curtis, of all people, should have merited more from Emily. He stopped himself thinking more on this subject. At the foot of the stairs, Emily let go of Cavendish's arm.

'We know the way from here. What time are we expected for lunch?'

'We'll have a light lunch around midday or after and then we will make ready for the carols singing afterwards. Reverend Simmons will be joining us once again with some of the villagers. Afterwards we'll serve mulled wine and mince pies.' He added innocently, 'I know how much you value this tradition, Emily.'

Emily smiled insincerely back at him and nodded.

Thirty-fifteen, Cavendish thought mischievously but not mean-spiritedly.

Henry passed by. He looked like murder.

Chapter 4

Kit lay on the large bed bent double with laughter. Miller stood before him with his arms spread wide. He was modelling his new livery. He was laughing, too. The merriment was loud and continued for a minute before Kit finally sat up. Taking another look at Miller, he lost it once more. Miller turned and walked to a full-length mirror. He turned this way and that.

'It fits quite well, don't you think?' suggested Miller.

Kit managed to splutter, 'Perfectly. You really must get the name of their tailor.'

'Yes, do you think he'd make one in white?' This set off another round of schoolboy laughter from the two men.

'Have to say, sir, I've done some things for you which were a challenge perhaps even foolhardy, but this really takes the biscuit.'

Kit looked more serious now.

'I know, old chap. I can only apologise. If you wish I can say something to Lord Cavendish.'

Miller shook his head and then gave a half-hearted shrug of his shoulders. He was not a grumbler by nature. His first instinct was usually to see the amusing side of any situation and he normally laughed at himself as quickly as he would make fun of others. Kit valued this. He, likewise, did not take life so seriously. How could they after what they had

33

experienced, he thought? They had both survived, many had not. There was nothing to complain about. Both recognized this; neither spoke of it.

Kit joined Miller at the mirror. He was wearing a tweed suit and a green woollen pullover, checked shirt and tweed tie. Miller couldn't resist one last smirk and shake of the head. His livery was a dark, long tailed jacket, matching dark trousers, silver waistcoat, a white shirt with stiff white collar and a black tie.

'I wish I'd given you better training for these situations,' said Kit apologetically causing Miller to laugh again.

'How difficult can it be, sir?' responded Miller.

'You'd be surprised, Harry. Listen carefully to what this fellow Curtis says. You can end up in all sorts of trouble when you're serving luncheon and dinner. Really, don't underestimate the challenges serving soup to lords and ladies.'

'I'll bear that in mind. You're sure you don't want me to spill some soup on Henry?'

'Oh, why do you say that?' asked Kit.

'I gather he's a real charmer,' explained Miller sardonically.

'Really? How interesting. I'll make time for this young man.'

Miller could not decide if this was for amusement or if he had more noble motives in mind. With Kit, both could sit easily alongside one another. It was one of the reasons why he liked him as much as he did. He recognized it was also one of the reasons Kit had employed him.

Miller had admitted to a past that had been on the wrong side of the law. Far from being shocked by this, Kit had found it both entertaining and useful. Although he rarely gave the impression of assessing individuals, Miller recognized in Kit an acute sense of people. He also had a belief in the fundamental good of human nature. Miller suspected Kit might use some of his time over Christmas to get to know Henry Cavendish better and, perhaps, act as a mentor.

All in all, it was going to be a very different Christmas to any that he had experienced before. He thought once more about Polly. However, before he could dwell on her, he realised Kit was addressing him.

'Perhaps you should re-join the rest of the staff, Harry. They'll need help with lunch, I suspect.'

'Right away, sir.'

Miller left the room and headed down the back stairs, to the kitchen. The food was sitting on the table ready to be brought upstairs. It was interesting, reflected Miller, that a light lunch at a country house would feed a hospital for a day. It looked wonderful and brought with it a comforting, gamey aroma. Curtis greeted Miller with a slow, priestly nod.

'We need to bring this up to the dining room. No need to serve; they shall do so themselves.'

Miller felt relieved. He was not looking forward to serving food. This was a stay of execution only. Even Devlin was dragooned into moving the lunch from the kitchen to the dining room. Only Elsie stayed behind. Her job was done, for the moment. She collapsed onto a seat. With the three men and Polly helping, the food was quickly transferred upstairs.

Once everything had been set out, Curtis sent Devlin and Miller back downstairs, but Polly remained, much to Miller's disappointment. On the way down the stairs, he shook hands with Devlin.

'Harry Miller.'

'Liam Devlin.'

Miller turned to Devlin when he heard the accent. 'You're Irish then. What part are you from?'

'Just south of Dublin; a town called Bray,' answered Devlin.

'My grandma on my mother's side was from Wexford.'

'Really? I know Wexford well. It's further down the east coast. Ever been?'

Miller laughed and shook his head.

'First time I left England was to go to France.'

Devlin smiled in acknowledgement but did not add anything more. By now, they'd arrived in the kitchen. Elsie was head down on the kitchen table snoring loudly.

Devlin looked down at Elsie as they entered. Turning to Miller he said, 'Just leave her, she's been flat out since dawn. I'm heading back out to the front of the house. I want to put more salt down. I wasn't anticipating so much snow. The carol singers will be coming in a few hours. At this rate they won't make it to the house the way the snow's falling. Help yourself to some of the food over there.' He pointed towards a smaller food preparation table near the larder.

Beside the table was the basket Miller had brought in earlier. Something was beginning to stir inside, Miller noted. He knelt down and looked through the wicker bars. Two small brown eyes opened and blinked up at him. This was followed by a light growl. Sam was awake. The barking started. As Miller had predicted, he was in a foul mood. Reaching up to the table, he grabbed a piece of chicken and showed it as a peace offering to the little dog.

'Well Sam, my lad, this can go two ways. You be nice to Harry, and you get this lovely piece of chicken, or you can be your usual bad-tempered self and starve.'

The little Jack Russell looked at Miller and then at the chicken with a slight tilt of his head. Incredibly, the growling stopped. Miller smiled triumphantly.

'Good boy, I knew we could reach an accommodation. You might be capricious little so and so, but you're not the stupidest, that's for sure.'

Reaching down, he handed Sam the chicken, which was gobbled down greedily.

'Do you want some more boy?'

Miller could have sworn he saw Sam nod assent. This definitely was not the stupidest animal in the house. He looked up and saw Curtis arriving back in the kitchen, clearly harassed.

-

Eric Strangerson was also wearing a tweed suit. He surveyed himself in the mirror. His jacket refused to button. He left it unbuttoned deciding it was not worth the risk of it popping at an inopportune moment. He clapped his expanding waistline. It would have been unfair to call him fat, but he was definitely running the risk. He reproached himself out loud.

'More bally discipline needed old chum. But not yet.'

A closer inspection of his face in the mirror brought a dissatisfied reaction. He took a pair of small scissors from his toilet bag and began to trim his, already, slim moustache. After a few moments he nodded with some satisfaction, then patted down his hair. Unquestionably it was beginning to recede at the front.

A rumble in his stomach reminded him that he hadn't eaten for a few hours and was now distinctly peckish. When would they bang the gong for lunch, he wondered? Reaching into his pocket he pulled out a hip flask. Sadly, it was empty. On the journey up from London, he had imbibed from time to time.

'This'll never do. Must have some rations. God forbid they're a dry lot here.'

He pulled out from his bag a bottle of Scotch. Carefully he decanted some of the contents into the hip flask. Finally, he was able to take a quick nip. All at once he felt warm inside. Magic, he thought.

The prospect of being in a country house with people he had never met was not something that greatly worried him. He was naturally gregarious and sociable. His only worry was not himself, but them. Thankfully, reflected Strangerson, Aston seemed to be a good sort. It would be easy to spend a few days in the company of this man. Then of course there were the beautiful Cavendish sisters. The prospect of meeting them also added to the appeal of the next few days. Although if he didn't miss his guess, one of the would be bound for Aston.

It was the first time Strangerson had met Aston. Although they had only been able to chat in the car from the station, he had formed an impression of a man at ease with himself and with a ready sense of humour. This corresponded with what he knew about Aston from mutual acquaintances.

They had both travelled from London, however, they were in different parts of the train. Strangerson had travelled second class on the train. Aston had travelled in first class. It was also interesting to note that his man, Miller, had also travelled first class with him. This seemed a bit odd, nevertheless, he realized things were changing. It would take a lot to convince him it was a sign of progress for servants to travel first class with their masters while a gentleman, like himself, had to travel second class due to economic necessity.

-

Lady Emily studied her reflection in the full-length mirror. She rarely over-indulged in any vice. She was temperate and did not smoke. Consequently, as her fortieth birthday loomed, she could easily have passed for someone ten years younger. Although quite vain in many ways, the way she looked was not something she thought about deeply. She was unquestionably beautiful. It had always been thus. There was little she could do to improve how she looked; there was no desire to do so and even less inclination to live a life that would age her unnecessarily.

Her contemplations were disturbed by a knock at her door. A voice said, 'Mama?'

'Come in Henry,' replied Lady Emily.

Henry walked in a moment later. He'd not bothered to change. His mother raised an eyebrow towards him. Emily Cavendish could say more with a twitch of a facial muscle than most could in an entire speech.

Henry was an expert reader of his mother's mood and understood immediately she was displeased. Lady Emily was even more expert at reading him, however. She could read beyond the surface façade that he did not care. He cared but did not want to betray weakness to people he loathed.

Although this did not make her despair, it saddened her more than she would admit. It also made her a little angry, but not with Henry. He was just at a certain stage in his life. Soon he would emerge from the place he occupied, deep within himself, to become a young man to be proud of. This was a matter of certainty not the blind optimism of a mother.

'You're ready?' she asked, knowing the answer.

'Yes.'

She made a great show of surveying him up and down, 'You could've made more of an effort.'

Henry snorted partly out of irritation for being treated like a child, partly because he could not see the point.

'For them? They don't like us. We don't like them. Obviously, I'm not going to come out and say this, but I'm sure they know.'

It was difficult to disagree. This was a silent protest from Henry, and he had every right. Robert's family had not been supportive since his death. If anything, they had seemed to wash their hands of both her and Henry. This was unforgivable. Lord Cavendish rarely wrote or called her. The girls never made contact. This was tantamount to abandonment. Robert's boy, the future Lord Cavendish, had been made an outcast by his own family. She looked at him unable to hide the sadness she felt.

'Very well. Remember, though, you will one day be lord of all you survey.'

Henry walked over to the window. What he could survey was quickly turning white.

'It's coming down pretty thick.'

'Yes, I've seen. I hope they've made adequate provision.'

'In other words, you think we could be stuck here for a while?'

This was good news as far as he was concerned but he did not want his mother to know why. Less enticing was the prospect of being stuck with relatives who did not care one jot for him. And then there were the other people he did not know. Almost certainly he would not like them. He knew they were just as likely not to like him, either. He was self-aware enough to know that he was awkward in company. This did not worry him particularly, or so he'd trained himself to think.

'Where is Godfrey by the way, did he unpack for you?'

'Yes, he was doing this when I came to you,' replied Henry.

'Very well, perhaps you should send him downstairs to meet the other staff and have some lunch,' said Lady Emily turning to gaze out the window again.

Henry took this as a polite dismissal. He left and returned to his room. Godfrey was there hanging up the last of Henry's clothes. He turned to see Henry enter.

'Will there be anything else, sir?'

'No, have some lunch Godfrey,' said Henry, not looking at him but going over to the window instead.

'Thank you, sir,' replied Godfrey, leaving the room.

Outside the Cavendish grounds were blanketed in white now. Even the trees had snow covering their branches. Henry felt oddly entranced by the scene and stood contemplating it for a few minutes. He had many happy memories here and he hoped they would return one day. It brought to mind his father. The wave of sadness, when it came, was heavy. Tears rolled down his cheeks as he thought of the father he would never see again.

-

At that moment Cavendish was also looking out at the snow covering the estate. Memories flooded back to him also. Two small boys in the snow throwing snowballs or sledging down Tarrant's Hill. It seemed like yesterday. How quickly the years pass. These reflections always left him feeling sad.

Enough, he thought. It was time to think to the future: to think of Henry and the girls. This Christmas he would endeavour to repair the bonds of his family. This issue had been left unattended too long and he blamed himself.

With this thought in his mind, he made a mental note to speak to the girls. It was important they tried with Lady Emily. They must find the resolve to ignore whatever provocation they faced from her. He glanced up at the portrait of Robert and made a silent commitment.

Leaving the library, he crossed the hallway to see how lunch arrangements were progressing. Curtis was with Polly arranging the table. On a sideboard was a selection of meats, soup, and salad. Curtis looked up from arranging the table and stood to attention. He was not quite sure why he still did this in the presence of Cavendish, something of the army air in the lord, he supposed.

'Everything's ready sir.'

'Very good. Please pass on my thanks to Elsie. It looks most appetizing.

'Thank you, my lord.'

'We should give our guests a few minutes more and then bang the gong.'

'Very good, my lord.'

A thought appeared to strike Cavendish and he asked, 'Have the staff of Lord Aston and Lady Emily eaten yet?'

'Yes sir, they're down in the kitchen, presently having lunch,' replied Curtis.

Cavendish nodded, Curtis took this as his and Polly's cue to leave the dining room. They both returned to the kitchen to find Miller and Godfrey in conversation, they had been joined by Agnes, Lady Emily's maid. Sam, meanwhile, was happily sitting on Elsie's lap being fed small pieces of meat.

'Sam's found a new friend,' indicated Miller to Curtis.

41

'Yes, so I see. I'm not sure, though, if it's advisable for the dog to stay in the kitchen,' replied Curtis in a tone of voice that made no attempt to betray its self-righteous sentiments.

'Don't worry about him,' replied Miller, 'He'll stay with his lordship in his room.'

Curtis raised an eyebrow at this but did not comment further. Both Polly and Agnes, joined Elsie in making a fuss about the little dog. Sam, an arch manipulator of humans, had long since worked out how to play the game. Experience had taught him that the humans with the higher pitch voices were more malleable and responsive to his tricks. Tactics such as rolling over on his back or getting on his hind legs almost always bore fruit or, better still, bacon. The deeper voiced humans, on the other hand, were often more difficult to bend to his will. Worse, they were often not to be trusted.

Curtis looked at the clock near the door. It was after midday. He turned to the rest of the staff in the kitchen and inhaled deeply. This was always a prelude to an instruction or an improving thought. The staff braced themselves.

'I think our guests will be getting hungry by now if they've had an early start. It's time for lunch. Polly, Agnes, will join me upstairs to assist, thank you.'

Rising from the table, he straightened his jacket and made his way up the stairs to the hallway with ceremonial dignity. He reached the gong and gave it three short raps almost causing Eric Strangerson to drop his hip flask which glued to his mouth.

'About bloody time,' he muttered. He pocketed the flask and went to the mirror to make one last recce. Deciding he did, indeed, pass muster, he opened the door and walked into the corridor. He was joined at this moment by Kit Aston, who was clearly also quite hungry.

'The old tummy has been rumbling for a bit now,' said Strangerson jovially patting his expansive girth.

42

'I know what you mean,' replied Kit trying hard not to glance downward at Strangerson's rather ample complainant.

They descended the stairs together in agreement that cold weather and long journeys boosted the appetite enormously. Curtis opened the dining room door for the two gentlemen. Cavendish was standing in front of the dining room table. He greeted them warmly.

Chapter 5

The dining room that Kit and Strangerson walked into was spacious and elegantly furnished. The table at the centre was long but not dominating and looked like it would seat ten people comfortably. Light flooded in through the tall French windows which bounced off the white walls giving a sense of air and space. Adorning the walls were a number of small genre and equestrian paintings from the nineteenth century. Cavendish moved to one side of the table and smiled to the newly arrived guests.

'Gentlemen, I trust you're well-rested following your journey.'

'Yes sir, thank you. The bedroom is very comfortable. Wonderful view, too. I'm sure there are beautiful gardens underneath the snow somewhere.' replied Kit, smiling.

'Indeed, it's come down rather heavily over last few hours. I hope our carol singers will be able to make it up to the Hall later.'

'Carol singers. Capital idea, sir,' said Strangerson.

'It is actually. We have a tradition at the Hall. The vicar and many of the villagers come up to the Hall and we serve mulled wine, mince pies, and give out presents to the school children.'

'Can we join in the festivities, sir?' asked Kit.

'Why of course. Traditionally it's myself and, in the past, my wife and boys who did the honours. You would be most welcome to help Mary, Esther, and myself.'

'I should be delighted, sir.'

'I'm always up for serving mulled wine. It sounds like a spiffing idea,' added Strangerson.

'Excellent, thank you very much, gentlemen. We can set up a few posts as there could be as many as sixty men, women, and children from the village to visit us this afternoon.'

Kit walked over to the painting hanging over the fireplace. It showed a horse and a foal. He recognized the artist immediately.

'This looks like a Stubbs, sir.'

'It is. My grandfather had an eye for these things. Probably spent a little too much on it in my view but there are many paintings around the house acquired by him over the years. Mostly equestrian, I should add, but some interesting portraits as well. We have a Sargent also. He painted Katherine.'

'I should like to see her portrait. I remember she was very beautiful.'

'You should've seen her when we first met,' smiled Cavendish but there was a melancholy in his eyes.

The dining room door opened. Lady Emily and Henry made their entrance.

'Emily,' said Cavendish. He took her hand and brought her over to Strangerson and Kit. 'Let me introduce you and Henry to our guests for Christmas, Lord Kit Aston and Eric Strangerson.'

Lady Emily held out her hand and they observed the usual introductory pleasantries. Kit could not help but observe the limpness of Henry's handshake and unwillingness to look him in the eye. He felt sympathetic towards the young man. He clearly lacked self-confidence and was uncertain in company. This could easily be changed with the right mentoring.

Cavendish had also noticed this exchange. There was much work to do.

'The idea is we serve food ourselves and allow the staff to make ready for the carol singers and villagers later. Please help yourselves and sit anywhere. We shall try to be as informal as possible,' said Cavendish.

The gentlemen allowed Lady Emily to pick a few items on her plate and then they followed.

'What a wonderful selection, Lord Cavendish. Your staff has excelled themselves. I hardly know where to begin,' said Strangerson. His solution was brilliantly simple, he put a generous amount of food on his plate from each of the offerings. Cavendish and Kit glanced at one another as they looked at the big explorer tuck in. Both smiled sympathetically. Perhaps he knew what extreme hunger was like.

'I shall make sure to tell Elsie, who prepared this feast,' commented Cavendish.

'Please do, sir.'

Neither Emily nor Henry made any comment on the food. Then she made a small show of looking around the table.

'Should we make a start, or do we wait for the girls?'

This was a split second too late for Strangerson who had already begun to eat. He looked up comically and laughed, 'Oh gosh, I'm afraid my hunger made me forget my manners.'

'Don't worry old chap,' reassured Cavendish, 'my granddaughters will make their usual dramatic entrance soon enough, I suspect.'

As if on cue, Esther and Mary entered the room, and for Kit, the oxygen left it. Esther was every bit as beautiful as he'd been led to believe. She seemed to glide rather than walk. Transfixed for a moment, Kit regained his composure and stood up. Strangerson finished off his mouthful, dabbed his chin with the napkin and rose in a movement that Cavendish found oddly impressive in its economy.

The girls went over to their Aunt Emily first. Greetings and kisses were exchanged. All of this was accomplished in a rather grand style by Lady Emily, thought Kit. Next was Strangerson. He performed his role to the hilt waxing lyrical about the beauty of the girls, making a great show of bowing to them and kissing their outstretched hands. Kit held his breath as they came towards him.

'Lord Aston, we're honoured to have you join us this Christmas,' said Esther.

She held out her hand and he shook it rather than doing as Strangerson had done.

'I'm the one who is honoured, firstly to have been invited by your grandfather and to be with the daughters, and son, of men I admired greatly.

'You met our father?' This was Mary.

He regarded Mary, for the first time. As he'd barely been able to keep his eyes off Esther, the appearance of Mary was almost a shock. She was slightly shorter than her sister and slenderer. Her movement had a different type of grace, but Kit was too entranced to analyse further. He noticed that she wore her hair much shorter than Esther. A Suffragette, he wondered? The blue eyes were those of her sister but where Esther seemed dreamy, inviting you to worship, Mary's crackled with an electric intensity.

'Our paths crossed on a number of occasions,' explained Kit.

'I should like to know more some time,' said Mary.

'Gladly.'

Cavendish, observing all introductions had been made, motioned for his granddaughters to collect their lunch and join the table. He was pleased by the impact Esther had made on Kit. The politeness of the meeting between Strangerson and Mary had told its own story. There was little prospect of romance there.

47

Kit was glad the two girls were sitting across the table from him. It would give him ample opportunity to view them. With some difficulty, he tried to dismiss the thought that this was a deliberate ploy by Esther or Mary. Nevertheless, he couldn't stop himself hoping.

'I say, it's fairly chucking it down outside,' said Strangerson. Cavendish silently thanked him for starting conversation at the table.

'We often have a white Christmas here,' added Cavendish.

'It's certainly very beautiful; romantic even,' said Kit.

'Are you a romantic, Lord Christopher?' asked Mary, putting her chin in her hands and fixing Kit with a look that would've passed muster in any Parisian bordello.

Kit laughed and avoided answering the question directly.

'My friends call me, Kit. I wouldn't go so far as to say I read Byron every day.'

Mary narrowed her eyes and smiled. Kit could tell she knew he had deftly avoided answering the question. He became aware Lady Emily had spoken, and he turned his attention towards her. His fears about her were quickly being realized. She was a little over-bearing and pompous. Henry seemed utterly disinterested in what she had to say as well as in more general conversation. Kit felt he should try and bring him into the conversation.

'Tell me Henry, are you at university yet?'

'No, Aston.'

'He will go next year,' interjected Lady Emily, 'Won't you my dear.'

Henry did not deign to reply so Kit added, 'Any thoughts on where you will go and what you would like to read?'

Once again Lady Emily jumped in.

'We would like him to read the Classics. I think that Greek and Latin provide such a good grounding for the mind and the soul? Don't you agree Lord Aston?'

48

'I read Mathematics and Modern Languages myself. At Cambridge,' replied Kit, realizing he was potentially making an enemy.

'I should like to have had the opportunity to go there,' said Mary.

'I agree you should be allowed to go, Lady Mary. There are so many things that need to change with regard to women and society,' replied Kit.

'The vote as well, Kit. Good Lord, they'll be driving next!' interjected Strangerson. Everyone laughed except Mary and Henry. Suspecting that his joke might offend Mary, he quickly recanted, 'Of course, I agree with Kit. It's a bally shame. Positively medieval really.'

Mary looked at Strangerson. Kit could not decide if she was warming to him or taking his measure. On balance he suspected the latter. Esther turned to Henry, realising he had not been given the chance to respond to Kit.

'I'm sorry Henry, but what would you like to do at university?'

Henry turned a deep red as all eyes turned towards him. Esther felt a tinge of regret for him, but her grandfather was very happy. He was very curious to hear what the young man would say.

He turned towards his mother and then looked at the table. His face was approaching crimson. Then with a surge of courage he spoke.

'Well, my grandfather has mentioned he would love that I read chemistry.'

Lady Emily turned to Cavendish and glared.

'Really Arthur?'

'I believe he's referring to your father, Emily,' said Cavendish innocently but his eyes were twinkling.

'I see,' said Emily in a manner which left no one in doubts that this matter was far from resolved. Cavendish was highly amused. He had a feeling that Cedric Blythe was going to get a rather severe verbal beating from his daughter. Poor fellow, he thought. It occurred to him that he should invite Blythe to visit soon. It had been too long; he quite enjoyed the old boy's company. The turn in the conversation appeared to embolden young Henry further.

'As it happens, I should be rather keen to study Chemistry, mama. Grandpapa and I have talked about it at length about this. He knows I have an interest and I've visited the plant in York a number of times.'

Emily looked like she was chewing wasps and remained silent. The lunch party took this to mean the subject, for the moment, was closed. Kit, however, was very decided on speaking to Henry, well away from his mother, on this subject. Both Cavendish and Mary were similarly determined.

'What languages did you read Kit?' asked Esther, to fill the silence which had descended like a raincloud onto a mountain.

'German, French and Russian,' replied Kit.

'And you did Mathematics also. Wherever did you find the time to do all this? You mustn't have had much of a social life,' probed Mary. There was no mistaking what her real question was.

'Thankfully I had a pretty good start on all but Russian. I began it at university. It meant that I didn't have to forego all of the fun to be had in Cambridge during my time there.'

'Have you been to Russia?' asked Mary, eyeing him closely.

Kit glanced at Cavendish who briefly shut his eyes and imperceptibly shook his head. The glance to Cavendish did not go unnoticed, however, by Mary who smiled and narrowed her eyes.

'Or perhaps I shouldn't ask?'

By way of an answer Kit replied, 'I've spent a little time with Kerensky. He's in London now. I've been able to practice with him.'

The rest of the meal passed off without any further diplomatic incidents. Strangerson proved to be very adept at keeping conversation light and instantly forgettable. Kit was able to enjoy the vista of the Cavendish girls who presented a fascinating study in polar opposites. He wondered how they were together. They seemed so different and yet there was no mistaking the facial resemblance, the beautifully modulated voices and also their laughter, which was frequent, sincere, and conspiratorial enough to suggest a genuine closeness.

Unquestionably, Esther was the most beautiful girl Kit had ever seen. He knew this from the moment she had entered the room. It was a relief to see that her beauty was not just an outward manifestation. There was no artifice about her. Her natural grace was both physical and metaphysical. To be near her was to feel a surge of good feeling for humanity. After the horrors of France, he could imagine no purer experience than to be with her. However, he was acutely aware it would become obvious if he stared at her too much. Instead, he tried to ensure he conversed with Lady Emily and Strangerson. From time to time he engaged Esther but for the most part focused his attention elsewhere.

Curtis brought some coffee in, and the lunch party stood to serve themselves. Cavendish joined Emily and Henry while Strangerson went over to the window. He was joined moments later by Kit, Esther, and Mary.

'I have to admit, I wasn't at my best this morning,' said Strangerson.

'Oh, why was that Mr Strangerson?' asked Esther.

'Well, at the risk of offending such beautiful and genteel company, I was with some chums last night and we were partaking in some games of chance until quite late. I must confess to imbibing a rather injudicious amount of alcohol. In fact, I think I splashed a bit too much brandy.' This revelation caused much amusement.

'I hope you're feeling better now, Mr Strangerson!' said Esther.

'Much better thank you, and how could I not in such lovely company,' laughed Strangerson in response.

'How did you get on in your game of chance?' asked Mary.

'On the receiving end of a bit of a rinsing, truth be told. I don't mind as they're good chums, but not the sort one introduces to one's mummy. Anyway, lesson learned. The grape and cards mixeth not.'

'Did I hear that you had some misfortune at the cards, Strangerson?' asked Cavendish.

Strangerson laughed and confirmed it was indeed so. Cavendish laughed sympathetically and said, 'I'm glad you've learned a lesson. I must admit, in my younger days I learned a similarly expensive lesson. Avoided gambling ever since.'

'Really Grandpapa?' said Mary, 'this is new and very interesting news. I should like to hear more.' Taking Strangerson by the arm, she steered him over to the side of the room where Cavendish, Emily and Henry were stood.

'Arthur is this really is a suitable conversation for Henry to hear,' said Emily rather stiffly.

Henry rolled his eyes in irritation and even Cavendish raised his eyebrows in surprise.

'I think, Emily, Henry will encounter all sorts of people doing many things that both you and I may not approve off. We do him no favour by protecting him from this knowledge. Would it not be better for him to hear of the sad outcomes resulting from such foolish behaviour?'

'And expensive,' interjected Strangerson.

'…and expensive experiences of our friend here?' added Cavendish, more in amusement than gravity.

'Well, I think it all sounds rather exciting, frankly,' said Mary. 'I would love to visit some illicit gambling den or hit the tables at Monte Carlo.'

'Trust you my dear. Ever the rebel,' smiled Cavendish.

'Where did you get involved in such illicit activity grandpapa? We want to hear more of this,' asked Mary mischievously.

'I was young once, you know,' he smiled, 'as difficult as that may be to believe, young lady. There was a lot of spare time in the army. I had many friends who gambled quite seriously. There were more than a few consequences, if I remember, often not to the benefit of those involved. I might've occasionally dabbled, but I was never so interested, and certainly had little aptitude.'

Mary smiled up at her grandfather with something akin to a newfound respect, but Emily's face continued to register disapproval. Cavendish felt it prudent to change the conversational tack to more commonplace topics.

Meanwhile, Kit and Esther were now alone, beside the window. Kit smiled at her.

'Was that deliberately stage-managed?' asked Kit.

'Knowing Mary, I would say yes. My apologies. What it lacked in subtlety was more than made up by the best of intentions.'

'You seem very different.'

'We are. But I'd add we're also the best of friends. I couldn't wish for a better sister than Mary.'

'I'm glad to hear it. I have a half-brother whom I don't see very much of, said Kit rather sadly. 'I've missed out, somewhat, on having a sibling rival or friend.'

'Siblings can certainly be both. I think with Mary and I it was mostly the latter. She's always been very competitive but not with me. Probably because I was never very bothered trying to compete with her, or anyone else for that matter, at school or the other things we enjoy.'

'Oh, why not?' probed Kit.

'It's different for women. We don't have your opportunities. I wouldn't get Mary started on this subject, by the way,' said Esther smiling. 'I always knew that, in the end, I would be expected to marry. Ideally marry well and have a family. Mary has been less accepting of this. I love this about her, but we're different in this regard.'

Kit was aware this was something of an understatement. Mary had caused a minor scandal in social circles when she had left Cavendish Hall and volunteered to become a nurse under an assumed name towards the end of the War. This had been done without the knowledge or consent of the family. Somehow, she had managed to convince various medical professionals that she was a nurse and ended up in France working near the front line.

'Where you aware of what Mary had intended?

'Yes, but I swore not to tell. She never told me her assumed name. This meant grandpapa was unable to track her. To be honest, I don't think he tried too hard. Not because he didn't care, I should say. It was hard for him. Losing grandmama and then papa, really took a lot out of him. He worried so about Uncle Robert. When Mary left, I think he felt more pride. Certainly not anger. He admired her spirit.'

'But I understand you also worked in London over this period.'

'Yes, but it was really nothing. I oversaw the work of some nurses in Voluntary Aid Detachments and worked on the buses, would you believe? Hardly like Mary at the front.'

'When I came back from France, I spent some time in hospital. The work of the VAD nurses was marvellous. I think it wonderful you both volunteered to help. You didn't have to.'

They were silent for a moment, as if realizing the subject was straying too close to things that neither was ready to talk about.

'Thank you for coming this Christmas. I'm not sure how it would have been with us, Aunt Emily, and Henry,' said Esther sincerely.

Kit smiled.

'Yes, I think I understand. Your aunt certainly has a strong personality. I hope young Henry will be allowed to make his own decisions.'

Esther did not reply but she seemed troubled. Kit did not pursue why. He accepted neither sister might not have much time for Henry for reasons he would not be privy to. They turned to less controversial topics. Kit was happy to let her talk about life at Cavendish Hall. He had no problem in playing the role of listener if it meant that he could gaze upon her.

Soon they joined the rest of the party. Cavendish looked over at Curtis who was trying to attract his attention. Nodding he turned to the rest of the party.

'I believe the carol singing will shortly begin. Curtis tells me that Reverend Simmons and the villagers are coming down the driveway.'

Everyone turned towards the window and, sure enough, a large party of men, women and children were heading towards Cavendish Hall. The snow had, temporarily at least, stopped falling.

Cavendish led his guests out into the main hallway, which had undergone some transformation whilst they had lunched. Serving tables and some chairs had been set out in the enormous hallway. On the tables were punch bowls full of mulled wine, heaps of mince pies, boxes of chocolates and Christmas crackers.

Under the big Christmas tree were piled all manner of dolls, bottles of sweets, bats, balls, boxes of toy soldiers, toy ships, toy aeroplanes, other charming mechanical toys, and books. Taking charge, Cavendish instructed his guests where they would go.

'Lady Emily and I will greet everyone at the front. Girls, please can you occupy tables one and two. Kit and Mr. Strangerson if you could be so kind as to go to tables three and four. I imagine, Mr. Strangerson you will have great experience in managing a punch bowl.' This brought much

55

merriment to all except Lady Emily and Henry. Finally, he added, 'Perhaps, Henry, you could join Kit.'

Orders given; all went to their positions. Curtis went to the front door, to anticipate the imminent arrival of the villagers. His timing was perfect as within moments of his arrival there was a loud rap on the oak door. With due solemnity, Curtis opened the door and was met by the Vicar, Tom Simmons. With a nod of his head, Curtis indicated that the carol singers could begin to sing.

It was difficult for Kit to judge how many there were from where he was standing, but he could see all ages. A warm feeling came over him despite the cold. This was one of his favourite Christmas traditions and he looked forward to the rest of the afternoon. He glanced over at the Cavendish girls. In fact, he was looking forward to staying in this company very much.

Chapter 6

God rest ye merry gentlemen
Let nothing you dismay
Remember Christ our Saviour
Was born on Christmas Day

The carol singers stood outside the hall, wrapped in large coats, scarves, and hats. The singers were led by a sturdy-looking man, in his late forties. Kit guessed this was Reverend Simmons. His complexion was ruddy with a largish nose that looked like it had been broken at least once. Kit detected what appeared to be a cauliflower ear, but he couldn't be sure as it was partially obscured by the dark hat. He wondered if he was or had been a rugger player.

The carol singers completed their first carol and then Cavendish stepped forward to greet Simmons.

'Tom, so glad you were all able to come,' he said shaking hands. 'I thought the weather might make it touch and go.'

Simmons laughed, 'You're not the only one Lord Cavendish. I think it would take more than a few flakes of snow to stop this lot coming up here though. They're a hardy lot.'

'I've noticed. Do come inside. I think you and the children deserve warmer surroundings and something for your efforts.'

The carol singers marched in first followed by the villagers and about a dozen children and toddlers. Once they were all in the main hall, Cavendish stood before them to give his traditional Christmas speech to the village.

'I feel there are a few of you who could probably give this speech you've heard it so often.' There was some laughter at this from the older villagers and carol singers.

'But no matter, tradition must be followed. I would like to think of this as a tradition that is as welcome to you as it is for us at Cavendish Hall.'

This was greeted by many saying, 'Hear, hear.'

'In fact, I hope this tradition of ours will go on for many generations to come.'

This was greeted with applause by all, although Cavendish could not help but observe, with dismay, that both Emily and Henry were not clapping. Neither seemed very enthusiastic at the prospect. Cavendish was not the only person to notice. Kit saw Esther and Mary look at one another grimly. He was surprised, however, when Mary turned, and looked directly at him with narrowed eyes and a half smile. He had been caught out and this made him smile. She didn't miss much.

Cavendish continued, 'As you know, we shall serve mulled wine, lemonade, and mince pies to you all. Doing so, as usual, will be my granddaughters whom you know very well. Joining Lady Esther and Lady Mary are our guests this Christmas. Lady Emily and my grandson, Henry, are with us again this year. And we are also happy to have Lord Christopher 'Kit' Aston and Mr Eric Strangerson.'

The guests were greeted with a round of applause.

'I should add, I met Lord Christopher during the war, where he fought with great valour for his country. Likewise, Mr Strangerson also fought for his country alongside my late son Robert. I hope you will give them a very special Little Gloston welcome.'

There was a murmured assent and further applause.

58

'I think it's high time we served you some food and drink, don't you think?' This was greeted with laughter. 'Then we can enjoy some more beautiful carols to get us into the Christmas spirit. Finally, we can get on with the key event of the day, at least as far as our younger guests are concerned.' A cheer rose up from the children, which added to the general happiness of the occasion.

After saying a final thank you to Reverend Simmons, the visitors dispersed to different tables to receive their drinks and mince pies. With some amusement, Kit observed how many of the men made straight for the tables where the two girls were serving. Meanwhile, the women of the village seemed to be making a beeline in his direction. The children had taken to Strangerson, and they were royally entertained. Much laughter ensued as Strangerson played the fool to an adoring gallery.

Once all the visitors had been served, the Cavendish family, apart from Emily and Henry, mingled freely and easily. Strangerson was now captive to the children and was performing magic tricks involving coins appearing from behind ears. This caused squeals of delight from the children who inevitably demanded more.

Kit was joined by Reverend Simmons. The removal of his hat confirmed Kit's suspicion that he had cauliflower ears. Although this was unusual for a parson, it made Simmons's appearance more interesting to Kit and he felt an instant liking for this man.

'Have you played a bit of rugger in your time?' asked Kit with a smile.

This was greeted by a roar of laughter. However, Simmons shook his head.

'No, more of a soccer man myself. I assume you're referring to the appearance of my ears.'

'Well, yes as a matter of fact.'

'I understand, your lordship. In fact, I wasn't always a vicar. When I first met Lord Cavendish I was in the army.'

'Really? Where were you?'

'South Africa during the Boer War. I was a Sergeant with the Northamptonshires. A few years after I returned from South Africa, I followed a different calling.'

'Is this how you met Lord Cavendish?'

Simmons smiled at Kit and touched his ears.

'Ah, well now we're back to my ears. I was a boxer, and I represented my battalion. Lord Cavendish came to one of the inter-army fights.'

'I've been to a few fights myself. In fact, I named my dog after one of my favourite fighters,' said Kit.

'Really, who would that be?' inquired Simmons.

'Have you heard of Sam Langford?'

'Heard of him? I sparred a few rounds with him when he toured England. It must be nearly ten years ago now,' said the man of God to an amazed Kit.

'It was – gosh what was he like?'

'A lovely man outside the ring but my goodness he could punch like angry a mule.'

Simmons rubbed his jaw as he relived the memory. Just as they were talking, Kit heard a familiar yelp and into the hall raced Sam, followed by Miller. This caused more amusement as they watched the spectacle of a very unhappy Miller trying to catch the tiny Jack Russell. Eventually he gave up but was rewarded with a sympathetic round of applause. Miller stopped, grinned to the audience, and made an exaggerated theatrical bow. Afterwards he immediately went over to Kit to apologise.

'Sorry sir, I couldn't keep him cooped up any longer.'

'Don't worry Harry. No harm done. Anyway, he seems to be making friends.' They both glanced over at Sam being fed snacks by Esther and Mary. 'Can't fault his taste.' added Kit. Miller noted the comment but made no reply. Kit returned his gaze to Miller and said, 'Help yourself, Harry. By the way this is Reverend Simmons.'

'Hello Harry,' said Reverend Simmons amiably.

Miller and Simmons exchanged handshakes. Kit caught Miller glancing at the Reverend's ears.

'He went a few rounds with the Boston Tar Baby,' explained Kit.

Miller and Simmons laughed and the three chatted happily for a few more minutes on the noble art. They were soon joined by Cavendish.

'Tom, I'm glad you've met Kit. I should add, Kit, that Tom will be joining us for Christmas lunch tomorrow.'

Cavendish glanced at Miller. Kit once again felt something had troubled him about Miller. He was very curious but decided that rather than ask Cavendish directly it would be more prudent to wait and see if he said anything.

'Yes, we have a mutual interest in the pugilistic science,' said Kit.

This made Cavendish chuckle. Then he went on to relate their first meeting in South Africa. After a pleasant few minutes Cavendish asked, 'Tom, do you think your carol singers are ready to perform?'

'I should say they are,' replied Simmons. Taking his leave from the group, he walked to the centre of the hall and clapped his hands to gain everyone's attention. A few minutes later the carol singers began again. This time accompanied by a few guest singers. Strangerson proved to have a very fine baritone, but Kit found himself listening closely to the beautiful harmonies coming from the two Cavendish girls.

The end of the first carol, 'Oh Come All Ye Faithful', was accompanied by an additional singer with a distinctly canine timbre. Sam's howling, of course, caused great laughter in the hall. With smiles all around, Kit went over to Mary and collected the little dog to bring him downstairs lest he should derail the rest of the singing.

He returned a few minutes later in time to join the singers in 'Hark the Herald Angels Sing!' The carols continued for another twenty minutes before Reverend Simmons brought an end to proceedings. The inhabitants of Cavendish Hall and the guests gave loud acclaim to the efforts of the choir. Soon the villagers were trooping out of the hall just as daylight was beginning to turn to grey and purple. Some flakes of snow were beginning to meander lazily through the air. Replacing his hat, Simmons bid goodbye to Cavendish.

'Merry Christmas, Lord Cavendish.'

'And to you. We shall see you tomorrow at the service. You'll return with us to the Hall for lunch as usual, of course.'

'Thank you again for your invitation.'

Turning he joined the villagers as they marched up the long driveway towards the nearby village of Little Gloston. Cavendish stayed to watch them until they were out of sight and then returned to the Hall where Curtis and the other staff were busy clearing up. Rather than getting in the way, he went into the library.

Kit, Strangerson and the two Cavendish girls soon joined Lord Cavendish in the library. Lady Emily went to her room deciding that she was fatigued from a busy morning. Eventually, after some deliberation, Henry decided to join his cousins in the library also.

'They're fine portraits, sir' said Strangerson, as Cavendish entered.

'Indeed. Sargent really captured Katherine.' The heartbreak in Cavendish's voice was evident. 'I remember when Lavery came to paint the boys. We had wanted two portraits, but he insisted it would be better they were together. He was right. They were such good friends, not just brothers.'

'You can see it in the painting.' said Strangerson. 'This is very much the Robert I remember. I never met John, sadly.'

'Oh, they were very different,' said Cavendish, 'in so many ways and yet unmistakably brothers. Both had such a sense of duty to family and to country. I was tremendously proud of them. John was much more serious whereas Robert, well, he had a streak in him certainly, but he was good for all that.'

Kit stood apart from the group with Henry looking at some of the books in the library. Over the years, the Cavendish family had built up an extensive collection of books on philosophy, science, and mathematics. He noticed Henry took down from the bookshelves a couple of books on chemical subjects. These were heavyweight tomes and it surprised Kit that Henry might even understand them, never mind be interested.

'I'm sure your mother has your best interests at heart but if this is what you would like to do…' Kit left the sentence unfinished. Henry glanced up at him. His face remained inscrutable. Persevering, Kit added, 'My parents were against me doing mathematics and modern languages, I insisted, however. They went with my wishes in the end. I certainly have no regrets in my choices. I learned a great deal and met some fascinating individuals along the way.'

This seemed to reach Henry. 'Oh. Who?'

'Bertrand Russell for one. A brilliant philosopher and mathematician.'

'And conscientious objector,' added Henry sourly.

'True but I respected his stance, even if I disagreed with him. I also knew Lawrence.'

For the first time, Henry seemed genuinely engaged in a conversation. 'Really?'

'Yes, we met at Cambridge and our paths crossed once during the war. I can't really tell you more, I think it will remain hush, hush for a few years, but maybe one day.' This disappointed Henry, but he let it go.

The group by the portraits looked over at Kit and Henry.

'What are you two talking about?' asked Mary conspiratorially.

'Well, we covered, chemistry, mathematics, philosophy and conscientious objectors,' responded Kit.

'Gosh, in only a few minutes. You clever chaps don't hang around,' piped up Strangerson.

Henry continued to review the books on the shelf, taking a couple down to leaf through. One of the books Henry chose caused Kit to raise his eyebrow but he said nothing. A voice from across the room called to him.

'Have you seen the portraits, Kit?' asked Cavendish.

Kit felt the room close in around him and begin to swirl around. His breathing became laboured, and the familiar cold sweat erupted like lava from his pores. Attempting to deal with this wave head on, he slowly moved over towards the group and looked up at the portrait of Katherine, avoiding the other painting featuring the Cavendish brothers. The attacks were usually at night. They came unbidden into his dreams. Rarely, did these waves come during the day. However, he had expected something. Spending Christmas at Cavendish Hall was always meant to be a signal to his mind that he would resist and refuse to submit.

'Beautiful, sir. She was very beautiful. Sargent has really captured her.'

'I know. Even the mouth.'

Kit smiled at Cavendish's joke about Sargent. Then he glanced at the portrait of the boys before returning his gaze quickly towards Cavendish.

'Remarkable likenesses of your boys.' He felt his throat tightening and he prayed the group did not hear the catch in his voice.

It had been a mistake to come. What had he been thinking? How he regretted this decision now. He gripped a nearby seat as his legs began to feel weak. His breathing became increasingly difficult, and he fought hard to give a semblance of control. Slowly breathe in, breathe out, he told himself.

Very soon he felt back in control. The tightness passed away and his breathing eased into its regular rhythm.

'Are you feeling well Kit? You look quite pale,' asked Mary.

'I'm fine really thank you, but sometimes my leg can trouble me.'

'Of course, Kit, we're terribly selfish,' said Cavendish regarding Kit with some concern.

'Nonsense, sir, I couldn't be with more considerate, indeed beautiful, company, and that's just Strangerson.'

Everyone in the room laughed and Kit felt this was an opportunity to escape the room, to escape the image. 'If you don't mind, I think maybe I shall take some air with Sam. I shall be down later.'

'Of course, old chap.' said Cavendish. With a nod to Esther and Mary he left the room. In the hallway, he was enveloped with a sense of relief. He took a deep breath and a few moments to regain his self-possession. There was nothing for it. He was here now and would have to make the best of this situation, but he knew the ghosts of the past few years would visit him again soon.

Chapter 7

Kit went out to the grounds at the back of the house accompanied by Miller and Sam. The little terrier was let off the lead. This was always an open invitation for him to go sprinting off and chase birds. The two men followed slowly behind. Snow covered the ground, but it was thick enough to make walking difficult. They tracked up the main path through the gardens towards the woodland created by Brown. Sam happily chased the few birds pecking at the snow in the field.

When they reached the woodland, they turned and looked at Cavendish Hall. They were now around four hundred yards away at the bottom of a slight incline. The fields and gardens seemed to be part of a white world. On one side of the Hall, they could see the stables in the distance. On another side there was a small cottage. There were signs of disturbance in the white canvas made by the footsteps of Kit, Miller, and Sam. It looked like there were also tracks from the Hall to the stables.

The air was cold and silver and seemed visible as both men breathed.

'It's not exactly the most beautiful looking house I've ever seen,' observed Miller.

'It's hideous. What on earth were they thinking?' agreed Kit

'The garden is quite nice though, I'm sure it's amazing in spring and summer. Look over there. Seems like a nice cottage,' said Miller pointing. In the distance was a small cottage with smoke coming out of the chimney. 'I wonder who lives there.'

'I should imagine an estate like this has other staff. Not everyone needs to live at the Hall,' said Kit.

He was glad to have come out into the air but still feeling a little angry with himself. It was always this way when the wave of panic came, and he despaired at how he could control it. Although very rare, he knew it was now a part of him since that night. This time it was particularly so because of where he was and who he was with. However, the walk was reviving his spirit and gave him the chance to reconsider his earlier fear that coming to Cavendish Hall had been a mistake.

When the invitation had come from Lord Cavendish, Kit's first instinct had been to send his apologies. The more he thought about it, though, the more he felt it was an opportunity to confront the anxiety that had been eating away at him since he'd come back from the War. For as long as he could remember, Kit lived by the principle that it was better to confront your fears than avoid them. Although he conveniently dropped this code when it came to visits to fearsome old aunts. An image of Aunt Agatha came into his mind. He smiled and shook his head.

Meeting the Cavendish girls had certainly been a consideration. They had certainly exceeded all expectations. However, he knew the challenge remained and he had no idea to whom he could speak about it. He sensed Miller was aware something was wrong. Equally, Miller was the last person in whom he could confide. Who knows what demons he had returned with? Specifically, he was there when it happened.

-

67

'Did you see Kit in the library?' asked Mary.

'Not until you drew attention to him. He seemed to turn very pale,' replied Esther. 'I hope he's not coming down with something.'

'I don't think he is, but it just seemed odd. One moment he was well, the next he seemed very off colour,' continued Mary.

'Well, hopefully he will be recovered for this evening and dinner. What did you think of him?' said Esther smiling.

'I hardly spoke to him,' pointed out Mary. 'I would be more interested in your thoughts Miss Cavendish. Operative word being Miss.'

Esther laughed. In fact, they both did. It had always been like this between them.

'He's certainly very charming,' mused Esther, scrutinizing her sister.

Mary laughed a little nervously under Esther's gaze and said, 'Good looking you mean.'

'Well, yes. You were right, he's certainly very handsome. I have a feeling he's very smart too, but he tries to hide it a bit.'

'Really, how so?' asked Mary.

'I can't really define it. It's just a feeling. I was asking about his chess matches with the Russians and Germans, but he just made a joke about his inferiority. Also, I thought it interesting how quickly he understood about Aunt Emily and Henry.'

'He seems to have taken to Henry.'

'I do hope so. Henry needs someone, preferably not female and middle aged, to guide him. For instance, I didn't know Henry was interested in reading chemistry. Did you ever hear him mention anything?'

'No, new one on me. I would've liked to hear more but Aunt Emily closed it down very quickly,' added Mary.

'I know, she's so overpowering. Poor Henry.'

'Poor Henry?' laughed Mary, 'You've changed your tune. Is this the Aston influence?

68

'Maybe, or maybe we haven't given him enough of a chance. Everyone deserves a chance, don't they? Remember, he wasn't always like this. He used to be quite good fun.'

'You're too pure, Essie. You should be evil like me,' grinned Mary.

'Hateful,' corrected Esther.

'Vile.'

The two sisters collapsed onto the bed in a fit of giggles. Finally, Mary said, 'Right ho, I'll be nice to Henry, but don't say I didn't warn you.'

-

Lady Emily glanced up as Henry walked into the room. His face was an unhappy combination of anger and fear. It did have the benefit of bringing some colour to his usually pallid appearance. Fearing his mother would begin a sally on the need for him to embrace his future rank, he decided to go on the attack.

'I know what you're going to say, mother. Perhaps you can spare us both the pain, for once.'

His mother looked up at him. She had not expected him to open up immediately and it took some of the wind from her sails. Instead, she remained silent for what seemed like an eternity. In truth she did not want to have this conversation.

She wanted Henry to be a self-assured, aristocratic man like Aston. Looking at him now, he was clearly a long way from this ideal. Yet he had such beauty. Yet this beauty, the surliness was only a disguise for the insecurity plaguing him. She desperately wanted Henry to leave the room. At this moment all she wanted to do was cry.

The anguish was like a stream of acid pouring onto her conscience. Each drop represented the evidence of her failure as a mother. How much was the Henry before her a reflection of her misdirected efforts to make him into something he didn't wish to be? Finally, she realized she had to say

69

something. Studying his hand, she noticed he was holding some books.

'Raiding the library?'

'Yes,' replied Henry cryptically.

'Can I see?' asked Lady Emily.

'No.'

'I see. I will hazard a guess they are not on Greek or Latin.'

'They are not.'

Lady Emily nodded absently. There was nothing she could think to say now. She decided to end their interview.

'I would like to lie down now. You should go to your room. Can you ask Agnes to come up, please?'

As he left the room, she saw with some alarm the title of one of the books he had taken from the library it was called, "*A Treatise on Poisons*".

-

Only Cavendish remained in the library. He was relatively pleased with how the afternoon had gone. Although he was no expert on romance and the attraction of men, he was convinced Kit would have made a good impression. There was much to admire in the man and recommend him as a potential spouse that went beyond rank. The fatigue Kit had felt in the library had not gone unnoticed by Cavendish, but he had given no more thought to it. Uppermost on his mind was the way Esther and Kit had naturally gravitated towards one another. It was a good sign although, he counselled himself, it still early in the game.

Strangerson was now completely dismissed as potential spouse material. A likeable chap but he would be utterly out of his depth with either Mary or Esther. However, he was keen to hear more of Strangerson's experiences with Shackleton at the South Pole. He also wanted to hear more about Robert.

This was a topic to be approached with caution. Firstly, he was not sure how the War would have affected Strangerson, notwithstanding the original letter of introduction. It wasn't an easy topic to talk about. Even he had tended to avoid talking about the War with Katherine. It was beyond explanation and only those who had been in there could truly understand.

Secondly, he didn't want to talk about Robert with either Emily or Henry around. It risked upsetting them. It would be best to speak outside Cavendish Hall. Perhaps he could suggest a walk to show him the grounds. Better still, perhaps they could go shooting. Strangerson was known to be a top-notch sportsman, and his War record indicated he was excellent shot. Yes, thought Cavendish, that might just do the trick.

Cavendish walked over to the bookshelves and lifted down an atlas. He studied a map of the world. Britain seemed so small and yet so much of the land mass was under its control. This made him feel proud. He'd played no small part in ensuring it remain so. There was no question in his mind that Britain was a force for good in the world. It had brought modernity, the rule of law and medicines to countries plagued by famine and lawlessness.

The extent of Strangerson's travels was impressive. Cavendish ran his finger from Britain over to South America and then down to Antarctica. An interesting man even if he did have something of the buffoon about him. It was difficult to reconcile the scholar, the much-
decorated soldier, with the man who was sharing their house this Christmas.

-

Devlin was sitting in the garage smoking a cigarette when Strangerson walked in unannounced. Strangerson took a cigarette box out of his jacket pocket. He was surprised to see Curtis fixing something under the bonnet. As if reading Strangerson's mind, Devlin explained, 'Mr Curtis has a genius for mechanical things.'

Strangerson raised his eyebrows but said nothing. Curtis looked up, 'Thank you Mr Devlin. I think you'll find everything in order now.'

71

'Thank you, Mr Curtis,' replied Devlin.

'Do you mind if I have a shufty at the Austin?'

'Of course, sir. Feel free,' said Devlin.

Curtis excused himself and left the Irishman and Strangerson together.

'I thought I detected an Irish accent earlier. Been over here long?' asked Strangerson.

'Long enough,' came the reply.

'This is a corking set of wheels. Must be a blast to drive.'

Devlin relaxed a little as the conversation dwelt on the car.

'She's handles a dream, there's no doubt about it. Would you like to get in?'

'I say, that's the ticket.' Strangerson hoped in and played at steering the wheel.

'Do you drive, sir?' asked Devlin.

'Yes, I learned before the War. I didn't have to do much over the last few years. It would be great to have a spin if the weather clears a bit. Not sure I fancy skating over the roads in a few tons of metal.'

Devlin laughed at the idea and reassured Strangerson, 'I'm sure Lord Cavendish wouldn't mind at all.'

The two men regarded the engine, with Strangerson asking questions about the engine. His next question surprised the Irishman, 'Does Lord Cavendish ever drive?'

'Yes, from time to time. Lady Mary also.'

'Lady Mary. Are such things really allowed? A lady driver? I say, we really are in the modern world. These Suffragettes have a lot to answer for. They'll be wanting to fly aeroplanes next or stand for Parliament. Where will it bally end?'

Devlin found himself taking a liking to the unusual guest. It was a rare occurrence for guests to spend any time talking to the staff. Lord Cavendish was friendly enough but his relationship with the lord was never anything other than formal. Lady Mary, on the other hand, was very informal and he admired her rebellious spirit. With her, he could let his guard down a little, but only so far. We all have our secrets, he thought.

You can't know mine.

-

Polly knelt down to put the last of the dishes into the cupboard. As she stood up, she had a momentary fright. In the doorway was Miller, smiling at her.

'Sorry, Polly, didn't mean to give you a fright.'

'Not a problem sir, sir.'

'Harry, no need to be so formal. We're all on the same side here, Polly.'

'Mr Miller, I would prefer if we kept it formal,' replied Polly. She motioned with her eyes towards Curtis who had just returned to the kitchen, no doubt, listening. Miller caught her meaning and nodded with a smile.

'Quite right Polly. We're here to work.'

Polly nodded her thanks. She turned and walked over to Curtis.

'Will there be anything more, Mr Curtis?'

'No. I think you should take a half hour to rest and then we'll begin to make ready for tonight's dinner, thank you.'

'Thank you, Mr Curtis.'

She walked out of the kitchen and headed towards the staff quarters. Curtis looked up from his newspaper at Miller.

'Mr Miller, I would appreciate it if you adopted a more appropriate mode of address with Polly.'

'What do you mean?'

'I think you know, Mr Miller.'

'I'm not sure what exactly this has to do with you.'

'Anything related to the staff at Cavendish Hall has something to do with me. Anyway, and this is friendly advice, I would advise you not to trifle with a young girl's emotions.'

He returned his gaze to the paper again but something in his tone had caught Miller's attention. Unlike his normal pious manner, this seemed a weary response from Curtis. Miller wondered what would have prompted such an unusually resigned reaction.

Unquestionably, this meant the subject was now closed. Whether Curtis was threatening him or if there was something else at play here was immaterial. The best thing to do would be to hold fire and scout the territory a little bit more. As he pondered this, Miss Buchan entered the kitchen in a flap.

'That Lady Emily has to be the most ill-bred, unpleasant women I have ever met!' stormed Miss Buchan. Miller remained quiet, but Curtis rose from his seat immediately to enquire what was wrong.

'She's with that idiot maid of hers and she was complaining about everything. If it isn't the food, it's the cleanliness of the rooms. I ask you, we spent hours cleaning her room specially. She goes out of her way to find fault. Horrible, horrible woman,' said Miss Buchan with real feeling.

Curtis raised his hands and cast his eyes towards Miller to indicate to Miss Buchan that she should be more circumspect in her comments.

'My apologies Mr Miller, it has been a difficult afternoon.'

'Quite understand Miss Buchan, say no more,' said Miller reassuringly.

'Thank you, Mr Miller,' replied Miss Buchan, 'But really, I could kill that woman sometimes.'

The door to the kitchen opened just at the moment Miss Buchan made this proposal.

-

Agnes left Lady Emily's room almost ready to weep. For the last twenty minutes all she'd heard was a litany of complaints. None were especially directed towards her, but the cumulative effect was depressing. Christmas at Cavendish Hall always seemed to bring out the worst in Lady Emily and this saddened Agnes greatly. There was another side to her few saw, and it pained Agnes when it seemed Lady Emily was

74

intent on feeding the prejudices of people who were unworthy of her.

Agnes had been with Lady Emily ever since she was a child. She had always been a headstrong girl. Unquestionably spoiled by her parents, she'd grown up to be wilful, self-centred, and volatile. Fortunately, she had met Robert. Her parents had been as delighted by her marriage to Robert as she was. For a few years, the better nature of Lady Emily took over because of the genuine love she had for her husband and the arrival of Henry.

Lady Emily and Agnes found out life is never so straightforward, however. Like the weather it has sunshine but also dark clouds. Then the storms come. A calm may follow but the damage it leaves can last a lifetime. Although Robert had sadly proved to be far from perfect as a husband, Agnes could see Lady Emily had never really recovered from his death.

Grief quickly turned to bitterness. This was increasingly directed towards Lord Cavendish and the two girls. Agnes found it difficult to comprehend how the Cavendish family could be so cold and unsupportive towards her. It was not just that they seemed uncaring about Lady Emily. Their coldness towards Henry was unfathomable. Could they not see he was turning inward? He was without friends, without a father figure and without family. How she hated them.

She descended the stairs in an angry mood. As she neared the kitchen, she heard Miss Buchan saying, 'I could kill that woman sometimes.'

Eyes ablaze, Agnes strode into the kitchen and faced Miss Buchan, 'How dare you say such a vile thing.'

Miss Buchan did not need Agnes to tell her that what she had said was abhorrent; she knew this herself. She'd over-stepped the mark and regret was immediate. However, just as she was about to apologize, Curtis intervened to bring patriarchal calm to a febrile atmosphere.

75

'Agnes, I am sure Miss Buchan did not mean…'

That Curtis failed was not a surprise. Sanctimony is a rarely used tool in diplomatic circles for a good reason. What caused wonder was the extent to which his intervention uncorked years of hostility and no small acerbity on the part of Agnes.

'I know exactly what she meant you pompous old fool,' snarled Agnes.

'Well really, there is no need to be so personal,' said Curtis, rather taken aback by the intensity of Agnes.

'Agnes, forgive me,' intervened Miss Buchan before matters descended further out of hand, 'I spoke out of turn. You are right. It was a vile thing to say. I was wrong and I apologise unreservedly.'

This succeeded in appeasing Agnes and might well have diffused an increasingly incendiary situation until Curtis's spluttering indignation took centre stage.

'This is intolerable! How dare you call me pompous!' he roared.

'You are pompous!' exclaimed Agnes. 'Don't think I haven't noticed the way you talk to me and the others here.'

Miller took a seat and made himself comfortable. This was becoming more enjoyable than an evening at the music hall. It was also, in his view, a mismatch. If he'd been able to place a wager, he would have put the house on Lady Emily's angry maid. She combined genuine grievance with a surprising knowledge of industrial language. By this stage Curtis was not getting a word in as the little maid let forth sally after sally on his demeanour, his lack of intelligence and unkindness. Miss Buchan felt it better to avoid getting into the line of fire by slowly withdrawing to allow Agnes a clear line of attack which she proceeded to engage in with gusto.

The battle was as one-sided as it was brief. It ended with a strategic withdrawal by Curtis. Observers later agreed that Agnes's devastating use of alliteration in describing Curtis as pompous, pretentious and a pantomime butler, cleverly weaving Christmas into her bloody narrative, left the poor servant emotionally battered and bruised.

Curtis stalked from the kitchen harrumphing about manners and breeding. Whatever Agnes may be, thought, Miller, she's no idiot. It had been a clinical dissection of Curtis. What was particularly impressive about Agnes was that she at no point raised her voice. There was a lot of pent-up anger against Curtis and the family. He wondered if this was the case with Lady Emily. Probably, he thought.

-

Curtis made straight for Lord Cavendish to relay all that had taken place. His objective was for Cavendish to make a formal complaint to Lady Emily. There was no thought to how this would put Cavendish in a difficult position in a relationship that was, itself, quite fragile.

Cavendish sought to manage the expectations of Curtis. However, at the same time, he realized this could present problems. He was sympathetic to Curtis, but only up to a point. Curtis had an inflated sense of his own dignity which Cavendish had noted over the years but chosen to ignore. Then again, he felt a duty of care to the man. It was not an easy situation, especially with Lady Emily, of all people.

'I understand your concern, Curtis. I shall convey my desire to Lady Emily that Agnes should act professionally and with courtesy to you and the rest of the staff at all times.'

'Thank you, sir. I'm sorry to have to bring this to your attention but if we are to manage over this festive period, we must all work together in an atmosphere of mutual respect.'

'I understand, Curtis. Is there anything else?'

Curtis understood this to mean the interview was finished. The curt ending to the interview meant he left the library suspecting, unhappily, no action would be taken. It did not feel as if Lord Cavendish had taken his concerns with the gravity they merited. On the whole, it was an unsatisfactory response

77

for someone who had been in service to the family for over thirty years. He deserved better than half-hearted reassurance. He returned to the kitchen in a foul mood.

Cavendish was astute enough to realize that Curtis was not entirely happy with the outcome of the interview. This was also a source of dissatisfaction to him. Although Curtis was staff, he'd been with the family a long time. Perhaps he deserved better but, as usual, something in the manner of Curtis had created an unnecessary dispute. Cavendish resolved to find a way of making amends with him. However, Curtis would have to accept that taking this up with Lady Emily directly would create a much bigger problem than a staff dispute.

He walked over to window. The snow had stopped but he knew instinctively there would be more to come on this subject. It was dark now and the snow gave a purple glow against the blackness of the trees. A dusting of stars peered out in a very clear sky. Just looking at the scene made Cavendish feel a chill but oddly comforted at the same time.

Walking back around to his desk, he glanced at the picture on the wall between the two bay windows. It displayed a photograph of Robert's battalion. It was very wide as there were over three hundred soldiers arranged in four rows. Robert was sitting at the front, in the middle along with the other officers. One soldier, seated at the front near the end, attracted his attention. His hat was on sideways. How odd, thought Cavendish. He hadn't noticed this man before. Reaching into his pocket he pulled out a pair of spectacles and put them on. He peered at the soldier in question.

'Good Lord.' said Cavendish out loud, 'I can't believe it.'

Chapter 8

Agnes updated Lady Emily on what had taken place in the kitchen. Having related the tale in forensic detail, Agnes folded her arms and said with a voice pitched somewhere between smugness and self-righteousness, 'He'll think twice about acting like he's the almighty again, in front of me.'

'Good for you, Agnes,' confided Lady Emily, although there was a little less enthusiasm than Agnes would have liked. How easy it is to forget. Perhaps she felt sorry for the fool. Then Lady Emily added, 'I will have to say something to Lord Cavendish. I want him to understand that you and Godfrey must be treated with respect.'

'Thank you, ma'am.'

'You may go now. Leave this with me.'

Agnes left the room and Emily went to the window. She looked out and considered how best to leverage what she'd heard. The beauty of the wintry scene outside made no impression on her. She was entirely focused on how to make Cavendish understand the level to which he and his staff were making them all feel unwelcome. That it was Curtis was no surprise. He had an exaggerated sense of his own importance. However, this troubled her, too. She felt a pain that had lain dormant for a number of years.

She spun around and left the room. There was a determination on her face that the sins of the past should not continue to betray the present. Descending the stairs rapidly, she walked through the hall to the library and entered without knocking. She saw Cavendish sitting at his desk holding a wide framed picture, studying it closely. Cavendish looked up from the picture and stood up immediately.

'Emily, I'm so glad you're here, I wanted to have a word with you.'

'And I you,' said Lady Emily quietly.

This doesn't augur well, thought Cavendish, his heart sinking fast. She did not look to be in a mood to reason. He decided to absorb the enemy attack. Hopefully her ammunition would run out after a few bursts rather than be a sustained artillery bombardment. His silence might act to quicken the engagement.

'That pompous idiot, Curtis, has upset Agnes, I demand he apologize immediately to her.'

Before Cavendish could reply, she continued in a similar vein, 'It's unacceptable. His treatment of her has been rude beyond belief. How dare he. This is a very poor show. I've already had words with Buchan about the state of my room. Curtis clearly has little or no control over your staff and he has the unmitigated gall to criticize Agnes, and in front of the other staff. I hope you can see that this is completely unacceptable.'

Thinking this signalled the end of Lady Emily's offensive, Cavendish made another attempt to sue for peace. Sadly, Lady Emily was just warming to the task. The heavy armaments were about to be brought into the action. Tears formed in Lady Emily's eyes. Cavendish accepted he had no defence against this type of weaponry. Defeat was not just inevitable; it would be complete with many casualties.

'You're all against us. It's not just Curtis. You've never made us feel welcome. You never wanted Robert to marry me and now he's gone, you and those girls isolate Henry and myself. He is your grandson, but you spend no time with him.'

Chance would be a fine thing, though Cavendish, but he decided not to throw this point out for consideration as it risked increasing the intensity of an already formidable frontal assault.

'He is the future Lord Cavendish. Yet you ignore him and devote all your time to the two girls. It's not fair. More than that, it is thoughtless and unkind. What have we done to deserve this? I am a widow. Your son's widow. You have given me no help, no consideration, no kindness. Nothing. Do you even think of us as family? Really, do you?'

Cavendish lowered his voice, aware the staff could be listening, 'Emily, please hear me out'

-

Outside the library, Miss Buchan had heard every word from Lady Emily. In fact, her ear had been pressed closely against the door. Sadly, she could not hear what Cavendish was now saying in reply. The appearance of Strangerson forced her to give the pretend to be putting things in order. She nodded to Strangerson as he walked past and up the stairs. 'Will you be needing anything sir?'

'No thank you Miss...er'

'Buchan.'

'No, I shall rest and get ready for dinner.' He continued up the stairs bounding two at a time.

Miss Buchan scurried down to the kitchen to update Curtis. She found him with Godfrey having a cup to tea.

'When you've had your cup of tea Mr Curtis, perhaps you could join me in your office.'

'Yes Miss Buchan.' Curtis immediately understood an important piece of intelligence was to be communicated. He quickly drained his tea and smiled to Godfrey, 'Duty calls.'

Miss Buchan was sitting by the small desk Curtis used for administrative tasks.

'Close the door please, Mr Curtis. I've accidentally overheard an interesting encounter in the library.'

Curtis doubted there was anything accidental about it, but he remained silent. It wasn't as if he had been above a touch of eavesdropping himself.

'Go on Miss Buchan, I'm all ears.'

Miss Buchan quickly related, word for word, all she had heard in a low voice. She concluded, 'I fear we are in a difficult situation whenever Lord Cavendish, and God forgive me for saying this, passes on.'

'Clearly Miss Buchan. This is troubling. I fear you're right. We may well have reached a point of no return with that witch.'

'She is a witch Mr Curtis and no mistake. How I would dearly love that…' She stopped herself saying anything more. Curtis nodded in agreement, he understood exactly Miss Buchan's sentiment. However, wishing was one thing but they were clearly facing a long-term problem.

'This is, indeed, serious.'

Lord Cavendish was not as well as he proclaimed. In fact, Curtis knew his heart had recently been giving enough trouble to warrant a trip to his doctor in Harley Street. Cavendish had requested that Curtis keep the trip to London confidential although he certainly had not shared with him the reason for going. A week later, Curtis had managed to read the notes from the examination when it had arrived in the post. He had been inducted into the art of steam-opening envelopes by his predecessor many years ago.

All of this had taken place in the last month. Curtis had not shared the information with Miss Buchan at the time. Now, it was clear that two heads were needed to address this very real conundrum. He took Miss Buchan into his confidence.

A few minutes later both returned to the kitchen. Godfrey and Agnes were both in the kitchen. Curtis recognized this would be a good opportunity to start building bridges.

'Agnes, I would like to take this opportunity to apologize to you for any misunderstanding earlier.'

He bowed slightly and gently clicked his heels, believing it might add a nice touch to the sentiment expressed. Having to do this sickened him enormously but the alternative was worse. Christmas was a taxing enough time for the staff without the added complication of trench warfare.

Agnes was taken aback by the surprising turn of events. She had been mentally preparing herself for a more attritional atmosphere in the staff quarters. This was a development she had not anticipated and, in the absence of an alternative strategy, decided there was no other choice but to accept the apology. She managed this with just enough feminine sense of hurt and injustice to ensure Curtis would have to maintain an air of sycophancy a little longer. It did not stop her feeling somewhat disappointed at such a quick a victory.

Miller had entered just as Curtis was displaying contrition. He raised an eyebrow at Godfrey who gave a hint of shrug to his shoulders. It was fairly clear there had been a resolution to the disagreement between Curtis and Agnes. He looked forward to hearing more. Perhaps he could quiz Polly about it later. A little bit of gossip and then, thought Miller, a chance to get to know her a bit better. Christmas was shaping up nicely.

Within a few minutes Polly returned to the kitchen with Elsie.

'Right, I want the kitchen cleared. Polly and I have work to do. Miss Agnes, can I ask for some help? I seem to remember you are a dab hand at desserts.'

'Of course,' said Agnes, always a pushover for a compliment. The next comment from Elsie, pleased her even more.

'Excellent, can the rest of you useless oafs, leave us now? Let's get to work girls, we have a dinner to make.'

The peremptory manner of Elsie was something Curtis was used to. It was as unwelcome as ever. Even more so given they

83

were in company. However, there was little value in having a second defeat inflicted on him by a female in the space of an hour. He beat a strategic retreat to his office.

Godfrey and Miller walked out together into the corridor.

'Have I missed something?' asked Miller with a smile.

'From what I heard old Curtis had something of an earful from Agnes. When Lady Emily heard about what happened, she went down to old Cavendish and gave him a bit of verbal,' said Godfrey.

Miller grinned at Godfrey, 'I could be wrong, but I suspect you wouldn't want to get on the wrong side of a certain lady.'

This was met with a grimace. 'You wouldn't, trust me. Tongue like a knife dipped in venom, that one.'

'Have you ever been on the wrong side of her?' asked Miller.

'No, she usually gets Agnes to wield the knife.'

'What about Henry?' probed Miller.

'He doesn't say much. Anything he does say to me is usually curt. I don't think the words "please" or "thank you" exist for him. He used to be a nice lad. You know how it is. He's at that funny stage.'

Miller grinned and nodded. They all went through similar. Thankfully, immaturity was a condition usually cured by age.

'Sounds like a charmer.'

'Honestly, out of the two of them, I would be more worried by him. I get the feeling he would think nothing of stabbing you in the front, and then stepping over your dead body to read a book.'

They parted at this point with Miller going upstairs to see Kit. He walked past the Christmas tree in the corridor and up to Kit's bedroom. A quick rap on the door was greeted by a voice inside.

'Come in,' said Kit.

Miller popped his head around the door, 'Just wanted to see if you needed anything sir?'

Kit was sitting at the desk writing a letter. He turned around and said, 'No thank you Harry. Oh wait, I don't suppose you have any idea what was going on downstairs between Lady Emily and Cavendish. I sense an atmosphere in the house which is none too pleasant.'

Miller reported all he knew before leaving Kit to his thoughts. His mind was chiefly given over to Esther and Mary. Conversations with mutual friends in London had prepared him to meet two beautiful women. In reality they were everything his friends had described and more. It was revelatory the depth of their friendship, the liveliness of their minds and, in Mary's case, a deeply independent nature.

The spirit of the two sisters brought to mind another. His mind wandered back to the War and his stay in the hospital. Thinking of her and this period always brought a bittersweet pain. He reluctantly dismissed the memory and returned to the task in hand.

Finishing the letter, he sealed the envelope to Alexander Kerensky. It was too late to send before Christmas, but he decided he would post when they all went to tomorrow morning's service in the village.

As there was still time to kill before dinner, he decided to go downstairs. Taking a deep breath, he walked into the library. If he tried to avoid the room altogether it would become obvious to his companions. Furthermore, he hated to be in a funk about anything. The only way to deal with how he felt was to confront it directly rather than cower in his room hoping no one would notice.

Much to Kit's relief, the library was empty. He strode over to the Lavery portrait of John and Robert. Forcing himself to study the picture, he stared at the young Robert. He had his arm draped lazily around the more serious John. They had the Cavendish nose, but both were fine looking young men. Kit looked into Robert's face. His eyes stung as tears clouded his view of the painting.

85

'Sorry,' he whispered and glanced around lest anyone had heard.

Finally, he looked away and walked over to the window. Outside, the night was lit only by the luminosity of the snow. He noticed a framed black and white photograph lying on the desk. Curiosity piqued, he walked over and picked it up. The picture was at least two feet wide and showed an army battalion sitting down in four rows. The name of the battalion was engraved at the front along with the date in 1914. They were obviously being photographed prior to their departure for France. He recognized Robert in the middle. The chance to examine it more closely was interrupted by the door opening. Turning around, he saw Strangerson peeking into the room. He looked surprised to see Kit.

'Sorry, old boy, I didn't mean to disturb you,' said Strangerson.

'You weren't. I was just going to have a nose through the library. It's pretty impressive.' Kit stood up and put the picture back on the desk.

'It is rather.' Strangerson wandered over to a decanter sitting on a trolley with some glasses. He raised a glass up to Kit, 'Fancy a bracer?'

'No thanks, I shall save myself for later. Don't let me stop you, though.'

'Well, under the circs, I'll make a start. Might need some courage for the evening. I gather there was a firefight earlier between Lady Emily and the Colonel. Not sure the old boy didn't get a bit of a drubbing,' said Strangerson.

'Really?'

'Yes, I heard it as I was coming in. The old boy was on the wrong end of a dressing down. I'll bet he hasn't had one like that since he was a private.'

'Any idea why?' prompted Kit.

'Not entirely sure. I think she missed her calling as a lion tamer that one. Anyway, she was in an impressive state of moral indignation from what I could hear. Poor fish had to stand there and take it on the chin. When the lady folk are like that it's best to exit stage left pretty sharpish.'

Kit laughed. Strangerson added a few more ribald comments about Lady Emily sotto voce, which amused Kit. Strangerson diplomatically avoided commenting on the girls possibly sensing there was some degree of attraction with Kit. Instead, he moved on to talk a little of his time with Shackleton. Kit was fascinated as he was a great admirer of the famed Antarctic explorer.

The conversation ended a few minutes later and turned to Strangerson's plans for the future. The erstwhile explorer expressed a desire to go to the Pacific Islands to write about the indigenous people there. Many of them had not seen Europeans. This subject was equally interesting to Kit and the time passed easily until Strangerson drained the last of the Scotch and said, 'You should've had a dram, very good stuff indeed. I'll say this for the old boy, he keeps a good cellar.'

'I'll take some later no doubt,' laughed Kit.

Strangerson stood up and left the library to get ready for the dinner. After he had left, Kit pondered a little on Strangerson. He sensed Strangerson had not expected him to be there. In fact, there was a hint of irritation, but it had been hidden beneath his well-practiced bonhomie. If it were the case that Strangerson had wanted to be alone in the library, Kit wondered why. Almost by instinct he found himself surveying the library. It could be anything in here, he concluded. There must have been at least a thousand books, various objets d'art and, of course the paintings. He then laughed at himself for feeling suspicious. Looking at his pocket watch, he saw it was nearly seven. Just enough time to get ready.

'It's Christmas, old boy. You're off duty. Time to enjoy yourself,' he said out loud. With one last look at the paintings, he left the library and returned to his room.

As he arrived, he caught sight of a lone figure walking through the snow from the back. It was hard to tell but it could have been Cavendish. The figure seemed to be heading towards the cottage he and Miller had seen earlier. Probably just a Christmas visit, he thought, and turned away from the window.

Chapter 9

All of the guests sat at the long dining table which had been elaborately laid with candles, cutlery as well as flowers and scattered holly leaves. There were also little reindeer and snowmen at each place. Strangerson rolled his eyes when he spied them, but Kit picked one up, brow-furrowed before breaking out into a smile. The room was lit by the warm glow of candlelight; silver cutlery glistened like jewels on either side of white porcelain plates.

Cavendish sat at the head of the table with his granddaughters either side of him. The gentlemen sat in the middle with Lady Emily at the opposite end of the table from Cavendish. The atmosphere was more relaxed than Kit had expected. The good humour of Strangerson, the vivacity of the sisters as well as the apparent ceasefire between Lady Emily and Cavendish created a happy feeling in the group that even the glum features of Henry could do little to dispel.

Kit took a look at the printed menu card. There would be seven courses. This struck Kit as somewhat excessive. Not all of them appealed either. Oysters were definitely something he regarded with suspicion. Evidently so did the girls, who made faces when they appeared, but Cavendish and Strangerson enjoyed them immensely. Curtis put on a great show of serving an excellent Bouillon. This was followed by salmon freshly caught that day, then quail with truffles. All of the meals were superb. Kit resolved to pay his compliments to Elsie.

Three dessert courses followed consisting of crackers with cheese, Nesselrode pudding and, finally, fruit with coffee. By the end, Kit was rather full despite his best efforts to avoid over-indulging. Throughout the meal, Curtis had ensured all of the wine glasses were constantly topped up although Kit observed all the ladies drank sparingly and Henry did not drink wine at all.

The gentlemen were determined not to be so temperate, and the atmosphere was convivial. Lady Emily maintained her good behaviour and chatted amiably to Strangerson. It was clear from occasional overheard snatches of conversation that Strangerson was telling her about his time with Robert. Naturally, he painted a very positive portrait of a brave officer loved by his men. Lady Emily was delighted to hear such a good opinion of her dead husband. Henry listened intently, said little and offered no hint of what he was thinking.

Once the coffees were finished the group stood up, whereupon Mary said, 'I hope we are not going to be so old-fashioned as to have the gentlemen retire for their brandy and ever so serious conversation about the state of world.'

'Indeed,' agreed Esther, 'I think the men should join the ladies for conversation about clothes, hairstyles and puppies.'

'Hats. Let's not forget hats Essie,' said Mary in a mock shrill voice and gesticulating with her index finger. 'We need to understand what's being worn in Paris this season. It simply won't do not to know.'

'We must know, Mary, otherwise how can we possibly be seen in public?' agreed Esther.

Cavendish put his arms up in the air to indicate surrender. 'An old soldier knows when it's time to make a tactical retreat. As it looks like the ladies are not going to permit us to escape to our brandy and cigars, I propose we go into the drawing room instead.'

'Hear, hear,' said Strangerson.

They all moved to the drawing room except Lady Emily who decided to retire early. This was the first time Kit had been in the drawing room and he liked it on first sight. A welcoming fire greeted all, and Curtis had laid out several glasses along with a full decanter of a fine brandy. Strangerson looked at it appreciatively as Cavendish lifted it and offered to pour the drinks

The room was large and was decorated with many fine paintings including, if Kit was not mistaken, a Gainsborough.

'I say, what a beautiful piano,' said Strangerson upon seeing the grand piano in the corner of the room. 'May I ask who plays?'

'Do you play Mr Strangerson?' asked Mary teasingly.

'Not a note, I'm afraid. Matched by my singing, really,' admitted Strangerson, untruthfully, but to everyone's amusement. Even Henry managed a smile. Kit looked towards Esther and Mary and raised an eyebrow.

In answer to this unasked query, Mary said, 'Well, I can tell you Essie plays beautifully, and her voice is angelic. Isn't it true, grandpapa?'

'Nonsense, Mary,' interrupted Esther turning red.

'It's true, gentlemen. Esther plays as beautifully as she sings,' confirmed Cavendish.

'Then I'm afraid, Esther, you are out voted.' said Kit.

'Hmmm, as usual, a woman is disenfranchised by the men,' observed Mary.

'You're right Mary,' agreed Kit. 'How would you vote if you had the franchise?'

'I vote Essie should play,' said Mary, turning to her sister with a grin.

'Whose side are you on darling sister?' laughed Esther but she duly sat at the piano as the rest of the party surrounded her. This brought a round of applause and a "Brava" from Strangerson.

91

'Well, I think a Christmas carol would be appropriate,' said Esther and she began to caress the ivory keys. Her voice was as angelic as Mary had promised. Kit was entranced.

In the bleak mid-winter
Frosty wind made moan;
Earth stood hard as iron,
Water like a stone.

The sombre melody and the singing captured the melancholy that hung in the air of Cavendish Hall. Kit also felt he could be carried away by the emotion and gripped his seat tightly to retain control. By the end of the carol, Mary had joined her. The effect of the combined voices was intoxicating. Mary's voice was exquisite but she let Esther lead and sang harmony except on keynotes when their voices soared in unison and became one. At the end of the hymn the performance drew rapturous acclaim from all. Esther broke into an embarrassed smile as Mary hugged her.

'I much prefer the Holst version also,' said Kit, before adding, 'Beautiful.' It was not clear if he was only referring to the singing. This brought a glance from Mary and a satisfied smile from Cavendish.

For the next half hour, the two girls played a selection of Christmas hymns and managed to rope Kit in to sing on a couple. He had a fine tenor and had clearly sung before, but not in Kings College, he added. With the end of the music, the party sat down on the two large sofas facing one another in the middle of the room.

'What shall we do now?' asked Esther.

'Well, I'm doing rather well with this brandy,' interjected Strangerson, causing a ripple of laughter.

'It's an Armagnac, 1870 I think, if you're interested,' replied Cavendish. 'Anyway, I think I have an idea for what we can do next, and it involves, you, Mary.'

All eyes turned to Mary. She rolled her eyes at what Cavendish was about to say. Esther clapped her hands delightedly, 'Great idea, grandpapa, we haven't done this in ages.'

'Well, we're all fascinated,' said Kit gazing into the eyes of Mary. In response, Mary narrowed her eyes seemingly to declare war which made Kit smile even more.

-

In the kitchen, a fragile peace existed as the staff enjoyed their dinner. Miller complimented Elsie on a wonderful meal and was seconded by Godfrey. Elsie beamed with pride and thanked everyone. It would be fair to say she had been beaming for most of the last hour. This was the inevitable consequence of her natural disposition towards sociability, aided and abetted by a fair quantity of wine then brandy. Curtis guessed another five minutes would see her sleeping head-first on the table. He glanced meaningfully at Miss Buchan who had also read the signs.

'Elsie and Polly, I think we should, perhaps, retire. Leave the gentlemen to their festivities. It will be a long day tomorrow,' said Miss Buchan.

Polly looked like she was about to object but a stern look from Miss Buchan dissuaded her from saying anything. However, she hoped her face communicated enough of the protest she felt. Rising up with a sigh she stropped over to Miss Buchan in order to help Elsie up from the chair and to her room. Curtis smiled benignly at Miss Buchan to acknowledge his foresight.

As a manservant treading a line between nobility on one side and domestic staff on the other, Miller had ample opportunity, which he rarely refused, to make sport of the people he encountered. Often these people would be blissfully unaware of what he was doing. With a wink towards Devlin and Godfrey he said, 'Very sensible move, Mr Curtis. I could see Elsie was perhaps over-indulging.'

'Quite so,' said Curtis with just the hint of a slur. 'I believe I have a duty of care towards the staff and must protect them; sometimes from themselves.'

'Your actions do you credit Mr Curtis,' continued Miller.

'Thank you, Mr Miller. Of course, I seek no credit, nor expect it. It's all part of the job,' he finished modestly, waving his hand airily.

Devlin, by this stage, was struggling to contain his laughter and excused himself under the guise of a coughing fit. He went outside. Miller took this as his cue to bring an end to his mischief. He also excused himself and joined Devlin outside.

'Hope you don't mind all that, just a bit of fun,' said Miller.

'No, I enjoyed it. Needs taking down a peg or two sometimes,' replied Devlin.

'Gets above himself then?' suggested Miller.

Devlin offered Miller a cigarette, 'He does with us. Not with the Cavendish family, though. He knows better.' He struck a match and lit both their cigarettes, then continued, 'If anything ever happened to Lord Cavendish, I wouldn't be sorry to see Curtis out on his ear.'

'Doesn't seem to be any love lost with Lady Emily and company.'

'None, that's for sure, I think there's a lot of history there though, so who knows? Not sure about the rest of us. I think we'd be all right, one thing or another.'

The night had a chill. Both could feel their skin freezing. They quickly finished their cigarettes and stuffed their hands in their pockets. Miller looked up at the moon. It shone clearly in the cloudless night sky. Snowflakes fell quietly onto his upturned face. They melted on his skin creating the impression of tears trickling down his cheek. He went back inside.

-

Mary smiled at the party then glanced at her grandfather who seemed to be enjoying the suspense he had created.

'I believe that my troublemaking grandfather is suggesting I tell you a ghost story.'

This brought laughter from Cavendish, excited clapping from Esther and a warm smile from Kit, who folded his arms and settled back into his seat. 'Comfortable my lord?' she asked archly.

Kit laughed and said he was very comfortable and looking forward to the tale while Strangerson added to the pressure on Mary by concluding that it was a capital idea. He, too, looked on expectantly.

Mary made a face towards Esther, who merely shrugged then grinned.

'I must add that I do this under mild duress. It's been a while since I've told one of these. I'm somewhat out of practice.'

'Objection noted,' said Esther without sympathy, 'Please proceed.'

Mary rolled her eyes once more. Although clearly reluctant, she began her tale.

'This story is entitled,' she paused for dramatic effect, but also to think up a suitably macabre title, '*The Curse of Cavendish Hall.*'

Chapter 10

The Curse of Cavendish Hall – A Ghost Story

It was, as far I can ascertain, Christmas Eve in the year of our Lord 1810. On a night such as this, a wintry wind blew, and snow fell heavily leaving all of the Lincolnshire countryside draped in white. It was so cold nobody from the village of Little Gloston dared show their face outside lest they suffer a very real danger of frostbite.

On this night, an old man, a tramp for over half his life, walked along the trail leading towards the village. Lights were visible not half a mile away. He trudged with difficulty through the thick snow. His feet were cold and wet; ill-protected by the old boots that had seen better days.

The intense cold burned through his meagre clothing and made tenancy in his bones. Worse was his hunger. It made him weak and ensured progress to the village was slow. Without access to heat and some food, he knew he was in serious risk of dying. This was no weather for a man, such as he, of over three score and ten years.

On and on, he trekked stumbling often. Each time he dragged himself up, it sapped a little bit more of his spirit. But give in he would not. With the last of his strength, he made it to the village.

Little Gloston has barely changed in the last two hundred years. Then, as now, it comprised no more than a dozen or two small dwellings, a public house, a village post office, and store. This is what the man encountered as he entered the village. He made his way to the public house praying it was open.

It was not. The doors were locked and, looking inside the front window, there was only darkness. Perchance he perceived a light in the village store. The door was locked but he knocked. For a few minutes he rapped at the door until he heard the noise of a man with keys grumbling on the other side, 'Who is it?'

'A traveller, please, help me.'

'What are you doing out on a night like this?'

The traveller was too tired to answer. Unable to stand any longer he collapsed against the door. However, his spirit rose as he heard the sound of the keys in the door. It opened whereupon he was met by the aggravated appearance of the shopkeeper Isaac Nettlestone.

'What do you think you're about then?' said the shopkeeper gruffly.

'I'm sorry sir. I'm lost and desperately in need of some hot food and a place to sleep. Could I trouble you for a little food?' said the old man.

Nettlestone was a crotchety man just past fifty years. However, he was not a bad sort and took pity on the plight of the old stranger. Helping him up, he brought him inside and gave him a seat.

'Wait here,' said Nettlestone. 'Mrs Nettlestone, we have a visitor.'

'A what?'

'You heard me Mrs Nettlestone. A visitor. Don't ask me what he's doing out on this night.'

Mrs Becky Nettlestone arrived to take charge of the situation. She was a formidable lady. Short but plump, she

97

contrasted with the tall, lean figure of her husband. She looked at the stranger and then at her husband. Nothing on her face suggested the sight of either of them gave her any pleasure.

'So, what do you want me to do?' she asked both.

'A little food madam, and I'll be on my way.'

'Where?' asked Mrs Nettlestone.

'Can you recommend anywhere I can stay? I have no money.'

'Well, there isn't any room at the inn, that's for sure,' laughed Nettlestone. 'Where do you think he could go, Mrs Nettlestone?'

'I'm sure I don't know, but we have no room here,' she emphasized, before leaving the front of the shop and going into the back. 'I'll bring you hot soup in a moment.'

Nettlestone raised his eyes in the universal way men do when they want to indicate how the distaff side has neither sense nor rationality when clearly the opposite is true.

'You're very kind,' said the man. 'I can never repay your kindness…'

'I know, but let's put our minds to where you can stay.' He eyed the stranger's attire. Clearly, he was at risk from exposure. A thought occurred to him. He had an old coat he had thought to throw away. It was not without holes, but it looked distinctly warmer than what the stranger was wearing. It would serve to be worn over the other coat allowing an extra layer of protection. He went to retrieve the coat from a wardrobe.

When he returned, the stranger was greedily partaking of a bowl of steaming soup. Liquid clung to his beard. It was clear he had not eaten ere a long time. He consumed the soup in a matter of seconds, wiped his mouth with his sleeve, began to offer thanks to Nettlestone and then to his wife. Nettlestone waved him away, graciously.

'So, do we have a solution to this problem?' asked Mrs Nettlestone, trying, unsuccessfully, to hide the edge in her voice. Her foolish husband needed to understand something that was quite plain to her: the old man was unwelcome, had chosen the life he led and needed to be on his way.

'What about the old stable at Cavendish Hall?' suggested Nettlestone, slapping the table as he was wont to do when Mother Nature gifted him one of his, all-too-rare, good ideas. 'It's hardly a quarter of a mile up the road. Best of all, it will shelter him from the snow, and it has plenty of hay to keep him warm.'

'Mr Nettlestone!' exclaimed his wife, 'You have arrived at an excellent solution.'

Her face beamed with delight, or was it relief? Excellent because it took away the problem of the stranger, thought Nettlestone, but he remained silent. The old man stood up and tried on the coat. It fitted snugly over his other coat. Nettlestone had also managed to find a hat. With expressions of gratitude from the old man, the couple waved him goodbye, wishing him a happy Christmas, with no sense of irony.

The old man felt refreshed, warmer if not quite full following his repast. He set off in the direction they had suggested. He tramped through the snow towards a large wooden building, a few hundred yards ahead. It had stopped snowing and the wind had dropped. However, it remained bitterly cold. There were no windows in the stable; protection against the cold would be a limited affair. As he neared the building, he could see, with some relief, there was a lot of straw. This would offer some protection and he gave thanks to the Almighty for this small mercy.

A few minutes later he spied, further ahead, Cavendish Hall. In the purple gloom he could make out the large silhouette against the sky and the luminosity of the snow. All of a sudden, he detected a light in a downstairs window. A part of him was surprised but he could not explain why.

Reinvigorated by the temporary stop with Nettlestone, he resolved to continue his progress up to the Hall with the intention of going to the back door and attracting the attention of the domestic staff. They might be able to find a warmer situation for him than the stable. Perhaps, dare he hope, there might even a bed in the staff's quarters. They may even find some food. His mouth watered at the prospect.

He turned and began to walk towards the large house. The wind rose and blew into his face. It was as if it was trying to prevent him reaching his destination. The cold had made it icy underfoot. At one point he fell. There was a stab of pain in his leg so strong it caused him to pass out.

How long he had been unconscious he knew not. Ahead the light was still on in the house. It seemed to sparkle. Rising with great care, he hobbled the last hundred yards; each step caused renewed pain in his leg. As he picked his way carefully towards the house, there was hardly a sound apart from his footsteps crunching through the snow. It seemed deserted, but his eyes had not deceived him; there was a light at the window. He crept up to the window and peered in. It looked like a drawing room. A fire burned, and two candles added additional light. Just as he was about to set off for the back of the house, he heard a door open.

Glancing to his left, he could see the front door was ajar. He was uncertain what to do. There was no one there. This was strange. He frowned and looked more closely. There was no mistake. Who could have opened it? Should he climb up the steps and attempt to attract someone's attention? He did not want to wake the household for fear of angering the inhabitants. Also, he did not want to be mistaken for a burglar. A life spent on the open roads meant he was used to sleeping in farm buildings, but he had never broken into a house.

A sudden gust of wind chilled him to the bone. The cold air seemed to find every hole in his clothing and attack his skin. This made him decided upon his course of action. He walked up the front steps and peeked his head through the door. The hallway was empty. Someone had to have opened the door

100

because he had noted it was shut on his approach. Peeking his head through the door, he called out, 'Hullo? Is someone there?'

No one answered.

The wind seemed to grow in intensity, as if it was forcing him inside. There seemed no choice, he hobbled into the hallway. As he did so the door shut behind him with a loud bang. He spun around and tried to open the door.

It was locked.

'Who are you?' said a frail, high-pitched male voice behind him.

The old man gave a half cry in terror and twirled around to find an old man, like himself, standing not two feet away from him, holding a candle. He recoiled in terror. The old man was very thin, almost like a skeleton. He could have been one hundred years old. His skin was a deathly pallor and drawn taught over his face. In the candlelight, his face seemed like a skull.

'I'm sorry sir, I saw the door was open. I was hoping to speak to the staff,' explained the stranger, perhaps shivering from something more than just exposure to the cold.

'I see,' said the old man. 'There is no staff here anymore. Just me.' The old man offered no introduction or explanation of the peculiar state of affairs. Instead, he stood staring at the stranger who had entered his home uninvited.

'I'm sorry, it was so cold, I wanted permission to lie down somewhere. Just for tonight,' added the stranger by way of explanation.

The old man of the house regarded him for a moment and then said, 'Follow me.'

He did as he was bid, and they entered into the drawing room. 'Sit down,' said the host. Without any further words, the old man then left him alone.

His seat was in front of the fire. Flickering shadows were cast by the fire burning in the hearth. The old man looked at the shadows when all of a sudden, he saw the shadow of a human figure rise up larger and larger. When he turned around, he saw that no one else was in the room. He gasped moments later as he looked at a table just behind him. On it was a glass with brandy and some cold meat. It had not been there when he had come into the room, of this he was certain.

Hungrily, he ate the meat and drank the brandy. All at once he felt warm from the inside. A newspaper lay nearby. He picked it up. It was nearly two years old and had a light coating of dust. It was too difficult to read but, in any event, he was beginning to feel drowsy. The sound of cries could be heard in the night. Perhaps it was an animal or perhaps the wind. He slept more soundly than he had ever before.

-

The next morning, Mr Nettlestone was at the front of the shop watching the villagers make their way to the church service. It was Christmas Day and trade had been good. They would soon shut and settle down to enjoy a Christmas dinner. Mrs Nettlestone had already begun to prepare a veritable banquet, or so he joked with her. She did this every year without fail. How Nettlestone laughed.

As he was about to go inside again, he saw the old stranger shuffling into the village. He waved to the old man, 'Sir? Sir? How are you this Christmas morn? You are limping.'

'Indeed, I tripped on my way to the shelter you recommended and hurt my leg, but I can still manage as you see,' responded the old man.

'Did you find the shelter?' asked Nettlestone.

'Indeed, I did good sir, but not the one you recommended.'

'Really you must tell me.'

The old man limped up to Nettlestone and joined him at the door of the shop. Mrs Nettlestone, having heard her husband in conversation, came out to see what was happening.

'Look who it is Mrs Nettlestone. 'Tis the gentleman from last night. He was just telling me that he found a place to stay.'

102

Mrs Nettlestone did not appear very pleased at seeing the stranger again. She was fearful that her weak fool of a husband might invite him for Christmas dinner. Looking around the shop, she could not find anything she could throw at him to attract his attention. She walked to his side in order to head off any unnecessary Christmas kindness from Mr Nettlestone. The old man began to speak.

'Yes, I went towards the stable as you had instructed me. However, I spied a light on in the big manor house.'

Both Nettlestone's looked at one another in astonishment but remained silent as the old man continued, oblivious to the reaction of the couple, 'I thought that it may be possible to ask the domestic staff for a warmer situation. The worst that could happen is they would say no.'

The old man proceeded to relate all that had happened. The next morning, sitting by his chair was a glass of milk, biscuits, and more cold meat. Thus, he had breakfasted well. However, when he went to search for someone to thank, he found the house empty. Of course, he had not gone upstairs for fear of disturbing the family. Instead, he had left the house from the back door and made his way back to the village.

Neither Nettlestone wished to continue the encounter and quickly bade the stranger a Merry Christmas and sent him on his way. If the old man had been more observant, he would have detected a look of fear in their eyes.

'How can this be Mr Nettlestone? Cavendish Hall has been unoccupied this last two years since his lordship died and the young lord went to fight Napoleon. Who did he meet?'

'I do not wish to think about who it might have been, Mrs Nettlestone. Some things are beyond our reckoning.'

'I'm scared Mr Nettlestone.'

'Hush now Becky. Let's go inside.'

As they turned to go inside, they heard a noise in the street. Nettlestone went to the door and saw Barney Brocklehurst, the coffin maker, riding his cart into town. The air was cold, and it

103

looked like snow was imminent. Barney had a blanket draped over his back and a hat covered his head. Examining the back of the cart more closely, Nettlestone thought he saw a body wrapped up in an old piece of canvas. He called out to Brocklehurst, 'Christmas greetings Barney. Why would you be working on Christmas morn?'

'Isaac, it don't matter what day of the week it be, when the Lord calls, ye must be ready. They found an old man dead this morning on the road out to Cavendish Hall. He must have tripped and fell for his leg was broken bad. It looks like he couldn't move any further, poor beggar. He died of exposure.'

Nettlestone turned to his wife who was at the counter. She had heard every word. Turning pale she began to whimper. Nettlestone quickly shut the door; fear gripped his heart. He strode over to Mrs Nettlestone, and they comforted one another.

'There, there my dear,' said Nettlestone.

'Who was this man Mr Nettlestone?'

Nettlestone shook his head in denial of the fear enveloping him.

'I don't know my dear, let's talk of it not.'

They stood there for another few minutes, finding solace in their embrace. Then Mr Nettlestone chanced to look out of the shop window. There, staring back at him was the old man. His face was blue and stamped with an expression of rage, fright, and mortal pain. Nettlestone gasped and tore his eyes away.

'What is it Mr Nettlestone?'

'The window. I saw him.'

Mrs Nettlestone forced herself to look at the window. No one was there. Outside the street was empty and snowflakes were sailing crazily in the wind. All of a sudden, the wind caused a slow whistle to creep through the house, chilling the husband and wife to the marrow. They slowly walked into the back of the shop. Their living quarters was warm, safe, and lit

104

by a roaring fire. The table was set for two. The smell of broth filled the air. It was snug and safe.

Neither spoke of their experience with the old man again.

Neither spoke of the guilt they felt.

Neither spoke of the nights in the future when they heard the cries of pain from all manner of animals, despairing wanderers and unseen people borne on the restless wind.

Chapter 11

Cavendish Hall: Christmas Eve 1919

A round of applause and many 'Brava' comments broke out as Mary finished the story. This prompted her to stand up and perform a mock curtsey topped off by an exaggerated bow. She sat down and received a warm hug from her sister who giggled with pleasure at the performance. Cavendish looked on with grandfatherly pride.

'Just one question, about your wonderful tale,' said Kit.

'Yes?' smiled Mary.

'What exactly is the curse, you refer to, of Cavendish Hall? I couldn't quite work that one out.'

'Me neither, actually, but capital story all the same, old girl,' added Strangerson.

Mary laughed and said, 'Well perhaps this was a little bit of artistic license on my part. I probably have a dozen stories like this. They could all be entitled, "*The Curse of Cavendish Hall*", or not, as the case may be.'

'I must say my good friend Monty would've been most impressed by this ghostly tale,' said Kit.

Mary sat up and looked at Kit, 'Monty? As in Montague Rhodes James?'

'Yes, the very same,' said Kit grinning.

This clearly surprised Mary. 'You know, M R James? My goodness. Now you've impressed me. I've read everything he's written. I'd love to meet him.'

'I'm glad to have finally impressed you, said Kit a slow smile spreading over his face. 'Well, it shall be so. Perhaps you could compile some of your stories into a volume, so he can read them. Although, I imagine he will be more impressed by the telling of them.'

'I shall hold you to that Lord Christopher,' said Mary before spinning around and walking over to her sister.

Strangerson stood up from the sofa and walked over to the sideboard where there were various decanters. 'Can I get you something Lord Cavendish? I see your glass is empty.'

'No thank you, Strangerson. I think I have had quite enough for today. Another one and I should be in danger of mild intoxication. Forgive me ladies.'

'Shocking,' said Mary.

'Well really,' added Esther in mock horror, 'the company we're forced to keep.' Both were smiling up at their grandfather affectionately.

A few minutes later the clock in the room chimed to indicate it was now midnight and therefore Christmas Day. Everyone stood up, clinked glasses, shook hands and wished one another a Happy Christmas. The sisters gave one another a hug and did likewise to Cavendish.

As the chimes faded, Cavendish said to the group, 'Well I think this old soldier will turn in. I shall leave you young things to your own entertainment. A reminder for those thinking about attending the Christmas service; I should like to be on our way around nine thirty in the morning. I must greet the villagers and it would be nice if those attending did likewise. In addition, Curtis has asked me to remind you that breakfast will be available from eight o' clock in the morning. There will not be a gong as I am conscious some of you won't be going to the service and may wish to lie on in bed.' He glanced at Henry

107

but said no more. As usual Henry was impervious to any veiled comment.

Disappointingly for Kit, the sisters also decided to take their leave. They left the drawing room accompanied by Cavendish who could be heard saying, 'No reason to leave on my account.'

Esther pointed out the need for the girls to have their beauty sleep causing Mary to laugh and roll her eyes. Strangerson inevitably took the bait to rebut such a necessity in their case. Henry, who had not been drinking, also took the opportunity to turn in and offered a curt goodnight. This left Strangerson and Kit alone in the drawing room.

'One for the road?' asked Strangerson sociably.

Kit contemplated his empty glass and replied, 'Why not.' He was not sure if he wanted to go to bed. Sleep meant dreams. Dreams always became nightmares.

They sat in silence for a minute or two contemplating the brandy. Then Strangerson asked Kit, 'Did you bring any presents old boy? I can't say I bothered. Perhaps I should've. Hope they didn't think me rude.'

'I'm sure they won't. Yes, I did bring some trifles. Perfumes for the girls and a first English language edition of War and Peace for Lord Cavendish.'

'And the grand dame with the foul child?'

Kit laughed. 'No, I knew they would be here, obviously, but felt the risk of causing offence, or worse, indifference, outweighed any conceivable benefits.'

'You obviously had first class intelligence. Clearly your métier,' said Strangerson knowingly.

Kit glanced at him but simply replied, 'Let's say her reputation preceded her.'

It was Strangerson's turn to laugh, 'She certainly is a tartar. I didn't bother to buy anything. Thank goodness. One dreads to think of how she would have reacted to something she didn't like.'

'Oh, how did you come to be invited?'

'The invitation was very last minute. I wrote to Cavendish several months ago. I'd meant to contact him long before - about Robert. I was there when, you know. Anyway, long story short, he contacted me at the end of the summer, and we corresponded. Then out of the blue he invited for Christmas. I hadn't any plans so thought, why not?'

Strangerson went on to relate the last moments of Robert Cavendish, but Kit was no longer listening. He felt his chest tighten and the heart pumping seemed to block out the sound of Strangerson's voice.

Kit turned away for a moment, was that an explosion? Who was shouting? Everything stopped. Then he was aware Strangerson was still talking to him.

'…it was clear he was a goner.'

Regaining his composure, Kit hoped his discomfort had not been noticed. Thankfully, Strangerson was so engrossed in recounting his story of Robert's death and its aftermath that he did not notice the reaction of Kit. The talk of the War was something Kit tended to avoid normally, but this subject, in particular, was too painful. Desperate to get away from the conversation, he emptied his glass and set it on the table.

'Perhaps it's time for bed.'

Strangerson finished his glass and they both headed out of the drawing room and up the stairs. Kit collapsed on the bed and looked at the ceiling. It was night in the Cavendish household; the house where Robert grew up. His wife and son just down the corridor. How desperately he wanted to avoid sleep. He went to the window and gazed outside. The clock said one o'clock. He felt so tired. Sleep was inevitable and before long he drifted off, reluctantly.

-

He lay in the crater. How long had it been? An hour? Five hours? He'd lost track. The night's chill hit him at every point in his body. That's what would get him in the end. Not the wound. Often it wasn't the bullet

109

or the shrapnel, the seeping of life from the rent in his body. It was the cold. He regretted discarding the overcoat, but what else could he do? He would have been mistaken for a German.

How much longer? Every time he regained consciousness, he hoped it would be to discover it was just a nightmare. What could he do? The situation was impossible, he realized. Trapped in No Man's Land, unable to walk. Why should they send someone out to him? The risk would be too great. It would be a waste of time anyway. He wondered how much the icy air was numbing the pain he should be feeling. The blackness returned.

When he came to again it took a few minutes for his eyes to become accustomed to the gloom. The ringing in his ears would not stop. Would he ever hear again? Then he laughed. No. He would not. A dull acceptance that this could be the end began to take shape. With each passing minute the form of it grew and became more distinct.

A flare went up causing the sky to turn a blinding white. He squinted upwards. His arm was trapped in a barbed wire stump, silhouetted against the lit sky. He felt numb. The cold enveloped his body once more. The layers of clothing seemed defenceless against its onslaught. With frustration he dug his fingers into the ground. The top surface was crisp with a wet frost that gave under the crunching force of his fingers. He felt the damp soil under his fingernails. The back of his throat felt dry. He was thirsty. The blackness returned.

He woke as he felt his body being tugged then dragged. It felt like a spear was stabbing him in his leg. A voice whispered in his ear, 'Don't worry, we'll have you back soon.' The blackness returned.

The flare woke him. He was being given a piggyback ride. How odd, he thought. Doesn't he realize there's a war on? An explosion nearby, the man carrying him collapsed to the ground. He collapsed on top of the man. Ahead he saw the British trench. It was so close. He could see some men climbing out of the trench. They were coming towards him. The fools!

Gunfire.

-

Kit bolted upright in the bed. His breath came quickly. He was sweating and shivering. After a few moments to gauge his whereabouts, he fell back onto the pillow and stared at the ceiling, praying he had not screamed, like those other times. The same dream: it never deviated. Yet it was just as he had remembered, so real. Was it trying to tell him something?

The clock on the wall was ticking loudly. Just after five in the morning. Like always; like then. Instead of trying to force sleep, he read a little. However, the thought that the dream was a message had fixed itself in his mind and he found he was unable to concentrate on his book. After an hour or so, he finally nodded off with the light still on.

Chapter 12

Christmas Day 1919: Cavendish Hall

The sun shone on Christmas Day. No clouds were visible in a cerulean sky. The snow was blinding white, and the air was crisp as the household stepped out onto the driveway. Only Lady Emily and Agnes were missing as the Cavendish family, their guests and the staff made the short walk into Little Gloston for the Christmas service.

They made the short walk towards tiny chapel, with each step the sound of the choir singing 'Hark the Herald Angels Sing' grew louder. Kit walked with Esther and further ahead, Cavendish accompanied Henry. Mary was busy pointing out parts of the village to Strangerson. Kit could not help but smile as they passed *"Nettlestone's Village Store est. 1702"*. He turned around to Mary and raised his eyebrow. She returned his look and winked slowly, 'It was a true story, of course.' she called out, smiling.

Sam, dressed in a natty tartan top, happily trotted alongside Kit until about halfway when he stopped and resolutely refused to move. Esther happily picked up and petted him for the remainder of the walk, much to Kit's disgust. Sam did not care, always happy to receive the attention of a beautiful girl.

They entered the chapel, which was named after St. Bartholomew. It dated back to 1659. The nave of the church contained barely a dozen rows of pews. They had all been filled by the villagers except the front pew which remained empty. This had clearly set aside for the Cavendish family. To the left of the altar were two rows of seats at a right angle to the pews. Behind the seats was a small organ. Here sat the choir comprising four elderly women and two men.

The stain glass windows were remarkably effective in blocking out light or perhaps were overdue a good clean, thought Kit as they entered. However, as the service began, the light began to stream through. It created a ray of light shining directly on the figure of Reverend Simmons. The effect of this and the choir's singing was quite heavenly, and Kit scolded himself for feeling uninterested. He hoped his good early impression of Simmons would not be dashed by a lengthy sermon from the pulpit. Kit wasn't in a mood for fire and brimstone being tossed far and wide.

Thankfully, this fear proved unfounded. Instead, Simmons treated the congregation to a short, heartfelt, but gently humorous sermon. It struck the right balance between the joy of Christmas for children, and the bittersweet recognition that the recent wounds of War would require a long time to heal. Kit nodded his head and felt a deep sense of guilt for those who had not made it back.

The service finished with several rousing hymns and soon the congregation was streaming into the sunny cold. Cavendish made a point of spending time with the locals and shaking hands. Both girls also joined him. Kit and Strangerson were joined by Reverend Simmons, who had had changed quickly following the service. He was wrapped up like he was ready to follow Shackleton across the icy tundra. Curtis, meanwhile, led the staff back to the house to make ready for

113

the afternoon's festivities upstairs and below. Their day would begin to get very busy soon.

'Beautiful day,' observed Simmons.

'Indeed, dashed cold though. I'm glad it's a small village,' said Strangerson.

'They shouldn't be too long,' said Simmons looking at three of the Cavendish family members chatting easily with different groups. Henry seemed unsure of what he should be doing. In the end, he forced himself to join some of the children. He knelt down and began to talk to one child, sitting in a makeshift wheelchair. The child began to smile. A man and a woman came and joined him. They were followed by a young woman who looked very much like the mother.

'They seem very popular,' remarked Kit, scanning the scene outside the church. Strangerson came over to join the two men.

'They are much loved,' confirmed Simmons, smiling his greeting to the new arrival. 'The family has always taken its responsibilities seriously and the people of the village recognize this.'

People were streaming past the three men now. Simmons nodded to a couple who walked with a small child holding each of their hands.

'Hello Stan. Happy Christmas Kate. And you, young Tom.'

Kit glanced at the man and immediately a chill descended on him. The haunted eyes told their own story. The man nodded to Simmons then looked away.

Seeing such despair made Kit yearn for something else. He turned and looked at Esther. She had joined Henry, kneeling down to chat to a bunch of the school children. She was laughing with them. As she laughed, she glanced at Kit. It was clear a thought had struck her. She leaned over to the oldest of the children, a boy no older than eleven or twelve, and whispered in his ear. She pointed to Kit and Strangerson.

114

'Get ready, Strangerson old boy,' said Kit laughing, 'I think you're on duty now.'

'Yes sir! Permission to engage enemy?' said Strangerson saluting.

'Granted,' laughed Kit.

Raising his arms as if he was a monster, he charged forward in a frontal assault, causing the children to run screaming. Strangerson played his part, spiritedly, for the next few minutes. This brought hoots of laughter from the onlookers and won him many admirers.

-

Activity in the kitchen of Cavendish Hall was at an elevated pitch under the unruffled direction of Curtis. So much so in fact, to cheers from Devlin and Polly, Elsie had chased him out of the kitchen wielding a bread knife. Consequences would follow, warned Curtis shrilly, as he adjusted his waistcoat and tie at the top of the stairs leading to the hall.

Miller groaned inwardly. He suspected the consequences might be directed towards him. Soon he heard Curtis shout down the stairs requesting his presence. With a wink in the direction of Polly he left to join Curtis. Arriving at the top of the stairs he recognized early signs of Curtis beginning to flap about something else. Probably the party was returning from church. Behind Curtis, through the open door, his assumption was confirmed.

A few minutes later they all stepped in, and Curtis helped with coats, hats, and scarves. Miller led everyone into the drawing room where tea and some light snacks were waiting. Miller tried to avoid Kit as he knew his master would be enjoying immensely his discomfort. Speaking to him would be unavoidable and he bowed to the inevitable, 'Will there be anything else, sir?'

'I believe everything is in order, Harry, thank you. You look very elegant.'

115

Miller escaped as quickly as he could, aware of Kit's half mocking, half sympathetic smile. Laughing to himself he swore he would find a way to get even.

Kit was joined by Mary. She smiled up at him and said, laughingly, 'Am I right in thinking Mr Miller is displeased with the livery.'

'Displeased barely covers it, Mary,' laughed Kit

'I can have a word with Curtis if you like, we're not so formal these days,' offered Mary.

'No, don't think of it. In fact, I'm enjoying every second of it.'

'Ahhh, I understand,' said Mary laughing. 'Poor Mr Miller.'

'Trust me, if the boot were on the other foot, Harry would be every bit as sympathetic!'

Mary nodded and then turned as Cavendish came over to join them. He looked at Mary, 'Mary, would you mind if I took Kit away for a few moments?'

'Of course.'

The two exchanged a look which intrigued Kit. Almost certainly it would be explained in the next few minutes. Cavendish led Kit out of the drawing room, and they crossed the hallway to the library. They went over to the desk and Cavendish moved the framed photograph of the army battalion, over to one side.

'I wanted to talk to you about one of the reasons why I had invited you this Christmas.' Kit raised one eyebrow and smiled. Noticing Kit's reaction, Cavendish smiled also, 'No it's not what you think, although do allow an old grandfather some hope on that score.'

Kit nodded and smiled, 'Please tell me what's on your mind.'

'It's quite serious, Kit or perhaps not. I cannot make up my mind about it and I've been reluctant to involve the police of late.'

'The police?'

'Yes, Kit. Take a look at this.' Cavendish handed him an envelope which was addressed to him. Kit eyed Cavendish who nodded his permission to open it and look at the contents. There was a Christmas card inside. It read:

Happy Christmas. I've killed you.

'Good Lord. Who would send such a vile message?' said Kit, in shock. He glanced down at the envelope and then glanced back at Cavendish. 'But this is four years old.'

Cavendish smiled. 'Very good, Kit. I see you noticed the post mark.'

'And it was posted in London. WC2. Not that this tells us much.'

'Why do you say that Kit?' responded Cavendish.

'The person who sent this may have had an accomplice who sent it from London, even unknowingly. The fact we're speaking now suggests this person either didn't try on your life or they failed.'

Cavendish reached into his desk drawer and took out three more envelopes. Kit examined each one. Each envelope contained a Christmas card with the same typed message inside, only the post mark date changed.

For the next few minutes, Kit carefully examined each of the envelopes, inside and out. He set them alongside each other and made comparisons. At the end of this inspection, he looked at Cavendish, 'I'm sure you've made all the same checks as I have. You've told the police about this but either they or you decided it was some sort of tasteless hoax.'

'Correct, I didn't show the cards from last Christmas or this. It seemed implausible this fiend would try to carry out his threat. In the end I decided not to waste any more of the police's time.'

117

'If you'll forgive me sir, but this was unwise. It could be that the person who sent these letters wanted to carry out his threat but was dissuaded from doing so because there was, I presume, police protection.'

'Only for the first two years,' admitted Cavendish, 'After...' he shrugged leaving the sentence unfinished.

'True, but it was still an unnecessary risk. Have you any idea who might want to send you such a wicked note?'

'Kit, I sent literally thousands of young men to their death. It could be anyone, their families, friends, I don't know where you would begin to look.'

'That is a vast distortion of the truth, sir. You did not send anyone to die.'

'Didn't I? You must understand, Kit, you and I know what it was like in Flanders. Decisions were made; orders were given. We knew we were sending those men to do the impossible and yet we did it anyway. There's hardly a day goes by when I don't think...'

'Sir. We all do,' interrupted Kit. 'But if it were the case that these letters are the work of some madman bent on revenge for the War, then why you and not the politicians? We went sleepwalking into a war. We were ill prepared and poorly led. They made us fight. Why you and not the other generals? They thought it was the Zulu War all over again. How could military strategy have advanced so little? How could they not have understood how deadly armaments were becoming? They had us walk into machine gun fire. No sir, this has to be different. Specific.'

'But who? I can't think of enemies outside of the War.'

'Let's start from the household. Is there anyone in the household who could possibly have a grudge against you?

'I don't think so. Apart from Devlin, they've all been with us for years. Curtis, Miss Buchan, and Elsie were here before we had the boys. They were broken-hearted, we all were. Polly came to us just before the War. She's still a child now. Devlin was in the War also. He served under John. Decorated a few times too. The Irish were great fighters,' acknowledged Cavendish.

'I know, sir.'

'Besides which, he only came to us last year,' added Cavendish.

'How did he come to join your household?'

'He wrote to me asking if there were any jobs.'

'Did you know him from the War?' asked Kit.

'Not personally, but I checked his references with army officers of my acquaintance. They all spoke highly of him. I needed a driver and a handyman. He demonstrated a good knowledge of motor vehicles and could fix things around the estate. I accepted him, and I must say I've had no regrets in doing so.'

'How does he get on with the rest of the household?'

'I believe he keeps himself to himself. Mind you, Curtis is not always the easiest of people. I shouldn't like to work under him; a little full of himself. Anyway, I'm not aware of any dissent between the two of them or the other staff.'

'And the villagers?'

'Again, I can think of no reason there should be any bitterness towards me.'

'Are there any new inhabitants?'

Cavendish laughed. 'Not really. Some of the young men leave, some come back with a wife. Some of the women leave but rarely return. I should imagine it's a story the length and breadth of the land.'

Thinking about seeing Cavendish walking in the grounds yesterday, reminded Kit about the cottage.

'Do you have any staff who don't live at the Hall itself?'

'Bill Edmunds,' said Cavendish after a few moments.

'Who is Bill Edmunds?' asked Kit.

'He tends the grounds of Cavendish Hall, but he doesn't live here. He and his wife have a small cottage just over the

119

hill. He lost his son in sixteen. I'm not sure of the circumstances as I was away then. He was in another regiment.'

'Oh yes,' replied Kit, remembering the cottage. 'I think I know the one. I saw it when we went for a walk yesterday. Was he at the carol service?'

'No, I think he rather fell out with God after he lost Ben.'

Kit nodded, 'I can understand. Do you think he could've blamed you in any way for his son's death?'

'I don't see why. I had no part in Ben signing up and he didn't serve in any regiment I was associated with.'

Kit picked the cards up again and looked at the typewritten notes. Although he was hardly an expert, it seemed like they could all have been written on the same typewriter. The quality of the type was poor, and Kit suspected the ribbon had not been changed since the first note was written. This could mean the typewriter was used frequently enough to deteriorate over time but not so often that it needed replacing. Sadly, there were no easily identifiable flaws in the type, however this was outside Kit's field. There was no reason an expert may not be able to connect the typewriter to these notes at a future point in time should the individual be apprehended.

It was difficult to know what to do next. As no obvious attempt had been made on Cavendish's life it was useless to continue asking the police to intervene. Besides which, Cavendish was a military man who had fought in conflicts around the world. He was certainly capable of taking care of himself, concluded Kit.

Sensing there was nothing else to be done, Cavendish said, 'Perhaps we should re-join the rest of the party, Kit. I've taken up enough of your time with this foolishness.'

They returned to the drawing room. Lady Emily had arrived bringing to the room a chill barely matched by the cold outside. Esther looked at her grandfather in the eye.

120

Cavendish immediately understood this to mean the situation was deteriorating due to Aunt Emily.

'Emily, I'm so glad you're feeling better. Happy Christmas,' said Cavendish. There was a no question it was warmly meant, and it appeared to have an effect of the lady's frosty demeanour.

'To you also,' said Emily generously. 'Why have you been keeping this good-looking young man all to yourself? I'm sure your granddaughters are missing him greatly.'

Cavendish resisted the temptation to reach for the seventeenth century musket on the wall. Thankfully Kit proved his valour in battle had not deserted him following the War by taking Lady Emily's arm, 'Perhaps you could give me a tour of the artworks in the room Lady Emily. I should like to hear your view on them. Lord Cavendish and the lovely ladies have been scandalously inattentive on this matter.'

Lady Emily looked at him archly, suspecting she was the subject of gentle chaffing but not seeming to mind too much. Doing as she was bid; they began to circle the room looking at the various objets d'art.

Out of the corner of his eye Kit saw Mary mime pinning a medal on his chest. This forced him to choke back some laughter. Thankfully, Henry did not see this. He was otherwise engaged with Strangerson in a discussion on tropical poisons. Kit tried to listen to this conversation but was aware that Lady Emily was demanding his opinion on a genre piece by David Wilkie. It showed a poor family mourning the death of an elderly grandparent.

-

Meanwhile, downstairs in the kitchen, Captain Curtis took a deep breath. He surveyed at his troops like a general before battle. Lined up in front of him were Elsie, Polly, and Miss Buchan. A quick inspection of dress was followed by a final look at the food to be served upstairs. Finally, accepting there

121

was naught else to be done, he lightly clapped his hands together and said, 'Are we all ready?'

'We are ready Mr Curtis,' came the reply from Corporal Buchan.

Get on with it, thought Miller. Curtis bowed to the men-at-arms, turned to the door, and went upstairs. Moments later the entrance hall echoed to the sound of Curtis banging the gong.

Christmas dinner was to be served.

Chapter 13

Christmas dinner went smoothly, under the assured stewardship of Curtis, ably assisted by Miller and Polly. At the end of a splendid meal, Cavendish asked for all of the staff to come to the dining room to present gifts to them. Then the party toasted their hard work. Cavendish made special mention of Elsie before allowing them the rest of the day off to celebrate Christmas. Curtis made a short speech exuding pontifical charity for Lord Cavendish and the family. They left the room to warm applause and a hip, hip hooray orchestrated by Strangerson. Sam remained, against Kit's wishes, with the party and was completely spoilt by the Cavendish girls. They were now, officially, friends for life.

The party retired to the drawing room to share out the presents lying underneath the small Christmas tree. Kit was delighted to receive a signed first edition book by the German World Chess Champion, Emmanuel Lasker, from the Cavendish family.

Strangerson was given a French army rifle dating back to the Franco – Austrian war of 1859. He was equally delighted with the gift and promised to try it out at the first possible opportunity. Cavendish happily took this as a hint to go shooting on Boxing Day and readily agreed although he

123

suggested that the new gun might not be quite up to the job, even for someone as accomplished as Strangerson.

Henry also received a gun. It was difficult to detect if this gave him joy or not. Kit suspected neither. It would probably never be used although Strangerson, manfully, offered to give the boy shooting lessons. This appeared to please Cavendish and even Lady Emily. Henry looked bored.

Even Lady Emily seemed genuinely touched by her present, a hat that had been imported specially from a leading Parisian milliner. She looked at the two girls and said, 'Well I don't have to guess who chose this. Thank you, girls. It's beautiful and I shall not only treasure it, but I shall also wear it often.' Esther and Mary both gave their aunt a hug.

The most delighted of the party was Reverend Simmons. He received, from the Cavendish family, the gift of a boxing glove reputed to have been worn by Bob Fitzsimmons, the last British man to hold the World Heavyweight Championship.

'How on earth did you ever get hold of this?' he said to Cavendish.

'I have my sources,' replied Cavendish smiling but added nothing more. Strangerson, inevitably, believed the sharing of gifts called for further toasts and he nobly offered to pour drinks for the assembled party. Both Cavendish and Lady Emily declined but even Henry had a small brandy after receiving a nod from his mother.

With the exchange of presents completed, the party sat down and chatted for the next hour in groups varying in composition. Kit managed to spend a little more time with Esther, content to listen to her. She spoke of life at Cavendish Hall. Although she clearly enjoyed living at the Hall, Kit detected a longing for something more. The life she had in London jobs during the War had, perhaps, created an appetite to join the vast movement of women in the country who were finding a voice and a purpose beyond the home.

The shortage of men meant there had been a need for women to fill posts formerly occupied by men. Much to Kit's amusement, she related her time as a bus conductor in the centre of London. It seemed so at odds with the exquisite woman sat beside him. Esther appeared to enjoy doing something in support of the War effort but laughed easily at how strange it appeared in retrospect.

Out of the corner of his eye, Kit saw Mary looking at him. How different she was: lively, playful, and rejoicing in impertinence. Underlying this was a seriousness that was well concealed behind a teasing facade. She was sitting with Lady Emily and Cavendish. Perhaps he was imagining it, but she seemed more interested in the conversation he was having with Esther.

Strangerson, meanwhile, seemed to be making progress in bringing Henry out of himself. They were both standing by the French windows. At one point, Strangerson gazing out the window said, 'My word, the snow is fairly pouring out of the sky.'

They all went to the window to look. It was true. 'I hope no one is out in this weather tonight,' observed Simmons. There was a murmur of assent to this remark.

There was a loud rap at the front door. This caused Esther to gasp. Mary turned to her sister with a grin, 'Just like one of my ghost stories Essie. I wonder who it could be?'

A few minutes later, the door to the drawing room opened and Curtis introduced an unknown visitor. It should be added that Curtis, at this point in the early evening, had enjoyed his break from servant duties so much that it was difficult to understand what he was saying.

'Mishter Wright,' he stammered. There were suppressed smiles in the room at the appearance of a rather intoxicated Curtis. Recognizing his faithful servant had indulged heavily, Cavendish decided to protect him from any further exposure.

125

'Thank you, Curtis, I don't think we will be needing anything else. Please enjoy the rest of your Christmas. We can manage from here.'

Curtis bowed unsteadily and swayed with immense dignity, from the room. The stranger looked at everyone and said, 'Actually my name is Doctor Richard Bright. I'm most terribly sorry to interrupt your Christmas celebrations.'

'Nonsense, please sit down and have a Brandy,' said Cavendish, who glanced at Strangerson. 'I'm sure you must be frozen from being out in this weather.'

Bright walked into the room. He was a shade over six feet and dressed in an old but well-cut tweed suit, that could easily have been worn in the Tattersall's.

'Well, I am to be honest,' laughed the Doctor.

'What on earth were you doing out on Christmas night, particularly when it is as bad as this?' asked Kit.

The Doctor turned to Kit, and they regarded one another. Bright seemed to be a similar age to Kit. His brown hair was pushed off his forehead and his eyes were a very clear grey. Invited to sit down by Cavendish, he continued, 'I was asked to locum for another doctor in the area, Doctor Stevens.'

'Yes, I know Stevens. He's getting on a bit. Like myself I suppose.' This brought, as expected, denials from the group.

'He asked me to stay with him over Christmas and do some work. His wife is unwell,' Bright looked up at Cavendish as he said this. Cavendish nodded in understanding, which Kit took to mean the prognosis was not good. Bright continued, 'He felt it would be too much, I suppose, to take care of Mrs Stevens and manage this area. Anyway, I received a call two or three hours ago to go to Leddings Farm, a few miles from here. Mrs Leddings was in labour. Happily, I helped her give birth to a baby boy. They say they're going to name him Richard.'

Everyone congratulated him on his good work with the men shaking his hand and a hearty clap on the back from Strangerson. When all of the compliments had ceased, at the

126

request of the two girls, Bright added more details on the baby before returning to complete his story.

'After I left the house, I could see the weather had turned for the worse. Mr Leddings insisted I stay over but I told him I had to get back. I suppose I was hoping I'd be back to the Doctor's before the weather became too bad. Alas, as you can see...' He held his hands out and left the sentence unfinished.

'Where is the car now?' asked Cavendish.

'About a quarter of a mile from the cottage in the middle of your grounds.'

'It sounds like Bill Edmunds' place,' added Cavendish. 'Well, if you're in a snow drift there, your car isn't going anywhere. It's at least three miles from Doctor Stevens's house. I think you'll be our guest tonight, Doctor Bright.'

'I really can't impose,' insisted Bright.

'Nonsense dear fellow, I won't hear of it,' asserted Cavendish.

Esther stood up and said to her grandfather, 'I'll tell Curtis to prepare the other guest bedroom.' Mary joined her and they both left the drawing room

Bright, who had not really had the opportunity to see the Cavendish sisters unexpectedly reddened and stammered a thank you. This amused Kit immensely and he sympathized with the poor fellow. Both sisters knew how to make an impact on a poor chap's senses. Another part of Kit felt a pang of jealousy. This seemed unaccountable to him, and he quickly dismissed it. However, he ruefully admitted to himself, Bright was a good-looking fellow, with an easy smile and a steady gaze: a head could easily be turned.

Sam went over to inspect the visitor. Unusually for Sam, he did not treat the stranger as his mortal enemy. Almost immediately the doctor began to tickle Sam under his chin. This was something Sam loved and within a moment he was lying on his back demanding to be tickled further. This brought much laughter from the assembled party, even Henry could not resist a smile. "*Et tu* Sam", thought Kit dolefully.

The girls soon returned and sat either side of Bright. Far from making Kit's mood grow darker, it actually amused him. At this point, he realized that both Cavendish girls were deliberately setting out to make him jealous. He speculated they had even planned the move while they had been out to brief Curtis. He caught Cavendish looking at him and he smiled back to reassure him that he knew the game. This caused Cavendish to roll his eyes a little by way of apology.

'How long are you to stay in the area?' asked Mary.

'I'm not sure. As long as Dr Stevens needs me, I suppose,' replied Bright.

'You don't have anyone waiting for you back home?' continued Mary shamelessly. This made Kit smile. He was beginning to recognize the mischievous nature of the younger sister.

Bright laughed sheepishly, 'I suppose not. I have rooms in London but, to be honest, I'm usually away on one thing or another, I've barely stayed in them since before the War.'

Cavendish asked him if he had served in the Royal Army Medical Corps. Bright replied in the affirmative. He refrained from adding he had been an officer and served in the frontline but shrewd questioning from Kit forced Bright to come clean on what appeared to be an exemplary war record.

It seemed very clear to Kit that Mary, herself a nurse during the war, was absorbed in listening to the new arrival. Esther, too. He had made quite an impression on the party in a short time. Even the glacial Lady Emily seemed to be interested in the young man's story. Kit was not entirely sure how much he welcomed this. Strangerson, insofar as Kit felt competitive, was unlikely to present a threat to the girls' interest in him. The new arrival, however, was a different matter. His foothold at the head of the pride felt distinctly shakier.

128

Cavendish mentioned about Mary's involvement with the Voluntary Aid Detachment, tactfully avoiding elaboration on the unusual circumstances that had led to her joining. Bright asked Mary, 'What made you want to become a nurse?'

'The option of being a Doctor, is still barred to women,' came Mary's sardonic reply.

'I agree, with you Lady Mary,' said Bright, 'We're long overdue a change in this and so many other areas related to women. I worked with countless nurses during the War who would've made very fine Doctors. I'm sure within our lifetime we'll see this happen.' He seemed in earnest and Mary nodded in agreement but added nothing more about her role, preferring to listen to Bright's account of his time in France.

Not long after Lady Emily retired to her room but not before taking Cavendish aside and saying, 'I believe Mr Curtis was inebriated.'

Cavendish merely shrugged and replied, 'I believe you're right Emily and I sincerely hope so. A very Merry Christmas, indeed. I suspect he's probably earned it – don't you?'

As he said this, Cavendish felt a stab of remorse. Was he reopening old wounds? In fact, while his answer did not please Lady Emily nor did she seem angered by it. This, thought Cavendish, was a welcome surprise. Perhaps she recognized how the sins of the past had affected Curtis. Or perhaps the Snow Queen was beginning to thaw. He certainly hoped so.

Simmons and Kit were enjoying each other's company immensely. They spent a good half hour in the period before Bright's arrival, chatting about the noble art of boxing. Simmons was interested to hear about Kit's own efforts in the ring when he was at school. This included the opportunity to share a ring with a ring legend, Jem Driscoll.

'How on earth did you ever end up in the ring with Driscoll?' Simmons exclaimed askance. The Cardiff man was one of the most accomplished fighters of the era to emerge from Britain. Notwithstanding the difference in size between the tall lord, who Simmons judged to be a light-heavyweight, and the diminutive Welshman, who fought at featherweight, Simmons would have considered it a great mismatch, and not in Kit's favour either.

With beguiling modesty Kit agreed with this assessment.

'A long story but it reflects no credit on myself as I believe I played truant from school in order to spar with him. He went very easy on me, which is more than I can say for my form master when he heard about my expedition. I think it was a day or two before I could sit with any degree of comfort,' smiled Kit remorsefully. Simmons left soon afterwards mentioning the weather was, if anything, worsening. Kit was sad to see him leave.

-

Incredibly, Miller's Christmas was going from bad to worse. He was stuck with an increasingly incoherent Curtis. Elsie had fallen asleep and had been helped to bed by Miss Buchan, who herself had also retired. Godfrey and Agnes were proving to be exceptionally dull company. They spent most of their time talking to one another. Miller wondered if there was something going on between them. Good luck to you both, he thought sardonically – you're well matched.

Worst of all, unless his senses were failing him, and he knew they were not, it was very clear Devlin and Polly were sweethearts. A little light amour with Polly would have been an ideal way to pass a cold Christmas evening. Now it looked like the highlight of his Christmas would be a bottle of Scotch and the company of a pompous bore, who was recounting his life year by year. However, something finally cut through the fog for Miller. Did he hear right? Had Curtis just said he'd been married? It was difficult to make out much of what the sloshed servant had to say. Miller stopped trying. Boredom and whisky were now his companions. How he wished for something to liven things up.

He would not be waiting long.

130

Around ten o'clock, Cavendish announced he his intention to retire and bid them goodnight. About ten minutes later, Strangerson also decided to call it a night, possibly suspecting there was one male too many circling the females.

Kit felt a stab of guilt at being glad Strangerson was out of the way leaving him, Bright and the two sisters plus Sam, snoring lightly on Esther's lap. For all his waggishness, Kit guessed Strangerson was no fool and could read the situation between he, Bright and the girls.

The remaining party looked down at the little Jack Russell. 'He's definitely a man for the ladies,' observed Kit.'

'So, I see,' grinned Bright.

'He's probably not used to being treated with kindness and gentleness,' kidded Esther.

'Indeed, his life is one of walks on cold moors, hunting and goodness knows what else,' chimed Mary looking to make mischief.

'I can assure you, Mary, quite apart from being one of the most well looked after pets in this country, he is, as you can see, profoundly untroubled by any kind of work ethic,' joked Kit. 'Don't be taken in by this display. It starts like this, then he wants you to feed him, then it's short walks and before you know it, you're doing all the walking and he's curled up in your arms enjoying the view.' The group laughed affectionately.

Mary stood up from her place beside Bright and looked out the window. 'My goodness look at the snow now. It really is getting worse. I think we shall be snowed in. How beautiful it looks though, and deadly. It wouldn't do to be out tonight.'

'I really am most grateful for your hospitality. It was getting rather cold out there.'

'Really Dr Bright, it's nothing. No more please,' smiled Esther.

'I promise,' smiled Bright.

131

Kit felt his stomach tighten a little as he watched the two of them smile at one another. Stop it, he almost shouted, but more for himself than to Esther or Mary. The thing was, he quite liked this fellow himself. He had clearly done his duty, as so many had, which made him a stout fellow. On top of this he had an easy charm; perhaps too much charm if the girls' reactions to him were anything to go by. As much as he had enjoyed the day and as much as he was enjoying the evening the correct thing to do now, with Cavendish gone, was to retire. However, there was no question of Kit leaving the field free for Bright: he resolved to wait until either the girls or the Doctor decided to turn in.

As it happened, they did not stay a great deal longer in the drawing room. The sisters perhaps understood that by staying they were prolonging a primal contest in which they had complete power of choice. So ended Christmas Day. It was a day when romance and jealousy danced their strange tango and death was just around the corner.

132

Chapter 14

Easter, 1916: A British Prison

The prisoner woke with a start. The cell was beginning to let in light, but the gloom would not give up its hold over the cell. He guessed sleep was over for the moment. Rising from the bunk, he listened to the noises outside the door. There were muffled shouts and the rattling of keys being put in doors. His corridor remained empty so there was nothing else to do but return to the bed.

And wait.

How much time passed he could not tell, maybe half an hour. The crash of keys in the door told him they had come. No welcoming smile or cup of tea. No please or thank you. Why should he expect to receive anything? He was the lowest of the low, a dirty prisoner. A man without rights, a man without hopes. A man who had fought for his country.

Of course, there had not been much choice about joining. You had to, didn't you? Everyone around you was getting involved. They would all see if you didn't join. It was a just cause with a clear enemy who had to be defeated. It was for your family, for your country: for freedom. Yet they were losing. There was no glimmering prospect of victory to lighten the heart of those who fought on.

'Up! Move!' shouted the guard.

'A "please" wouldn't hurt,' responded the prisoner.

This was greeted with a shove out of the cell. 'You won't be laughing soon.'

'I'm not laughing now, trust me.'

The guard recognized that trying to bully with words was probably not going to work with this prisoner. Instead, he resorted, inevitably, to his one and only weapon. He struck the handcuffed prisoner across the back of his head.

'Temper, temper,' responded the prisoner but his head was spinning.

Another guard saw what was happening and shouted down the corridor, 'Leave it. They won't be happy if they see he's been beaten.'

The guard stopped the assault and contented himself with kicking him in the backside as the prisoner made his way down the corridor. The other guard glared at him, so he stopped.

The two guards and the prisoner made their way into the open air. The prisoner drank in the sweetness of the air. How had he never realized its beauty before? The honeyed, rain-washed fragrance caressed his senses. The cold moistness bathed his skin, cleansing him of weeks locked and chained in the dank, depressing dungeon.

It was dawn. The sky was a tender pink mixed with another colour. He stared up at the sky as he was marched along trying to decide what the colour was. Yellow, he thought. Yes, it's a soft yellow.

All around him he could see army men, like him. They were not looking at him. He tried to make eye contact with one of them. Nobody took him up on the offer. Shame, he guessed. Utter shame for what they had to do. Every one of them was tending to their weapon or chatting to a friend. He noticed the guard was no longer shoving him. Perhaps it would be unacceptable, in front of these men. They would know what he'd been through. He was like them. At this moment, he felt his power returning. Stopping he turned to the guard who had been his tormentor for the last two weeks.

'Not so tough, now, are you?' said the prisoner.

The guard said nothing. This made the prisoner laugh and he began to walk again. His back straightened. It was almost funny. He was leading the way but was not sure where he was supposed to be going exactly. They rounded a corner and then the destination became all too apparent. He saw for the first time the wall where it would happen. Bullet holes pockmarked a section in the middle. The thought of some soldiers deliberately missing *amused him. There were some signs of blood on the ground. Someone had kicked over the traces. They couldn't even do this properly.*

They led him to the wall. Their hands on his arm irritated him because he hadn't intended making a scene. His stomach rumbled. No breakfast even for the condemned man. Are they so hard up? Execution on an empty stomach seemed positively barbaric.

Behind him he could sense the army men filing in to do their ghastly duty. A quick glance confirmed this. There were other onlookers standing looking sombre. The weight of justice on their shoulders; all were army, clearly senior. One or two of them looked familiar. In truth, it was difficult to see without his glasses. The clergyman who had come to him the night before was there too; he was not difficult to recognize. The prisoner nodded to him. But the clergyman looked away, taking refuge in his prayer book.

At the wall, he was brusquely turned around. He refused the offer of a cigarette but thanked the guard anyway. Manners are so important. There was no choice regarding the blindfold, and he did not bother to argue. Perhaps because he had displayed good manners or possibly out of a hitherto unrevealed sympathy, the guard put his blindfold on less roughly than he was expecting. Gently the guard made sure he was unable to see the firing squad, or perhaps they, him.

The sound of their footsteps walking away told him it would be over soon. As they crunched through the gravel, the sound grew fainter. In the last few moments, he examined his own feelings: to his surprise, he felt calm. His fate was decided. There would be no last-minute reprieve. But what did it matter anyway? Since he began to witness the slaughter of war, a part of him had never expected to survive. Perhaps there was a relief that the end would be quick; it would not be the slow lingering agony he'd always feared, gargling blood, or drowning in gas.

A voice he did not recognize called the firing squad to make ready. There was a collective clacking sound as the weapons were loaded. He wondered how many of the bullets were blank. They were ordered to aim.

They shot him as he made a silent prayer to a God.

Chapter 15

Boxing Day 1919: Cavendish Hall

Curtis awoke slowly. As his eyes cleared, he realized a number of things rapidly. His head felt like it contained a fifty-piece orchestra comprised solely of energetic child percussionists. In addition, he became conscious that he was still dressed in his livery. Also, the kitchen table had, somewhat surprisingly, been his pillow last night. Finally, and perhaps most seriously, the rest of the domestic staff were having their breakfast around him.

There are times in life when one should lose it. Properly and irrevocably lose it. People need to understand when you're not only displeased but actually pretty miffed. Looking around the table at everyone suppressing smirks, Curtis felt his temperature gauge rise to dangerous levels. Everyone, that is, except Miss Buchan. When he finally caught her eye, the true nature of anger was revealed unto him, although she spoke not.

There are also times in life when it is important to recognize, both privately and publicly, when you have erred. One look at Miss Buchan was enough to confirm to Curtis, this time had arrived. Rising with great care, he straightened his coat. Regarding each member of the staff in turn he said, with as much dignity as was possible to fashion in such disadvantageous circumstances, 'I believe that I was somewhat inebriated last night.' A final realization began to dawn on him

136

as he spoke. He felt ill, very ill. His mea culpa would, of necessity, have to combine sincerity with brevity.

'I recognize I have let everyone down. Forgive me.' He bowed his head at the end more by instinct than calculation.

This was greeted with assurances from everyone that this was not the case, and they were glad he had enjoyed himself.

'If you'll excuse me, I shall make myself ready for the day. Please continue.' This speech ended with Curtis leaving the kitchen slowly before sprinting to his room as quietly as he possibly could.

The suppressed smiles were on the point of erupting into outright hilarity, but it was clear as Miss Buchan rose with what could only be described as having a face on her, this would not be appreciated.

This is how Boxing Day started at Cavendish Hall. A day none would ever forget.

-

The flare. He was being given a piggyback ride. An explosion nearby, the man carrying him collapsed to the ground. He collapsed on top of the man. Ahead he saw the British trench. It was so close. He could see some men climbing out of the trench. The fools! Gunfire.

This isn't right. Why isn't it right? Kit was no longer lying on top of the man as they surged towards the trench. He was an observer now. Something was wrong, and yet this is what had happened. Now he was floating around the scene. Nobody was moving, only he. It was all clear, but nothing made sense. He knew he was going to wake up any second. One more moment, I need a little more time, please.

Then he woke.

This time he was not sweating nor screaming. He was thinking about the question that had woken him. Why was the scene wrong? The dream had not changed in substance. The dream was just how it happened. He remained sitting up in the bed for a few more minutes repeating the word 'think' over and over again. It would not become apparent for some time, but the fear had diminished.

137

The dream would never return.

Replacing it was sorrow, anger, and frustration. Not about what had happened to him. Sorrow for those who had died; anger and frustration at himself for not understanding what was wrong about his memory. Rolling out of bed he rubbed his eyes and looked for his pocket watch. Another day ahead with the sisters to look forward to but now with a complicating factor in the shape of Dr Richard Bright. He dismissed the thought quickly and set about dressing for breakfast.

-

All of the guests were in the dining room breakfasting when the Cavendish girls arrived. They served themselves some tea and toast and sat down. Esther turned to Polly who was waiting at table, 'Where is grandpapa? Is he having breakfast in his room?'

'He's not come down yet ma'am,' said Polly

'Has Curtis not been to him yet?' continued Esther.

'Mr Curtis is a feeling a little indisposed this morning,' responded Polly.

This brought a snort from Lady Emily. 'I think we can guess why.' Polly made no comment, but she could not disguise the hint of a smile. This caused grins around the table with all except Lady Emily and Henry, who was not listening.

'All the same, I think someone should get him up,' said Lady Emily somewhat sniffily. 'He has guests to entertain.'

'I think we can manage for a morning, Lady Emily,' spoke up Kit. 'If he wishes to rest then I would feel much happier if we let him.'

'I'm inclined to agree, Lady Emily,' added Strangerson.

Nothing more was said on the subject and soon the guests went outside to see how much snow had fallen overnight. It had been extensive.

'I'm not sure you will be moving too far today, Bright old fellow,' said Strangerson.

'Looks like it,' agreed Bright. Kit could not help but notice how Bright seemed far from disappointed at this prospect. 'Is this normal for the time of year?'

'I've never seen it so bad,' admitted Esther. 'I hope the people in the village aren't too inconvenienced.'

'I'm sure they are used to it Essie, don't worry,' reassured Mary. 'It's still freezing, though. I'm not sure it will melt any time soon. You could be here for a day or two yet Dr Bright.' The smile on her face when she said this also wounded Kit enough to make him smile at his own discomfort. These girls certainly know how to twist a man's senses hither and thither, he thought.

Kit went back inside to look for Miller and Sam. It was time the little terrier had a walk, although how practicable it would be for him in the deep snow remained to be seen.

He heard Miller before he saw him. He was having his daily argument with Sam. Upon seeing Kit, the dog ran happily to his master. Kit knelt, and Sam pounced, giving Kit's face one almighty licking. Miller laughed, 'I think we're definitely getting on better.'

'So, I heard,' grinned Kit. 'Shall we go for a walk? Come on boy.'

The three of them walked out via the kitchen. The back yard had been relatively shielded from the snow. However, as they reached the main gardens they had to wade through the drifts and Sam was being ferried by Kit. They took the same route from two days previously. It was the same and yet so different. A blanket of snow clung to the house and the land. The air made their faces numb. Smoke still came from Edmund's cottage, but it was now enveloped up to the windows by a drift.

At the head of the rise, they were able to survey the grounds. Fresh tracks had been made in the snow from the cottage to the stables and from the stables to the house, so someone had been out earlier. There was no sign of life anywhere now. All was still.

Kit turned to Miller, 'I hope Lord Cavendish is up. He's had quite a sleep in.'

'That's funny, he was down in the kitchen last night,' replied Miller.

'Really, must have been after he left us,' said Kit. 'Did he speak to you?'

'It was late, not sure when. I think he was a bit surprised to see me. He was still looking at me a bit strangely. Anyway, he came down and wished Curtis and me a happy Christmas. Then he did a strange thing. He went over to where the room keys hang on the wall and took a key with him. I supposed it was his bedroom key. He didn't explain what he was doing and naturally I wasn't about to ask him.'

'How odd.'

'Nothing else to report. Soon after Curtis passed out. He's not really a drinker that one.'

Kit laughed, 'We noticed.' They were picking their way back, retracing their footsteps from the hall. As they neared the house Sam decided it was time to resume his walk.

'Lazy little beggar,' said Miller.

Inside the house, chaos reigned.

Chapter 16

'Lord Cavendish is dead,' said Miss Buchan.

These were the words that greeted Kit and Miller as they entered from the back. They could see Miss Buchan comforting a tearful Polly. Elsie was sitting with her head in her hands. The water on the stove was boiling over but nobody seemed interested. Miller walked over and reduced the heat.

Recovering from the shock of this announcement, Kit asked Miss Buchan, 'Where are Lady Esther and Mary?'

'Upstairs in Lord Cavendish's room with Dr Bright.'

Kit said nothing more but went upstairs to the room. Arriving outside the room, he could see the door had recently been forced open. Curtis was sitting outside the room. Seeing Kit, he scrambled to his feet but could not say anything. His red-rimmed eyes spoke of grief as much as the hangover he was unquestionably suffering.

'The ladies are in with Lord Cavendish, Mr Strangerson and Doctor Bright.'

He knocked the door and went in. On the bed lay Cavendish, only his head was showing. It was pale but very peaceful. Both girls were crying, face down by the bed. Only Bright was aware of Kit's arrival.

'I can't believe it,' said Kit, 'Esther, Mary, I'm so terribly sorry.'

Both looked up, but neither could say anything. Bright motioned for Kit to join him outside the room so that he could fill him in the about the events of the morning. Speaking in a low voice he said, 'I know it's such a shock. He seemed in fine fettle last night. As far as I can tell he seems to have passed away peacefully in his sleep. It's difficult to establish an exact time but I think, given the progression of rigor it couldn't have been more than a few hours ago.'

'Are you sure he died from natural causes?' asked Kit

'Good Lord, Kit. What an extraordinary thing to ask,' said Strangerson.

'I have my reasons,' said Kit but added nothing more.

Bright responded, 'We can't assume anything of course without a post-mortem. But I should add, the room was locked from the inside. As far as we can tell nobody, except Lord Cavendish could have entered the room last night.'

'I saw the door had been forced,' said Kit.

'We did that when there was no answer from the room,' added Strangerson, who had joined them also. 'The ladies were becoming concerned for him,' he added by way of explanation.

'Do you believe there was foul play?' asked Bright.

'Possibly, but I accept this is something that must wait for a post-mortem. Have the police been informed?'

'No, there is no telephone line at the moment, perhaps the weather. I understand Devlin has gone into the village to see if there's a way of getting in contact with the police in Lincoln,' confirmed Bright.

'Obvious question perhaps, but Esther and Mary, how are they?'

'Distraught as you may imagine,' answered Bright.

'Where is Lady Emily?'

142

'She retired to her room. The old girl looked fairly cut up to be fair. I haven't seen the youngster,' said Strangerson.

The three men spoke for another few minutes and then Kit went in to see the girls. Bright went to the kitchen with Curtis to update them on what had happened and what to expect over the next few days.

Esther and Mary were holding one another as Kit returned to the room. He told them again how sorry he was. Then Mary asked, 'What do you think happened? It's inconceivable he could just pass away like that. I don't believe it.'

The emphasis she put on the word 'believe' and the way she looked at Kit told him that Lord Cavendish had shared the strange Christmas cards with them.

Mary continued, 'You saw those vile notes?'

'Yes, Lord Cavendish showed them to me. I agree they were despicable.'

'And now he's dead.'

Mary began to cry again, hugging Esther even harder.

'Yes, we can't rule out foul play,' admitted Kit reluctantly.

'We should tell Richard about the notes,' said Mary.

Kit noted Mary's familiarity with the Doctor but refocused on the death of Cavendish.

'Forgive me Mary, I'm not sure that's a good idea just yet. I spoke with him just now and alluded to circumstances that suggest we are dealing with a murder here, but I didn't go into detail.'

Mary seemed to see the sense of this, but Kit could also recognize her unwillingness to accept he could be involved. She looked at Kit and said, 'I understand. We need to get the police.'

'I gather Devlin has gone into the village, to see if there is a telephone line working.'

'Is this wise?' asked Mary.

143

There was a steely look in Mary's eyes as she said this. Kit understood what she was thinking because he had felt the same when first told of Devlin's mission.

'If your grandfather was murdered then you're right, Mary. We're all suspects.'

-

In the silence of the kitchen, the dripping of the tap was deafening. Miller felt uncomfortable in an atmosphere as heavy as it was cold. Not the sharp cold of outdoors but rather a damp intense sensation. Around him sat Miss Buchan, Elsie, and Polly. All were shocked beyond tears, most probably fearful of the future, concluded Miller.

To move from his seat, it seemed to Miller, would be to intrude on the grief around him. Therefore, he remained seated, unable to say anything. He could think of nothing to say that would console or reassure. It was unbearable. He prayed Kit would come down soon and release him from the torment of inaction.

Cavendish's death was suspicious. The threatening notes sent to Cavendish, had been brought up by Kit the previous evening and he was under instructions to keep an eye out for suspicious activity. It seemed implausible there was not a connection between the sudden death of Cavendish and these notes. For the time being he waited. The tap continued to drip.

The door of the kitchen opened. Curtis with Dr Bright walked in. Everyone looked up, thankful for something to break the oppressive atmosphere. Curtis sat down but Bright remained standing. For the next few minutes, he briefed them on what had happened and what to expect next. Following this, Miller used Bright's arrival as an excuse to escape the kitchen.

-

Mary walked over to the window of Cavendish's room with Kit and looked out. The whiteness of the snow was unbroken

144

save for some distant hedges and trees. She turned to Kit saying, 'We must assume he was killed.' Tears welled in her eyes as she said this. Kit moved towards her, she shook her head and regained control quickly. 'It may be another day before the police are able to come. You've done this before. We all saw the newspapers. Can you make some inquiries, Kit?'

'This means questioning everybody. The key is to understand, where everyone was last night. Who could have gained access to the room? Did anyone hear any suspicious noises during the night? We also need to understand possible motives. Mary, you must understand how this places everyone under a degree of suspicion. Your staff, never mind Strangerson and Bright, may be offended by being even the lightest of investigations.'

'I realize this. Will you help us?' asked Mary.

'Of course, I'll try to help.'

'I want to help also. I want to catch this person.' A thought struck her, 'Do you think they might attempt to kill someone else?'

'Once I start to interview people, it will put whoever did this on their guard. The first thing we need to do is understand motive. Why would someone do this?'

Mary looked troubled but could offer no ideas. Then a thought occurred to her, 'When you spoke to grandpapa, did he have a view on who had sent those Christmas cards?'

'No,' replied Kit, 'he was mystified although he wondered if it could be someone who had a family member killed during the War.'

'Why wait until now?' said Mary.

'My thought also. I asked if it could be someone closer to home.'

'What did he say?'

'He thought it unlikely either here at the Hall or in the village.' Mary nodded in agreement. After a few moments Kit

145

added, 'He mentioned a man named Edmunds, do you know him?'

'Yes, he's been with us for years. He lost his son. Difficult character.'

'So, I gather, but even with him it brings us back to the same point, why wait until now?'

'Unless it's to divert suspicion,' suggested Mary although she seemed sceptical.

'We need to understand motive,' affirmed Kit. 'But we also need to understand what has changed. Why now?'

Esther came over to join them. She wiped her cheek with the heel of her palm. 'What are you two cooking up?'

'Kit will start an investigation into what people were doing last night while we wait for the police,' said Mary.

'Investigate? Why? You don't think he was murdered?' responded Esther, clearly astonished.

'I don't know but we can't ignore the threats. Nor can we sit idly by if we do have someone in our midst who is a murderer.' This made Esther gasp involuntarily. Mary hugged her, and they returned to their grandfather.

'I will convene everyone downstairs in the library to tell them what we're going to do. There's no need for you to come down. It may be upsetting. I suggest you remain here for the time being,' said Kit, heading towards the door. The sisters nodded but said nothing more.

-

Kit walked into the library. Miller was already there, which surprised Kit. 'Oh, I'm glad I found you Harry, can you ask everyone to assemble in the library? The girls have asked me to make some preliminary inquiries. I mean everybody, by the by, guests also, please.'

'Yes, I'll get to it,' replied Miller, happy to be active.

A thought struck Kit and he asked Miller as he was leaving, 'By the way Harry, why were you in here?'

146

Miller greeted this with a rueful smile, 'I wanted to escape from downstairs. It's rather depressing down there.'

'I can understand. Are Bright and Strangerson still down there?'

'I think they're in the drawing room now. Do you want me to ask them to come here?'

'Yes, thanks Harry and then the staff.' Miller left the room and Kit went immediately to the desk to retrieve the threatening notes.

They were nowhere to be found.

He checked the drawers and around the table. Someone had taken them. If it proved not to be Esther or Mary, then this would throw an entirely new complexion on Lord Cavendish's death.

The next thing to strike him was that someone had replaced the framed photograph of the Robert's battalion back onto the wall. Kit was certain it had been left sitting on the desk the last time he had been in the room. Before he could take another look at the photograph the door opened. Strangerson and Bright entered.

'Hello old chap. What's going on?

'All will be made clear soon. Please have a seat. I'm waiting for the others.'

Within a few minutes all the staff and guests were assembled in the library. Esther and Mary remained with Lord Cavendish and Devlin was still absent. Kit stood up and addressed the household.

'I know everyone is in shock over the tragic death of Lord Cavendish. Firstly, my sincere condolences. You will have known Lord Cavendish for many years. I have known him but a few; he was someone whom I admired greatly. I will not detain you long. Lady Esther and Mary are with him at the moment, and I think it would be a kindness if you do not disturb them much as I am sure you wish to express your sympathy. The death of Lord Cavendish was unexpected. We

147

all saw him in such good humour last night. In circumstances such as these it's natural that the police will wish to investigate in order to dismiss any possibility of foul play.'

'Good Lord' exclaimed Lady Emily, 'Are you really suggesting he could've been murdered?'

'I'm afraid this will only be confirmed following a post-mortem. But we cannot ignore anything at this stage. There will need to be an inquest of course.'

'But what makes you think someone would do this?' pressed Lady Emily.

'There are reasons that I cannot disclose at this point,' responded Kit.

'But how?' she continued.

'Dr Bright has made an initial examination and there are no obvious signs of violence. This would suggest two possible causes of death. Either natural causes or poison.'

Lady Emily gasped unconsciously and grew visibly paler. Kit saw her reaction and reacted immediately, 'Curtis, water for Lady Emily please. I'm sorry Lady Emily, I recognize how upsetting this must be.'

Kit continued, 'The police will speak to all of you to understand your whereabouts last night or if you heard anything unusual. I need hardly tell you how it is of critical importance that you speak truthfully. I have no doubt Dr Bright will have conveyed this to you. However, because of the weather, we cannot be certain of when the police will be able to get here. I would hazard a guess it will be tomorrow morning at the earliest. This is assuming, of course, that Devlin has successfully made contact. In the meantime, and at the request of Lord Cavendish's granddaughters, I will undertake some initial inquiries in advance of the police arriving here. I have had some experience in these matters. I hope you won't take offence at my questions. No one is being accused of any crime. In fact, we can't be certain any crime has taken place. Until this is confirmed, we must proceed with an open mind.'

'One question Kit.' This was Strangerson. 'The implication of what you're saying is that one of us could be the blighter that murdered Lord Cavendish.'

Kit groaned inwardly. This was unhelpful and predictably, it brought mild panic among the assembly. Holding his hands up Kit said, 'Please, please can I have your attention? I repeat, we cannot be certain any murder has taken place. However, it would make sense if we all take certain precautions.'

He then proceeded to outline some specific things for everyone to do, 'Please do not go anywhere in the house on your own. If you're in your room, please lock the door. With regard to preparation of food and serving, this should be done in pairs. Elsie and Polly will continue to prepare food, Curtis, and Miss Buchan, if I could ask you to serve. Harry Miller will be helping me in making inquiries. Please give your full assistance to him.'

There was no escaping the fact that one of the people in the library was potentially a murderer. This would cause mutual suspicion which would not cease until it was proven if a murder had taken place and the murderer brought to justice. Kit looked across the library, he saw everyone glancing surreptitiously at everyone else. All except Bright, who calmly kept his eyes firmly on Kit.

'I will spend some time with each of you over the course of today. Thank you for being so patient.'

The gathering broke up with most returning to their rooms. Evidently no one welcomed the prospect of making conversation with a potential murder suspect. Strangerson and Bright remained behind.

In a corner of the room, Kit spoke quietly to Miller in order to brief him on key questions to ask the staff. The key would be to ensure a consistent approach so a timeline of everyone's movements could be constructed and used to cross check

149

responses. Following his briefing to Miller, Kit re-joined Strangerson and Bright.

'Did you mean to scare the horses like that?' said Strangerson lighting a cigarette. His tone was light-hearted, but Kit suspected his mood was not. In fact, the question was a legitimate one if misplaced.

'Strictly speaking it was you,' smiled Bright.

'Fair point, I hadn't thought of that,' acknowledged Strangerson.

'Don't worry. They would've worked it out without your intervention,' said Kit.

'What happens now that we are openly discussing the possibility of murder?' asked Bright.

'I start to interview…'

'The suspects?' smiled Bright.

'The household,' responded Kit smiling at Bright. 'May I start with you?'

Chapter 17

Richard Bright graduated from Oxford a year after Kit had left Cambridge. When the War started, he immediately volunteered but was turned down on the grounds that he could be needed in a medical capacity at an unspecified future date. He didn't have to wait long. Within a year he was in France working near the front. Over the next two years he gained the experience of a doctor twice his age.

The intensity of this period almost came at the price of his reason. Several times he was at breaking point as he dealt, on a daily basis, with the horrendous impact of the War on the young men who fought. It was almost unbearable, but he knew if he relinquished responsibility, the misery would not go away from those injured or tasked with repairing, rebuilding, and caring. He chose to push on in the hope that his sanity would outlast the madness of war.

Following the War, he took several months off to recover. He spent time travelling in North Africa and the Greek Islands as far away from the blood-stained landscape of Flanders. As the youngest son of a comparatively wealthy family, he had a comfortable income but one that still required him to find a profession, hence his choice of a career in medicine.

All this he related to Kit briefly. Reluctantly, Kit probed more on the War. Intuitively he felt the death of Cavendish, if it was murder, might be motivated by the War rather than money. The key would be to use the War, money, and

151

inheritance as a lens through which to view the stories, motivations, and actions of everyone at Cavendish Hall.

Bright confirmed he had not met any of the Cavendish family during the conflict. This could easily be checked with the War Office and Kit's instinct was to believe Bright. However, he was also conscious that any personal feelings towards Bright should be kept in check. Incontestably, Bright was a good fellow. Kit recognized this was someone who, in other circumstances, could be a good friend. They were of a similar age, both sporting men, cultured and Bright was clearly a gentleman. It was difficult to begrudge his attractiveness to the girls either, even if it represented a threat to him.

Since returning from his travels, he had been happy to act as a locum in various parts of the country. Again, both recognized this was easily checked and Bright happily supplied Kit with a list of names, places, and dates for his employment over the last six months. None of the places, at this stage anyway, put him into contact with the Cavendish family.

'Incidentally, before today, have you been in this room?' asked Kit.

'The library, no, just the drawing room and my bedroom' responded Bright.

The rest of the interview was confined to helping Kit understand what would happen next with Cavendish. Following the conclusion of their interview, Kit reflected that Bright, ostensibly, had no obvious motive for killing Cavendish. Their paths had not appeared to cross, and he had nothing to gain from either trying to threaten Cavendish or from killing him. The next meeting would be Strangerson.

-

'A damned bad show,' said Strangerson by way of initiating the interview.

'Indeed,' responded Kit non-committedly. He proceeded to inquire about Strangerson's association with the Cavendish family.

'I knew Robert but had never met the old man until this trip. Robert was a Captain in my battalion. I was a sharpshooter for the unit along with Teddy Masters; we all had chums we worked with. One would look and the other would take a pop. We made a very effective team. By the end of the War, the Boche were after me, that's for sure. I fancy I had a price on my head.'

Kit nodded; he was familiar with the role Strangerson performed but was uncomfortable with it, too. Both sides had used sharpshooters extensively throughout the War. They had been responsible for many deaths and maiming.

Sensing that Kit was not in favour of such tactics, Strangerson added hastily, 'But of course Fritz started it.'

'Did Teddy make it all the way through?'

'No,' said Strangerson and he stopped for a moment to compose himself then continued, 'He caught one at Cambrai.'

Kit looked up at this, 'Like Robert.'

'Yes, by a sniper also. Sadly, an occupational hazard, you might say.'

'You said you were there when Robert was killed. Can you tell me more about what you saw?'

'Certainly, old boy. Remember it vividly. The main stuff at Cambrai had stopped, just the odd empty beating of the gongs by the Hun. I think they were waiting for Christmas like ourselves. Anyway, there seemed to be something happening on this particular night out in No Man's Land. A few flares were going up and we could see one of our boys was being dragged back into the trench.'

This made Kit start. 'Could you see who?'

'No, too far away. Anyway, as the chaps neared our lines, all hell breaks loose. First there was a flare, then a bomb went off near us and Fritz started firing. I let of a few back in the direction of the gunfire. Doubt I hit anything. When I looked back, I could see a few of our chaps coming out of the trench

153

and dragging some bodies back. A few minutes later, the word came down the line that Robert had copped it. Poor blighter.'

'You went over to see him?' asked Kit.

'Yes. Immediately. The sniper had caught him in the head. Professionally speaking I have to say it was a bloody good shot, but my God, who would do such a beastly thing? There are rules, you know. Well, there are no rules but even so, it's just not done that sort of thing. Typical Hun trick,' concluded Strangerson.

Strangerson's post war activities had been limited to writing scholarly articles for various presses about his experiences in South America and searching for a lecturing job at a university. There were not many in supply as the War had severely drained university intakes.

They chatted for a few minutes on Strangerson's experiences in both South America and the Antarctic but neither seemed material to the current circumstances to make them worthy of detailed discussion. If it were the case that Cavendish was poisoned then the source of the poison, assuming it could be identified, might require further inquiry with Strangerson.

The last part of the interview checked on Strangerson's movements over the previous twenty-four hours. They parted soon after and Kit met up with Miller to discuss progress.

-

'I have spoken with Polly, Elsie and Miss Buchan,' related Miller, 'But it's still too early yet for them. They're all a bit traumatized and scared now, thanks to your pep talk.'

'Yes, I was unsure how far to push it then Strangerson pipes up and panic sets in.'

'It seems unlikely any of them could be involved. Polly has never been outside of Lincolnshire, and I gather has no relatives in London, so how could she have arranged threatening cards? Both Miss Buchan and Elsie could've had someone send the cards as they have family down there, but

154

why? And why wait until now? Of course, working in the kitchen means they certainly would've had the opportunity to poison Lord Cavendish.'

'Yes,' replied Kit, 'But then how did we avoid being poisoned? Neither Elsie nor Polly served much of the food on Christmas Day. Curtis did most of the serving and I have racked my memory to think of an occasion when he could've slipped Lord Cavendish anything but avoid giving it to us. Surely someone would have seen this happen anyway.'

'I see what you mean about Elsie and Polly. Was there no other occasion when he might've taken something without us seeing?'

'Of course, it's very possible. But then we are in the realms of a slow acting agent. At this point I don't see how any of the ladies would have developed enough expertise in toxicology to kill Lord Cavendish. It seems utterly implausible.'

'So, we've neither motive nor the ability to carry out the murder then as far as the three ladies are concerned,' said Miller.

'There are no motives?'

'Not really. They would all possibly lose their jobs if Lady Emily took over the Hall. She's not well loved. Now if it'd been her who was killed…'

'Harry, careful with the comments on Lady Emily, it's a touchy enough situation here without you putting me in hot water,' laughed Kit.

'Anyway, it's not obvious what they'd gain from his death. Besides which, and I'm not an expert, but they all seem genuinely grieved. I think they liked the old boy, so I'd be surprised if any would want to harm him.

'What about this room? Has anyone been in here to tidy up?

'No, nobody has been in here since yesterday before lunch.'

'So, nobody moved the photograph?' continued Kit.

'I asked. Nobody.'

This was strange and potentially material. Moving on he asked, 'Anything else you could pick up from them?'

'Nothing I can put my finger on but maybe you should speak to Curtis. I'm certain there's something they're not saying about him. He was around for all of the interviews. They might be holding some things back.'

'Very well, let's see what he has to say.'

-

Miller was right about the sense of grief. It was like a black curtain falling down, blocking out all light, creating a void. Curtis walked into the room absently; stripped of pretension, lost without purpose. Kit found it difficult to believe the man was acting. His eyes were tear-stained red, his voice choked with emotion despite his efforts to control it. Kit invited him to sit down and take a few moments to compose himself.

He spoke of a life of service to the Cavendish family. It seemed he had known barely any other life. His education had finished when he was thirteen. He had lived in country houses since then working his way up through the ranks.

Speaking to Curtis, Kit found himself thinking about his own staff. He preferred to spend time either at his flat in London or on his frequent travels abroad. This kept him away from his father and half-brother, which was probably for the best. With a pang of guilt, he realized how rarely he saw the old staff now. He wondered if he still commanded the same degree of affection with them.

Curtis had seen many changes over the years at Cavendish Hall. When he had joined there was a large family in the house and staffing was double the current level. Never a great country house, it had once upon a time been enjoyed some degree of importance, at least in the county. The War and its aftermath had changed things, observed Curtis. When Kit probed about John and Robert, he immediately detected a change in tone from Curtis. He transformed from the grieving manservant into a diplomat. Kit was reminded of Talleyrand's maxim that speech was given to man to disguise his thoughts.

'How did you feel about the loss of the two boys?'

'Shocked. How else would one feel? It was a great loss.'

'Did you like John and Robert?'

'It's not for me to say, sir. I was here to serve them.'

Kit felt there was more he might have said on this, but he dropped the subject and dwelt more on the whereabouts of the staff over Christmas Day. He and Miller would cross check the answers to these questions later on in the evening.

'Oh, just one other thing,' asked Kit, 'Did you visit the library yesterday to tidy or arrange things?'

'No. I was not in the library all afternoon.'

'Did you see anyone go in here?

'I'm fairly certain I did not.'

'Very well. I think we've covered everything, Curtis. If something else comes to mind, you can speak to me any time, in complete confidence.'

Curtis stood up and thanked Kit as left the room. Looking out the window, he considered his next move. Although he was not looking forward to it, he realized he needed to interview Lady Emily and Henry, ideally separately. He went up to Lady Emily's room.

-

Agnes tidied up the room for the third time in the space of an hour. Lady Emily, meanwhile, stared vacantly out of the window. Tears were still running down her cheek. She turned to Agnes finally and said, 'Agnes, I'm quite sure the room is tidy now. If you're finished, I think you should join Mr Miller and help with whatever inquiries he sees fit.'

'Yes ma'am,' replied Agnes and she left Lady Emily to her thoughts. She continued to gaze emptily at the wintry grounds, seeing nothing, feeling numb. Her thoughts were of Robert and of Lord Cavendish. She knew how the last few years had been hellish for all of them. Yet the anger she had felt towards

157

Cavendish was gone. Just at the moment he seemed to want to atone for the past, he had gone. The anger was now replaced by fear.

She thought about her wedding to Robert; was it really twenty years one ago? He was everything she had wanted. When Henry had arrived so early in the marriage, she had felt complete. She'd brought into the world a boy. Robert was delighted, their happiness was sealed. Happiness is momentary though. She soon found this out. Of course, she loved him. She always had. As the years passed and no more children came, she understood his frustration. It was natural, wasn't it?

The time away from home on duty was part of their life. It was accepted and understood. When did it first seem to her that he preferred to be away? Was it her or was it Henry? The child was so different from Robert in temperament, in his interests and in his health. She sensed Robert's difficulty, not in loving him, but in his ability to conceal his contempt. He despised weakness because he thought himself strong. But in the end, he was the one who had been weak. She had forgiven him but how could she ever forget?

From then on, the marriage existed in name only. Her life was built around Henry. Robert's life became increasingly devoted to the army, partly because he desired it so, partly out of necessity as the War loomed. Emily grew to recognize Robert's concerns in her son. As the years passed, she saw more clearly the things that had dismayed Robert and, reluctantly, began to share them.

His detachedness, his lack of interest in the future was a constant worry and source of friction between them. She needed help, but Robert and Lord Cavendish were fighting an unending war. Neither seemed interested in the child, the young man, the future Lord Cavendish. So, it was left to her and the school. The boy hated school from the start. Emily had no idea what he wanted.

158

Neither school nor being at home seemed to please him although she noted, unhappily, how he seemed to relax more during the summers at Cavendish Hall with the sisters, the stable girl and, of course, the Governess. While Henry enjoyed these summers at the Hall, they also revealed to Emily the extent of the disappointment in him felt by his father and grandfather. It was unspoken, of course, but Henry's absence at shoots, or his disinterest in their discussions on the War seemed unnatural in a boy. The feeling that the two men were somehow responsible for Henry's vulnerable nature grew in Emily. It became the guiding narrative for hating the Cavendish family long before she lost Robert.

The death of Robert had merely acted as a respite from this hatred, but a new element was added. Guilt. She withdrew from the Cavendish's as much as they avoided her. Her own family was sympathetic, but she only had her father. He was too immersed in the family business to provide the consolation she craved for her loss. Furthermore, his desire to involve Henry in the business went against her wishes. It added to her sense of isolation. She began to avoid contact with her own family also for fear it could interfere with her ambitions for Henry.

He was the future Lord Cavendish. Her son would be a lord. Henry's disdain for the rank he would inherit was unfathomable to her. This place in society seemed, to her, to be irreconcilable with commerce. Of course, it would be painful for her father, who adored Henry and always hoped he would one day run the family business. This Christmas had made her realize the extent to which Henry's interests lay with the business rather than fulfilling the role destiny had provided. Anger and frustration had built up in her, and in Henry, too. His future was an increasing source of conflict between the pair.

And now Cavendish was dead. Fear overwhelmed her. The questioning would begin soon. The picking away at motives;

159

the speculation around method, the proof that he was poisoned. She knew where the trail of questions would lead. There was no avoiding it. She knew what had to be done.

-

Kit knocked on the door. He heard Lady Emily say, 'Enter.' She was sitting by the window, and it was clear she had been crying.

'Lady Emily, I am so sorry to intrude. May I tell you how sorry I am for your loss. I know this is upsetting but would you mind if I asked you some questions? This will help provide a clearer picture of what has happened.'

She nodded in response. He recoiled at the banality of his words but what else was there to say? Grief cannot be repelled by the kindly meant words of another. The words act more as a comfort for the consoler than the consoled. Sitting down opposite her he was about to speak when Lady Emily held her hand up to stop him.

Calmly, in a quiet voice she said, 'I killed him. I killed him with poison. I wish to confess, Lord Aston.'

Chapter 18

Devlin returned to Cavendish Hall in the early afternoon. He sat down at the kitchen table and had some lunch. Miller saw him return and joined the chauffeur. He related to Miller his busy morning as he was eating. The phone lines were not working at the village either. Rather than returning to the Hall, he'd borrowed a horse from the undertaker and rode several miles to the nearest town, Louth.

Upon reaching Louth he went straight to the police station and informed the Duty Officer of the death of Lord Cavendish. They informed him that there were too few policemen on duty due to the weather; none could be released. It would be tomorrow before any police officers could come to the Hall. In the meantime, they undertook to contact the County Police in Lincoln because it would have greater resources for any potential investigation. Having accomplished his mission, he returned to Little Gloston.

Miller updated him on what had happened since his departure. Devlin was surprised to learn of the possibility that Cavendish's death might not have been by natural causes. He accepted readily the need to account for his own movements over the previous days. Miller added to the notes already made with the other members of staff. He couldn't help but smile inwardly when Devlin drew a veil over his activities on

Christmas night. It was almost certain he had spent a romantic evening with Polly. This was not likely to remain secret for long if the police became involved.

Devlin's story was consistent with the other stories told by the staff. It was clear he liked working for Cavendish. Of course, it was scarcely credible that Devlin would try to incriminate himself, but it seemed he did hold Cavendish in high regard. At no point, despite his death, did he refer to him as anything other than Lord Cavendish. Miller guessed the Irishman felt a debt of gratitude for being given the job. Therefore, it was difficult to detect what direct motive he would have. Instead, Miller decided to look further back. Devlin guessed immediately where Miller was heading.

'I see. You're thinking because I'm Irish…'

Miller held his hands up and said, 'Hang on, I have to do this. You're not accused of anything. The police will ask you all this anyway.'

'Why should I tell you then?'

'His lordship has been asked by the ladies to make initial inquiries. He's done this before.'

Devlin told him in more detail about his life leading up to his employment by Cavendish after the war. He had arrived in England in the late 1916 with the intention of volunteering for the army upon arrival. In the aftermath of the Somme offensive, the army was desperate for new recruits, and they had readily accepted Devlin. Miller would like to have understood more about his reasons for joining but he knew, from experience, that many Irishmen had volunteered and fought with great bravery.

His first action was not until early 1917 as the British pushed forward following the German withdrawal from the Somme. Within a few weeks he had received the first of several decorations for his actions. By the summer of 1917, he'd been promoted to Lance Corporal. He was a Corporal by the time of Cambrai.

He did not go through the War entirely unscathed and received minor shrapnel wounds on two occasions. Neither were serious enough to remove him from the conflict. As a soldier in the Irish Guards, he had not come into contact with either Robert or Lord Cavendish. In fact, he claimed not to have heard of either of them until towards the end of the War.

Devlin's demobilisation took place in early 1919. He joined thousands of former soldiers looking for a job. Following demobilization, he kept an eye on any newspaper articles about ranking military personnel returning to the country. He sent letters offering his services as a chauffeur. There had been only one reply. Miller nodded sympathetically. He also had returned to civilian life in early nineteen. He went to jail.

Miller ended the interview soon after. Devlin had provided a detailed account of his War record. All of this could be verified without difficulty and Miller had no doubts that Devlin had performed his duty in the War with courage. They chatted for a while about the War, something Miller rarely did, but Devlin's experience was similar to his own and he identified with the Irishman.

The War and his employment with Cavendish did not point to any motive. If anything, as with the other domestic staff, his death went very much against their interests. However, as comprehensive as his story of the War had been, his recounting of his time before 1916 had not been very detailed. Specifically, it was unclear to Miller what role, if any, Devlin had in the conflict in Ireland. However, as Lord Cavendish had not been involved with Ireland, there was no obvious connection. This meant Devlin had no obvious motive to kill his benefactor.

Miller went to the library but found no sign of Kit. He returned to the hallway and went upstairs and found Kit coming out of Lady Emily's room. Although he could not see her, it was clear she was crying. Kit shook his head at Miller

163

and led him down to the library to update him on his conversation with Lady Emily.

'She confessed to killing him,' said Kit as they both sat down.

-

'…I'm confessing,' said Lady Emily to Kit.

'Go on, Lady Emily,' responded Kit. It was difficult to hide his surprise and the scepticism was easily readable on his face.

'It's no secret, I suppose. We disliked one another. They have treated Henry and me like pariahs. Henry will be the next Lord Cavendish and yet that man has never had any time for him nor those two girls.'

'So, you killed him?'

'Correct. With poison.'

'I see, Lady Emily. What type of poison did you use?'

Lady Emily was taken aback. Why should any further questions be required? 'What do you mean? Does it matter? One poison is like any other I imagine.'

'Lady Emily,' said Kit patiently, 'there will be an inquest. Part of this inquest will be evidence from the doctor who performs the post-mortem. Clearly, this will establish the cause of death beyond doubt. If, as you say, it was poison then you will be expected to answer certain questions regarding the selection of the poison, how you sourced it and how you went about giving it to Lord Cavendish to consume, when you did so, etcetera.'

This was unexpected news to Lady Emily. Her assumption that an admission of guilt from her would prompt no further investigation was proving to be somewhat wide of the mark. In fact, Lady Emily's career in murder was singularly devoid of any actual, real life, experience. This meant she could not call upon any prior knowledge on poisoning to disguise her obvious innocence of the crime.

In such situations, where she lacked either competence or knowledge to deal with human obstructions, her default

164

approach was high-handedness. With social inferiors, this approach was devastatingly effective and had emboldened her over the years. Facing Lord Kit Aston, war hero, scholar and, well, a genuine blue-blooded lord, was another matter. In Lady Emily's favour, however, she had genuine courage and no small reservoir of righteous indignation that could be called upon when required. She chose to attack.

'Forgive me Lord Aston, but are you insinuating that I'm not telling the truth?' In any other situation, Kit would have found her hauteur at not being appreciated for the murderer she was, amusing.

'I'm implying nothing, but you would need to prove to the satisfaction of the law officers if you did, indeed, execute this crime.'

'But my word is…'

'Not enough Lady Emily,' interjected Kit. 'The law requires proof of guilt in cases of murder. As it stands at the moment, we have no proof a murder has taken place and, if you'll forgive me, you have not convinced me that you're guilty of anything other than lying to protect Henry.'

'This is outrageous!' Lady Emily leapt to her feet. 'Are you questioning my integrity?'

'You've just admitted to a murder, Lady Emily. You would agree a murderer is likely to be somewhat deficient in this area.'

Lady Emily stared down at Kit, speechless. This was not going as she had planned and if anything, she was beginning to look foolish. Then she remembered what Kit had said and found new reserves of energy.

'How dare you bring my son in to this!'

She was in a rage now and Kit genuinely wondered if she would attack him.

'I saw the book he took from the library.'

This silenced Lady Emily immediately. She collapsed into the chair and began to cry. Kit immediately went to her side

165

and comforted her. He waited for the first wave of tears to subside and then he returned to the seat opposite her. She wiped the corner of her eyes with a handkerchief and looked at Kit. Resignation and fear were etched on her face.

'What do you intend doing?'

'I wish to speak to him, in private. The book means nothing unless a crime has been committed. Even if a crime has been committed then we need more evidence before any case can be made against Henry. I'd like to understand why he chose this book. You have to admit, it's a somewhat strange choice.'

'I can see how this will be perceived, Henry killing his uncle in order to inherit this ghastly title. He didn't do it. He's just a boy.'

'I am inclined to agree with you, but it is imperative he and I speak. In private.'

'He's just a boy,' she replied pleadingly before breaking down again, seemingly beyond comfort. Kit left soon afterwards promising to send Agnes up to the room. As he shut the door, he saw Miller outside in the corridor.

-

After Miller and Kit had finished updating one another on the latest developments, Miller went downstairs to send Agnes up to Lady Emily. Then he returned to his room to get his overcoat. His next interview was with Bill Edmunds, and this meant a walk in the cold weather to the cottage.

Kit, meanwhile, went to see the girls in Lord Cavendish's room. As he entered, he was struck by how cold the room was. This made sense, of course, as it was unclear, at this point, when the body would be taken to a mortuary. All of the windows had been opened. Mary and Esther were sitting by the window, dressed in overcoats. He walked over and joined them.

For the next ten minutes he brought them up to date on the interviews and what he would do next. Both of the girls were more composed now and Kit felt it was appropriate to ask

166

them some questions. Both understood and answered freely, desperate to help. Their answers helped fill in some of the gaps as well as verify other stories. It confirmed, in Kit's mind, how it would have been very difficult for one of the guests to poison Cavendish without someone witnessing the moment when they had done so.

Finally, he asked the same question he had asked all the other interviewees, 'After yesterday morning, were either of you in the library at all?'

Both answered no. 'Why do you ask?' said Esther.

Kit did not answer her question immediately, asking instead, 'Did you ask anyone to tidy the library yesterday?'

Again, the response was no. Mary looked at Kit directly and raised her eyebrows. This was his cue to reveal the disappearance of the threatening notes. The implications were not lost on Mary.

'Gone!' exclaimed Mary. 'But this means...' she left the sentence unfinished.

'Yes, it was someone or some people in this house who sent the notes,' finished Kit.

'But this is extraordinary, who would do such a thing?' said Esther.

'The same person who may have killed grandpapa, Essie,' pointed out Mary.

Kit stayed quiet. What Mary said was undeniable. He mentioned some of his other observations including how the photograph of the battalion, which had been sitting on the desk, had been replaced on the wall.

'This is very strange,' observed Mary. 'I glanced at it the other day to look for Mr Strangerson. It was probably the first time I have looked at it in years. It's always just been there, in the same place.'

'Yes, he's sitting front row,' said Kit. 'I was looking for him, too. I wonder how many of them came back. Not many I suspect, poor blighters.'

Mary held Esther's hand and then looked at Kit. 'Who're you going to speak to now?'

'Henry. Harry's off to see Bill Edmunds.' Kit thought for a moment then asked, 'Can you tell me a little about Mr Edmunds?'

Esther answered, 'He's been with us for years. He's of a somewhat taciturn disposition, to put it mildly. Not the nicest person but not the worst either. The family has changed a lot since they lost Ben. Can't blame them, I suppose.'

'Does he have a key to the house?'

'Yes, I imagine he does,' said Esther, 'You don't really think he would do anything?'

Kit looked at Esther and Mary. He could tell how much they were putting all their hopes on him coming up with answers. Yet he found himself groping in the dark. If Cavendish had been murdered, then finding the killer would not alter the fact: he was gone. Any comfort would be momentary. At the moment, far from providing comfort and reassurance, he sensed he was adding to their unease and fear. Yet lying to them was indefensible and short sighted.

'We can't jump to any conclusions yet, Esther. I'll continue to speak to people and see if something emerges.' He stood up, indicating he would talk to Henry. Mary rolled her eyes, but Esther looked tearful. He desperately wanted to hold and console her.

Chapter 19

Kit walked along the corridor to Henry's room. Several portraits, variable in quality, adorned the walls featuring descendants of the Cavendish family. Interestingly it was possible to see, in the more recent portraits, the family resemblance to the later Cavendish men, including the Roman nose. The sisters were very different.

The house was unusually quiet, his footsteps echoed on the parquet. Henry's room was at the end of the corridor. He gave a couple of sharp knocks without identifying himself. Inside he could hear the sound of a drawer opening and closing. Finally, after knocking again he heard disdainful, 'Yes? Who is it?'

'Henry, it's Kit, may I enter?' Kit waited to hear if Henry did anything else. There was no sound apart from his answer.

'Yes.'

The room was also very cold. Henry had left the window open. Kit remarked on how cold the room was. Without replying, Henry stood up and closed the window. He turned around to Kit and asked, 'Better?'

Kit merely nodded in response. Give him a little of his own medicine, he thought, and sat down. Henry also sat down. They regarded one another for a few moments. Deciding to unsettle him, Kit went straight to the matter in hand.

'Your mother just confessed to murdering your grandfather.'

'What?' exploded Henry. 'Never. I've never heard anything so ridiculous in my life. It's inconceivable.'

'Do you mean confessing or murder?'

'You know perfectly well what I mean.'

Kit remained silent for a few moments waiting to see if Henry would add anything. Henry said nothing, so Kit added, 'She says she poisoned him.'

'Preposterous,' snorted Henry.

'Why would she confess then, or do you not believe me?'

Henry regarded Kit silently then said, 'I don't know what to believe apart from one thing, my mother is not a murderer.'

'As it happens Henry, I agree with you. Yet here we are. Your mother has confessed and whether it is true or not, if Lord Cavendish was murdered and she persists in this claim, she will hang. I ask you again: why do you think she would confess?'

'You tell me,' said Henry sulkily.

'I shall. She did it to protect you. She thinks you killed him.'

'My mother would never say something so absurd,' exclaimed Henry.

'She didn't have to,' replied Kit. 'For the third time of asking, why do you think she's saying she killed him?'

'This is getting boring. Why don't you tell me as you're so smart?'

'Don't patronize me you fool,' snapped Kit. Indicating the drawer, he continued, 'What did you put in the drawer before I came in?'

'I don't know what you mean.'

'I'm not an idiot Henry, nor is your mother. We both saw the book you took from the library. It's in the drawer.'

Henry face turned red. Sullenly he opened the drawer and took out the book, "*A Treatise on Poisons*" and put it on the

170

table. He no longer seemed so defiant and rather than look at Kit, stared out of the window instead. Turning the book over in his hand, Kit spent a few minutes flicking through before placing it back on the table. The book was not for the layman. One look confirmed in Kit's mind - this was written with an expert reader in mind. If Henry was able to read and understand such a work, it revealed how the young man had much greater intellectual capacity than he had previously thought.

'Just because I was reading this book doesn't make me a murderer.'

This was a fair point, accepted Kit, but not one that would go well with everyone.

'Why are you so interested in this subject?' asked Kit. His tone was softer. He hoped it would encourage the young man to open up. It was important he understand how seriously this would go for him if it turned out Cavendish had been poisoned. More silence save for the sound of the clock ticking. Finally, Henry looked at Kit.

'I'm interested in toxicology, but not with a view to killing my grandfather. The last thing on my mind is being the future Lord Cavendish. I would happily pass on inheriting, thank you.'

'Then why, Henry? This is serious.'

'Believe it or not, I have grasped this point. The truth is, I'm interested in this subject because my grandfather has a problem.' It took Kit a moment to register that Henry was referring to Lady Emily's father. Henry continued, 'We've lost some of our workers at the factory through illness. I'm sure it's related to airborne poisons. I was researching this. My mother, you may have noticed, is somewhat antagonistic towards my interest in science, generally and my grandfather's business, specifically. I didn't want her to know.'

Kit believed him. However, even if he was telling the truth, the appearance created a problem not easily be ignored. At

171

best it was a circumstantial point in terms of evidence, but in a public inquest, it would portray Henry in a bad light. Looking at the boy, it was clear he was angry and fearful. Rather than scare the young man senseless, Kit adopted a different tack.

'There's no certainty your grandfather had been murdered. Furthermore, there is another factor that might discount you being involved but I cannot go into this at the moment.'

'Really?' said Henry scornfully, 'I mean, it's absurd, the whole idea.'

'One more question. Do you have a typewriter?' said Kit ignoring the derisive tone Henry had adopted.

This bemused Henry, but he answered, 'At the house, no. My grandfather's business no doubt has one. In fact, many.'

There was a knock at the door, Lady Emily entered. Henry looked up at his mother, he could see the eyes still red from the tears. For the first time in ages, he looked at her with tenderness. How could he have forgotten that she loved him? The shame burst over him like a flood. There was anger also, the feeling that her response was driven by the belief he was a child rather than an adult. He wanted to hug her and scold her simultaneously. However, he stopped himself, partly because Kit was there but also because he was not sure how to console her.

'How could you be so silly mama?' said Henry, perhaps more angrily than he had intended. He softened his tone a little and said, 'I would never do such a foul deed.'

'I'm sorry Henry, it was when I saw that frightful book.'

This was an opportune moment for Kit to leave the room and he bid them goodbye. The interviews proved nothing one way or another about the possible guilt of Lady Emily and Henry in Kit's view. There was much yet to ascertain. One thing was now certain: he was hungry. He went down to the kitchen to steal some food.

-

172

Now fully protected against the bitter cold, Miller made ready to visit Edmunds. Sam looked up at him with a slight tilt of the head. It was evident the little terrier was bored cooped up in the house and fancied a little fresh air. Reluctantly, Miller gave in.

'Little so and so. Come on.'

Sam gave a yelp of delight and, for once, did not object to Miller putting a coat on him. The pair made their way out into the afternoon chill. Glancing down at the little dog Miller began to chat, 'Let me know when you want to be carried.'

The little dog barked in response. A few minutes later when they reached the deeper snow in the garden he barked twice. Although not a trained linguist in canine, it was apparent the little dog would need to be carried at this point. Pushing through the snow to the cottage Miller could see fresh tracks in the snow, leading from the Hall to the cottage. Someone had clearly been to the Hall and returned this morning. It would have been early this morning before Miller had risen. He was surprised no one had mentioned any visit. Perhaps no one was aware. This would put an entirely different complexion on the tracks. At the side of the house, he also saw footprints in the snow. They seemed to lead towards the stables.

They made better time across the field with Sam being carried. Within a few minutes Miller arrived outside at the door of the Edmunds cottage. It was a striking cottage from the outside. Clearly very old but well maintained. It was made from limestone that had darkened over the ages. Through the window he could see a roaring fire and two fairly elderly people sitting in front of it drinking tea. He knocked the old oak door.

The door was unlocked from the inside after a few moments. A woman, who Miller supposed to be Mrs Edmunds, greeted him irritably. Up close he realized she was younger than he had first supposed. The hair was grey and the lines on her face betrayed not so much a long life as one that

173

had been hard. It was clear she had once been a handsome woman but now he could only see loss in her eyes.

'Yes?' Well, she gets straight to the point thought Miller. The best thing in his view was to be equally to the point.

'May I come in? I've come from Cavendish Hall. Lord Cavendish is dead.'

The look of surprise on her face was genuine. She opened the door wider and walked away. Miller took it as his cue to walk in. In the background he heard Edmunds say, 'Who is it?'

'Someone from the Hall.'

Edmunds stood up to meet, if not exactly greet, the visitor. He was tall, easily six three or more. Miller suspected his willowy frame disguised great strength. Like Mrs Edmunds, closer inspection revealed him to be younger than he had first thought, around fifty.

'Who are you?' Clearly Edmunds was as welcoming as his good lady wife.

'The name's Harry Miller,' he decided against attempting a handshake. 'I'm the manservant of Lord Christopher Aston who is a guest at the Hall. As I was saying to Mrs Edmunds, Lord Cavendish died overnight.'

The couple looked at one another. Edmunds turned away and went to the fireside chair and sat down. His wife joined him. He studied Miller for a moment then pointed to the seat.

'Sit down.'

The cottage was small inside with barely a few seats and a dining table. On the wall was a photograph of a young soldier looking into the camera intently. There was little decoration in the house. It felt as though they were still in mourning. How many households across the country were like this, wondered Miller?

Doing as he was bid; Miller sat down and began to relate more of the circumstances surrounding Cavendish's death. The news that the police would also be involved did not seem to disturb them. Why should this or Cavendish's death mean anything to them, reflected Miller? They had lost everything they cared about.

'How did he die?' asked Edmunds.

'We're not sure if it is foul play yet.' explained Miller.

'Why the police?' he continued.

'There will have to be an inquest. He was here yesterday; we saw him come out. The police will want to speak to everyone who was in contact with him over the last few days.'

'I see. He always visits at us at Christmas.'

'How did you get on with him?'

'I liked him well enough.'

Miller noted the emphasis on 'him' and asked, 'But not his sons?'

'Hardly knew them. They never had much interest in the estate.'

Miller was not sure where to go on the subject of John and Robert so left it. 'Did you visit the Hall yesterday?'

'No,' said Mrs Edmunds. It was clear she had to be lying but Miller saw no value in drawing to her attention the tracks in the snow. Edmunds shifted in his seat uncomfortably and there was silence for a few moments. They knew he suspected them of lying but it did not seem to Miller that the deception related to Cavendish. Again, it seemed better to move away from this topic.

As they spoke, the door flew open. Miller swung around. In walked a young teenage girl. She was tall and slender like Edmunds but with striking green eyes like Mrs Edmunds, who she resembled. Miller thought her beautiful. Striding down towards her parents and Miller, she looked at her parents for an explanation. As garrulous as her parents, thought Miller. Sam began barking at the visitor for a few moments but then went quiet when she looked down at him.

'A visitor to the Hall. Lord Cavendish is dead,' explained Mrs Edmunds.

175

Tears welled up in the young girl's eyes, but Miller sensed something else also: anger.

'Good.'

She turned and stalked out of the room, quickly followed by her mother.

Miller turned to Edmunds for an explanation. Staring into the fire Edmunds remained silent, wrestling with how he should respond. Finally, he said, 'She blames the family for a lot of things.'

'The death of your son?'

Edmunds looked at Miller in the eye. Then after a few moments he asked, 'Where you there?'

'Yes, I joined in fifteen,' replied Miller.

'You came back.' It wasn't a question.

'I was lucky. Nearly bought it a few times,' responded Miller, then added, 'I'm sorry about your son.'

'What made you go?'

It was Miller's turn to feel uncomfortable under the penetrating gaze of Edmunds. The truth, where Miller was concerned, lay somewhere between anger at the Germans and a desire to evade the law which was getting perilously close to catching him. He held the gaze of Edmunds and told him the truth. Edmunds nodded and returned to looking into the fire. For a few minutes neither said anything. Finally, Edmunds turned to him and said, 'I didn't try to stop him. My son was a man. He chose to go. It was nothing to do with them, at the Hall. I don't blame them.'

Chapter 20

It was early evening when Miller returned. Curtis told him he would find Kit upstairs in the drawing room. Without bothering to take off his overcoat, Miller bounded up the stairs and burst in on Kit who was sitting with Strangerson and Bright. All three looked up with surprise as Miller burst into the room. Kit caught Bright's eye. He could see wry amusement on the doctor's face.

'I say,' said Strangerson, somewhat taken aback.

'My apologies gentlemen,' said Miller quickly, 'I though his lordship was alone.'

Strangerson looked like he was shaping up to toss a rebuke in Miller's direction, so Kit sensed he should step in and rescue the situation.

'Don't worry Harry. I'm sure these gentlemen have faced far worse than over exuberant manservants.'

Bright laughed and added, 'Well, there've been a few matrons that certainly put the fear of God into me.'

Getting into the spirit of the joshing, Strangerson added, 'A few aunts too, I warrant.'

'Ye Gods. Aunts,' agreed Kit. 'I have an Aunt Agatha who could've had the Boche cowering in their trenches asking for their mummy had we had the good sense to deploy her in a direct assault.'

The atmosphere relaxed considerably.

'Join us, Harry,' said Kit turning to the two other men, 'if this is acceptable.' Both agreed readily. 'How was your visit with Edmunds household?'

Miller glanced at Kit who nodded back. For the next ten minutes he related most of the details of his interview but did not mention the tracks in the snow or about the daughter. When he had finished, Kit thanked him. Miller took this as his cue to leave. Strangerson stood up also and announced he would go to his room, and he followed Miller.

In the hallway Strangerson clapped Miller on the back and apologized for his reaction, 'Sorry old boy, you caught me by surprise. Last chap who did that is lying in an unmarked grave in Cambrai.' Both laughed and parted company as Strangerson went up the stairs.

-

Kit and Bright sat together and chatted on general topics. Both steered clear of any mention of Lord Cavendish, the girls, or the War. They felt comfortable with each other, and Kit hoped Bright was not implicated if something was amiss in the death of Lord Cavendish.

The conversation turned to Bright's future in the area. He was not sure how long he would stay but admitted that, after an unhappy start with Dr Stevens, he was beginning to enjoy his time in Lincolnshire and getting to know more people. His biggest problem was the unrelenting and single-minded desire of most of the mothers he met to marry him off either to one of their daughters or someone else.

Kit laughed and replied, 'Yes, I know a thing or two about these things. What did Jane Austen say?'

'Ah yes, well, unless I miss my guess, Kit, you're unquestionably a man of good fortune. I wish I could say the same for myself.' The thought appeared in Kit's head, much to his regret, that the Cavendish girls could solve this problem rapidly. The same thought occurred to Bright also and he

178

added, 'Although I'm keen to avoid being marked as a fortune hunter also.'

The topic was moving dangerously close to the Cavendish sisters. Recognizing this, Kit gently steered it in another direction. This topic was for another time, hopefully never.

-

Miller took off his coat, gave it a shake and deposited it in the cloakroom located beside the kitchen. Returning to the kitchen he saw Elsie busy making a simple evening meal for the household. Creeping up beside her, he tapped her on one shoulder and dipped around the other to try the broth cooking on the stove.

'Mr Miller you're the devil incarnate,' cried Elsie but without malice.

'Very nice Elsie. You'd make a wonderful wife. What do you say you leave this place and run away with me?'

'You're just after a cook. Now if it was me body you were after…'

Miller viewed the ample frame of Elsie and grinned, 'You're all woman Elsie, and no mistake.'

'Too much woman for you, young man,' laughed Elsie. 'What do you want?'

'I've just been to the Edmunds cottage,' he told Elsie.

'Oh really, why did you go there?' There was an unmistakable note of caution in the cook's voice.

'I wanted to ask them some questions about his Lord Cavendish's death. It turns out they didn't know he'd passed away.'

'Why would they know?' asked Elsie, genuinely surprised. 'None of us went to tell them. The shock, I suppose.'

'Well, there were tracks leading from the Hall up to the cottage. Fresh tracks. I thought someone must have either visited them or one of the family came here.' Miller could not be sure, but he sensed hesitation in Elsie's response.

'Not sure what you mean Mr Miller.'

'Look if we're to be married my darling, you'd better start calling me Harry.'

Elsie laughed uproariously at the little Londoner's cheek.

'God love you Harry. You'd cheer an old woman up.'

'Less of the old, young lady,' smiled Miller. It was apparent Elsie was hiding something, but it was doubtful whether the direct approach would reveal much so Miller dropped the subject and left Elsie to her work.

Godfrey and Agnes were both in the kitchen by this time. Miller took each one aside, separately, to understand their whereabouts over the last day. Each corroborated the stories of all the staff. From their interviews, Miller found it difficult to see how they could have done anything to poison Cavendish without killing everyone in the household or being seen by another person in the kitchen. Neither held much love for the Cavendish family probably out of loyalty to Lady Emily but also because of their perceived ill treatment by the staff at Cavendish Hall.

Following the interview, Miller returned to his room. As he made his way along the corridor, he saw Curtis in his room staring into distance. He knocked on the door and Curtis looked up. His eyes showed how much he was still in shock from the events of the day. They seemed absent of life or purpose.

Miller went into the room. It was larger than the other rooms downstairs but sparsely furnished: a double bed, a wardrobe, drawers, a desk, and an armchair. A lifetime of service thought Miller, and this is what it amounts to. There were some pictures on the wall including one depicting a young woman. Then Miller recalled Curtis drunkenly mentioning that he'd been married. Miller asked Curtis if he needed anything.

'Nothing, thank you.' He motioned for Miller to sit down. In his position, Miller guessed, it was difficult to have anyone

180

with whom he could talk. It looked like he wanted to talk to someone.

'My condolences again, Mr Curtis,' said Miller.

'Thank you, Mr Miller. It's very difficult at this moment to take in. Have you made any progress in your inquiries?'

Miller updated him on the various interviews but revealed nothing material. He mentioned the meeting with Edmunds and asked if he had been to the Hall. Curtis shook his head absently then asked Miller, 'Did you meet Jane?'

'Yes, I did meet a young girl, very briefly. Their daughter I presume?'

'Probably,' said Curtis vaguely.

'Probably? Why would there be any doubt it is their daughter, or do you mean it might be someone else?'

Curtis looked at Miller with some remorse. 'Forgive me. Please forget I said that. I have no doubt Jane is their daughter. She's quite striking now.'

Miller accepted the answer and decided against probing further on the subject of her parentage. It was a surprise to him, however, there could be any hint of doubt. Physically, she seemed to be the image of her parents. Changing tack, he asked, 'Jane didn't appear to have much love for Lord Cavendish.'

'Probably not. It's her age. I can't think of why she should be antagonistic to him. She seems to get on well enough with the ladies, though.'

'Does she work in the estate?'

'Yes, she's the stable girl. She looks after the family horses, spends all day with them. We're all convinced she prefers horses to people.'

'You don't see her much then?'

'No, not much. She's tended to avoid contact with the Hall lately. When she was younger, she would come here a lot. She spent time with Lady Esther and Lady Mary and Lord Henry. She was included in their schooling.' His voice appeared to

181

choke with emotion, which Miller put down to recent events. Regaining control, Curtis added, 'I wonder what she'll do.'

'How do you mean?' asked Miller.

'What will we all do Mr Miller? What will we all do?' His voice tailed off.

Further questions seemed pointless to Miller, and he offered an apology for interrupting him. Rising he nodded towards the photograph of the young lady on the wall. 'She's a beautiful girl. Who is she?'

Curtis looked at the picture on the wall. It showed an attractive, fair-haired woman probably no older than thirty. He was silent for a moment then looked up at Miller.

'It's a picture of my wife, Christine.'

-

The afternoon turned into evening and then night. The snowdrifts gave off a purple glow glistening against the darkness of the trees. The silence was all consuming and Kit was happy to have some time outside in the cold air. It seemed to Kit the chill had lost a little of its bite. Perhaps the roads would be more passable tomorrow.

As he walked with Sam around the grounds, he felt a few drops of rain drumming gently on his hat. The arrival of rain caused Sam to whimper.

'Fair-weather dog,' admonished Kit. He picked the little terrier up and walked back to the Hall. As he did so, he saw a solitary figure emerging from the Edmunds cottage. A strand of hair emerged from underneath the hat. Kit guessed this was the daughter Miller had mentioned. The girl moved quickly through the snow, clearly headed in the direction of the stables away from the cottage and where Kit was standing. He watched her for a few moments then continued inside to the warmth of the house.

Kit found Bright sitting opposite the Cavendish sisters in the drawing room. A fire danced in the hearth bringing warmth and light to the room. In any other circumstances the situation would have looked positively romantic but on this evening the low light matched the mood of the household.

'I hope I'm not interrupting you,' said Kit as he and Sam entered.

Mary looked up and smiled, 'No, don't worry. We've been boring Richard about our childhood here.' This comment was met with a denial by Bright.

Esther looked miserable. She seemed particularly affected by Cavendish's death or, perhaps, her nature was more sensitive than Mary's, thought Kit. She looked up at Kit and said, 'I'm so sorry. All of this has ruined Christmas for you both.'

Bright responded very quickly, 'Please Esther this is nobody's fault, least of all yours.' Kit agreed and said so. Sensing her desolation, Sam immediately made a beeline for her and hopped up on her knee. This seemed to revive both girls and they focused their attention on the little dog.

Kit turned to Bright and remarked, 'I've noticed I'm invisible to young women and children when Sam appears.' This made Bright smile. Mary looked at him in the eye, an eyebrow raised and nodded slowly to confirm this.

There was silence for a few moments and then Mary asked how the interviews were progressing. This was a welcome distraction and Kit was happy to fill in everyone on what he and Miller had found out.

'Harry and I have mostly established where people were over the last day, but some questions clearly remain unanswered. As to motive, assuming we are dealing with,' he hesitated a moment, then continued, '…murder, we do not have anything that seems plausible.'

'The telephone is working again,' said Mary.

'Good, I want to make some calls tomorrow to London, if I may,' said Kit. Both girls nodded. Then he added, 'It seems less cold tonight. With luck the roads will be passable tomorrow, so I suspect the police will finally be able to visit.'

183

Mary took Esther's hand. 'It also means they'll take our grandfather away.'

'Yes,' said Bright. 'I imagine they shall want to conduct a post-mortem soon. We should know more about what we're dealing with when they've finished.'

Following a few minutes more of conversation, the sisters rose and retired to their room. As much as Kit longed to console them, he realized they needed one another at this moment. The last thing he wanted to do was to intrude on their private grief. Bright seemed to read his thoughts and said, 'Nothing we can do at this point.'

'I know,' agreed Kit.

Kit decided to turn in also. As he left the room, he met Strangerson who was just coming into the drawing room, 'Thought I'd have a little glass of cheerfulness. Definitely needed. It's been a rough day.'

Kit heartily agreed.

Chapter 21

The next morning Kit pulled his bedroom curtains back to reveal a silvery grey sky and sheets of rain falling steadily onto the ground. It pleased Kit to see this. Rain meant that the snow would clear, and they could make progress on what killed Lord Cavendish. It meant also he would be taken away, for the last time from Cavendish Hall. This would be a symbolic break with the past for Esther and Mary.

Unquestionably it would be emotional. He felt sad for the two girls as they faced a life without both their father and their grandfather. He did not doubt they were strong individuals who would cope in these circumstances. However, there was no question of the bond existing between the sisters and their grandfather. They would miss him greatly.

Many questions remained unanswered and one more person remained to be seen, Reverend Simmons. It would be better to see him first thing in the morning, if only to give him fair warning about the possibility of the police needing to interview him. Seeing the clergyman again would be a good excuse to get away from the sad atmosphere in the Hall.

Kit was the first to arrive for breakfast. Curtis seemed to have regained control after the turmoil of yesterday. However,

Kit could feel, not just see, the void behind his eyes. It was important for Lady Emily to clarify her plans for the future of the staff soon. Kit made a mental note to approach Esther and Mary about this.

After a rapid breakfast, Kit retrieved his overcoat and hat. Sam appeared looking very bright.

'Walk?' asked Kit. Sam readily assented, and Kit put his lead on, feeling a little guilty. His little dog disliked the rain intensely and he would be a little put out at having been taken for a fool.

They made their way through the rain to Reverend Simmons. The snow was becoming a brown-grey slush and began to soak through Kit's boots. Sam, as Kit surmised, had not realized it was raining and was making his feelings clear. A remorseful Kit picked him up and carried him to the Rectory.

Reverend Simmons was delighted to see Kit. The delight turned to sadness in an instant when Kit revealed his sad commission. They both sat down in the drawing room.

'I'm sorry we couldn't come down yesterday to inform you. In truth, I became wrapped up in some elements related to his passing and I forgot. The girls were probably too distraught to think of asking someone to come down and inform you.'

'Think nothing of it, Kit. I understand completely. But may I ask one thing?' said Simmons looking at Kit, 'Are you implying the circumstances of his death are suspicious due to its suddenness or is it something else? '

Kit replied, 'Both, but I can't talk about the latter. I think it's best left to the police to decide how to handle.'

Simmons nodded his head, 'So it will be a matter for the police?'

'Yes, it must be so.'

'Of course. The poor girls,' said Simmons shaking his head. 'How are they bearing up?'

'Esther has really taken it hard. Mary also, but I sense she is stronger in controlling her emotions.'

186

This caused Simmons to smile, and he nodded his head and smiled, 'I wouldn't disagree with you there.'

A faraway look entered the eyes of Simmons and Kit guessed the news was beginning to sink in. Not wanting to impose too much, Kit limited his questions with Simmons and took his leave after a short visit. They parted with Simmons thanking Kit for coming specially to relay the sad news.

Stepping out of the Rectory, Kit was relieved to see the rain had stopped and sunshine was threatening to break through the heavy cloud above. It was still icy, so he put his hat on and walked with Sam back towards the Hall. The air was damp, and Kit was keen to return to the Hall as quickly as possible. However, a familiar feeling in his leg forced him to slow his pace.

As he walked towards the Hall, he passed a middle-aged lady and a young girl coming from the direction of the Hall. Both looked at him and he returned their look. He raised his hat and addressed the older lady.

'Good morning. Would I be right in thinking that you are Mrs Edmunds?'

'Yes,' came the reply.

Kit remembered Miller's description of the Edmunds family as a charming mixture of hostility and taciturnity. He doubted if they would be interested in a conversation about the inclement weather, so he confined himself to saying, 'My name is Aston, I'm staying with the family. I hope you'll accept my condolences for the loss of Lord Cavendish.'

Sam clearly took a shine to Jane and was muzzling her shin. A smile burst onto the lips of the young girl, and she knelt down to stroke the shameless little terrier.

'This is Sam,' added Kit.

'We've met,' said Jane, not looking at Kit. 'Aren't you a beautiful boy.' Her voice was very different from her mother's. It would not have been out of place at a debutante's ball. Then

Kit remembered something about her having been educated with the girls at the Hall.

Mrs Edmunds tapped Jane, 'Come along.' She nodded to Kit and said, 'Good day sir.'

Kit tipped his hat again and they parted company. It was difficult to reconcile Miller's description of the antagonistic young girl and the person he had just met. In any company she would be considered a beauty. She was tall, slender with wide set green eyes and high cheekbones. Only her clothes betrayed her humble origins because the gaze that met Kit suggested nobility.

Ever the man for the ladies, the meeting with a pretty girl seemed to perk Sam up and he trotted along happily to the Hall without demanding a lift. This did not pass unnoticed by Kit who rebuked his little friend for such barefaced attempts at wooing impressionable young girls. Sam merely barked a carefree riposte.

The morning walk to the village had taken its toll and Kit was relieved to be back at the Hall. His leg hurt, and he needed to rest. At the door he met Strangerson on his way out from a walk.

'Making a break for it,' said Strangerson with a smile, 'Don't tell the law, guv.'

'Your secret's save with me. Where are you off to?'

'A walk into town, I think. Don't worry I'll be back to face justice.'

They parted company and Kit led Sam downstairs to see Miller. He knocked on the door and Miller invited him inside. Sam hoped up onto the bed and settled on Miller's knee. This was staggering, and Miller looked at Kit for an explanation.

'I think he's in love.'

'With the sisters?' laughed Miller, 'Well, we finally have something in common then mate.'

'Actually, I think his new favourite is the daughter of Edmunds'.'

188

'Really, where did you see them?'

Kit related his encounter with the two ladies. Both acknowledged the young girl was beautiful. Miller then updated Kit on his conversation with Curtis.

'Does he really think Jane is Robert's daughter?' asked Kit.

'Apparently Robert a bit of a cad,' confirmed Miller. 'I checked with Elsie and she told me that he couldn't be as he was in South Africa at the time Mrs Edmunds would have become pregnant.'

Kit nodded and congratulated Miller on following up on this. Miller looked out of the window at the grey skies and the rain falling gently onto the snow.

'What is the plan today, sir?'

'Wait for the police. They need to take over this case if it is a case, of course. I'll stay involved, though, but in the background.'

'Anything you want me to do?' asked Miller.

'Dig a bit more into the tracks in the snow. If the staff are telling the truth, then could it have been someone from the Hall going to the cottage? There are also tracks from the Hall to the stables. Those might be from Esther and Mary, so I'll check with them. To be honest, it's all conjecture at the moment. None of this may be relevant but it's a loose end and, until it makes sense, it'll drive me crazy,' laughed Kit.

Kit went upstairs after his meeting with Miller. He heard the sound of the sisters in the library. They were talking animatedly but in low voices. It also seemed to Kit that they were talking to someone on the telephone because a burst of chat from them would be followed by a few moments of silence.

Miss Buchan came out of the dining room at this moment. They looked at one another and Kit was uncomfortably aware how his presence by the door gave the appearance of his eavesdropping on the girls. However, Miss Buchan either did not notice or was too tactful to notice what he was doing. She

189

seemed to have recovered from yesterday and this was confirmed by Kit's inquiry into how she was.

'By the way, Miss Buchan, did anyone from the Hall go to the Edmunds cottage on Christmas Day? I saw tracks between the Hall and the cottage. They looked fresh.'

Unfortunately, Miss Buchan was unable to shed any light on who might have gone from the Hall. She seemed to be telling the truth, insofar as Kit was able to judge. They parted after this, and Kit decided to go the library to see the two sisters. He knocked on the door but received no answer. Assuming they had not heard him, he tried a second time. Still no answer. Rather than wait he pushed the door open. The room was empty. Seems odd, he thought, where have the sisters gone?

-

Miller squelched out towards the cottage. The ground underneath his feet was a pleasant combination of sludge and ice. Up ahead he saw Edmunds walking towards the stables. Changing direction, he trotted over to join Edmunds as he walked towards the stables.

'Are you a groom as well?' asked Miller indicating the stables.

'No, just Jane. There's a barn behind the stables. I want to check on the equipment.'

Miller also noticed the trail of footsteps through the snow leading from the Hall to the stables. There seemed to be two sets of prints, but it was just as probable that it had been made by the same person returning. Miller could sense Edmunds looking at him. He turned and faced Edmunds.

'Apart from Lord Cavendish, did anyone from the Hall come to visit your cottage over Christmas?'

Edmunds eyes narrowed, 'What makes you ask that?'

Miller explained about the tracks in the snow. They continued to walk without Edmunds replying. Miller decided to wait for a reply. They reached the stables and Miller saw

190

the horses for the first time. There were three horses, two greys and a chestnut. Edmunds went over to each of them and patted them. Each of the horses seemed to recognize Edmunds and, in Miller's estimation, were pleased to see him.

The smell of manure in the stable was something Miller found eye wateringly pungent. Edmunds smiled at the reaction of Miller.

'You're from the city then.'

'Born and bred.'

'This is Queenie,' said Edmunds, indicating one of the greys. 'The other grey is Frisco, and the chestnut is Phantom.'

'They're beautiful. Your daughter looks after them well.'

'They're family to her.' It was apparent Edmunds was not going to answer Miller's earlier question so there was no point in this line of inquiry pursuing any further. After ensuring the feed and water containers were well stocked, Edmunds indicated he was finished in the stable. They went behind the stable to a large barn containing various items of farm equipment, feed for the horses as well as bales of hay. The smell of the manure now co-mingled with the sweeter smell of hay and petrol. It still gave off a stench that Miller knew he would never get used to.

'You get used to it,' said Edmunds, reading Miller's mind.

'Not sure I would, but there you go,' said Miller with a laugh.

There seemed no prospect of getting anything useful out of Edmunds, so Miller bade him a farewell and retraced the existing footsteps back to the Hall. There was no doubt both Edmunds and the staff at the Hall were hiding something. If it were relevant to Cavendish, then it would be up to the police to establish what they were trying to conceal as he and Kit were at the limit of what they could reasonably establish.

-

Where had they gone? There was no doubt they had been in here, thought Kit. He checked the windows, but none had

191

been opened. No other door was visible. Then he noticed something peculiar. The photograph of the Battalion was no longer on the wall.

Kit walked over to the desk to see if it had been placed inside one the drawers. They were empty except for some paper documents. Checking under the desk he could see that it had not fallen down. The only possible conclusion to be drawn was that the sisters had taken it. This brought him back to his original question: where on earth had they disappeared?

A thought occurred to Kit and went to the opposite wall from the where he was standing. He began to tap on the wall to check the relative thickness. Moving slowly on the along the wall he tapped it every few feet. After a minute he found a part of the wall that was potentially hollow behind. He looked around for something obvious to press or pull in order to reveal a hidden door. This seemed to be the stuff of children's stories, he thought to himself, before remembering the Aston household also had a number of priest holes and secret passages.

Another few minutes elapsed as he pushed various parts of the wall and even, after a mumbled apology, had a quick look behind the paintings. Eventually he walked back to the table. At the corner of the table was a button. He pressed it. A door in the wall near where he had been tapping: a secret room. This was not just the stuff of a "penny blood". There was no doubt, in Kit's mind, the girls had escaped using this door. He decided to follow them.

The door led into a tiny corridor that was dark save for the light from the library. Groping in the poor light he felt around the wall and found another door. He opened the door and stepped in another small room. Inside he found the Cavendish sisters. Esther was seated at a small wooden table. On the table was the framed photograph from the library. When he entered, Esther looked up and seemed unsurprised by his arrival. Mary, who had her back to Kit turned her head and said, 'I told you he'd find us.'

'It wasn't easy,' admitted Kit.

'It wasn't meant to be,' replied Mary. Then she turned around slowly. To Kit's speechless amazement, she was holding a gun. It was pointed directly at Kit.

Chapter 22

The police arrived at Cavendish Hall just after midday. Inspector Leopold Augustus Stott of the Lincolnshire police was met by Curtis and invited to sit in the drawing room. Accompanying Stott was Constable Christopher Coltrane who was in his second week on the force. Stott gave no impression of having the slightest confidence in the new recruit. The result was that young Coltrane's nerves were completely shot. This was a source of no little satisfaction to Stott.

The estimable Stott was a very experienced officer in the Lincolnshire police. He had joined straight from school and for nearly two score years had kept the streets of Lincoln as free from the tentacles of crime as could reasonably be expected. Regrets were few although he would always harbour a lingering question as to whether he should have exercised his, not inconsiderable, skills on a bigger stage than Lincoln.

Ambition and energy go hand in hand. From an early age, Stott recognized one without the other would result in certain disappointment. Similarly, insight into oneself went hand in hand with understanding the criminal mind. Such objectivity had long since helped him realize that his undeniable ambition would always take second place to an inherent predisposition towards idleness.

194

Stott's indolent nature informed his approach to criminal investigation and his management of subordinates. His primary objective, when presented with a case, was to prove as early as possible in the investigation, there was no case to investigate. It never ceased to amaze him how the young bloods in the constabulary were always in such a lather to turn the most innocent of circumstances into a full-blown manhunt.

The unexpected arrival of Stott created a problem for Curtis as he had no idea where to find the key principals. The sisters had disappeared earlier in the morning. Lord Aston had arrived back and then promptly disappeared. Strangerson had indicated a desire to walk into town. Meanwhile, Henry was walking in the grounds and Bright had last been seen in the drawing room.

Sensing Curtis was at a loss on what to do, Stott suggested a visit to the late Lord Cavendish might be a prudent next step. In the presence of such a sensible idea, Curtis was more than happy to assent. They all proceeded up the stairs to the bedroom. It was empty save for the dead body. It was also very cold as all of the windows had remained open for the previous twenty-four hours.

'It's a bit parky, sir,' offered Coltrane.

This was met by a glare from Stott. Ignoring Curtis and Coltrane, he set to work. The former offered to look for the good doctor in order to assist the Inspector with his preliminary investigation.

By the time they had reached the room, Stott had already slipped into his well-practiced modus operandi. His initial impressions suggested Cavendish's death may not have been by foul means. Stott's goal was to confirm, prior to any post-mortem anyway, such a hypothesis. Sadly, on first inspection, it seemed improbable this case involved suicide. Had the worthy Lincolnshire police force captured performance statistics on their personnel it would have revealed an unusually high incidence of suicides and correspondingly low

195

murder rate in the cases investigated by Stott. However, he retained strong hopes that death by natural causes may provide the answer his lordship's early demise.

When Curtis left the room to find Dr Bright, Stott made some cursory efforts to inspect the room. First, he checked the doors and then the windows for signs of forced entry. After completing this, he was somewhat at a loss as to what to do next.

Coltrane looked at Stott. He found the Inspector disagreeable and was already having doubts about his chosen profession. Stott presented a figure who seemed an alarming portent for what could happen to him. The man he was looking at was short, rotund and had as red a face as he'd ever seen. The ruddiness of the visage was obscured by a large moustache which would have looked dated ten years ago and now looked positively mid-Victorian. Stott, however, was immensely proud of his moustaches and stroked them often, particularly when asked a question requiring him to buy time before answering it.

Coltrane caught his eye in the hope that he would be asked to do some, detecting. Realizing he had better delegate Coltrane something useful to do, he sent him to round up the domestic staff for an initial interview.

This left Stott alone in the room with the deceased. He spent a few moments looking at Cavendish before casting his eyes around the room without the foggiest idea of what to look for. The room was sparsely furnished. If Stott had not already known, he would have guessed this was a military man or a widower. There was a lack of ornamentation and personal touches. It spoke of a man who had spent much of his life on the move. The window showed no signs of forced entry, but the view was very pleasant.

There was a leather armchair by the window and Stott tried it for size. It was a pity it was so cold as he might have enjoyed sitting there longer. Pondering what to do next he

196

looked out the window. He could see a young man in the grounds walking alone. The young man seemed familiar, but he could not place him and gave it no more thought.

The return of Curtis with Dr Bright was a relief to Stott. He had run out of things to do and was now a little bored. After formal introductions, Stott dismissed Curtis. Taking in the doctor for a few moments, he asked Bright for his professional opinion on what had led to the demise of Lord Cavendish.

Bright related the events of the previous two days. His description tallied with what Curtis had told him earlier. This gave hope to Stott. A locked room with no signs of forced entry, aside from the previous morning, was always good news. Whilst it may speak to the highest form of fiction, in Stott's experience, locked-room murders were rare bordering on non-existent. He listened intently as Bright continued to speak about Cavendish.

'I haven't been able to do a full examination, clearly, but I can detect no signs of violence on his person.'

'Meaning?' asked Stott.

'No wounds or bruising. In the absence of a post-mortem to check for the presence of any toxic agent, it would appear, on the face of it, to be a death by natural causes.'

'I see. Any other thoughts? Please feel free to offer an opinion here. No one else is around; we'll keep it to ourselves,' said Stott conspiratorially.

'Cavendish was not a young man. Even though he appeared in good form on his last night, for all we know he may have had a heart condition or some other illness that he was hiding from his family.'

This seemed a good moment as any for Stott to stroke his moustache. He turned away from Bright and walked over to the door. Having already ascertained it had been forced from the outside by the family, this served no purpose other than to buy time for his next thought. Thankfully it came to him soon.

Looking again at Bright he asked, 'Based on what you've seen of Lord Cavendish, your recommendation would be to progress to a post-mortem?' Bright confirmed this with a nod of his head.

'Very well. I'm not sure there's anything more to be gained by staying in this room unless you've a desire to contract hypothermia.' As they left the room and walked into the, distinctly warmer, corridor, Coltrane reappeared. Glancing at Bright he reported to Stott that all the staff had assembled in the kitchen.

'Excellent, we can kill two birds with one stone. I don't suppose you noticed if the cook was preparing lunch. I must confess I'm feeling a little bit peckish.' Coltrane gazed at the large stomach of the venerable Inspector.

'I believe she was, sir,' responded Coltrane.

'Excellent, let us interrogate the staff. Lead on Coltrane.'

The three men walked down the stairs into the main hallway. Stott looked at the grand Christmas tree and wondered how long it would remain given the tragic circumstances of the last few days. Bright turned to Stott as they descended the back stairs to the kitchen.

'May I ask you a question Inspector?'

'Of course, Dr Bright.'

'Why has an Inspector from Lincoln come all the way over here for what may have been death by natural causes?'

'Good question,' replied Stott, more passionately than he had intended.

In fact, Stott heartily agreed with the sentiment. How he wished he was in a nice warm station, at this moment, rather than moving from one cold room to an equally cold and drafty corridor. He might soon need a doctor himself. However, he felt Bright was owed an explanation for his presence and it might be an opportunity to check his reactions to the news. Sadly, he could not entirely ignore duty because, no matter how remote the possibility might seem, there was a chance he was talking to a murderer.

'Lord Cavendish was in receipt, a few years ago, of threatening messages. They were delivered by post at Christmas. He reported them to the police. We even went as far as to send some officers out to patrol the grounds in case an attempt was made on his life. Evidently, nothing untoward took place. In the end, Lord Cavendish thanked us for our preparedness but decided no further action was necessary.'

'Good Lord,' exclaimed Bright, 'I think I understand now why Kit wanted to question everyone.'

'Kit?'

'Kit Aston,' said Bright before adding, 'Lord Christopher Aston.'

'Lord Aston is here? I must have missed this from er…'

'Curtis.'

'Indeed, Curtis. Well, this is very interesting; I've heard a lot about his Lord Aston. I look forward to meeting him. Where is he exactly?'

Chapter 23

The answer to this question would have surprised the estimable Inspector. Kit Aston was staring down at the gun Mary Cavendish was pointing towards his chest. After the initial shock, a smile spread slowly over Kit's face and he said after a few moments, 'Am I supposed to put my hands up?' The casualness in his tone of voice suggested that he did not view his life to be in imminent danger.

Dismayed, Mary pulled a face and turned the gun towards Esther who was holding a cigarette. Pulling the trigger on the gun caused a tiny flame to emerge, sufficient to light the proffered cigarette.

'You're no fun,' pouted Mary.

'I assure you; I can be tremendous fun in the right circumstances,' replied Kit. Mary shot Kit a look but made no reply. Kit continued in a more serious tone, 'How are you feeling?'

Esther still looked tearful, but Mary was more in control and replied, 'It'll be a while before it sinks in. I try not to think of what life will be like without him. I want to know what happened. Have you had any more thoughts Kit?

'I still don't want to speculate too much. I walked into the village earlier to see Tom Simmons. No one had told him. He

200

was quite upset. Clearly, he had a high regard for your grandfather.'

Esther grimaced slightly and said to Mary, 'We should've called him.'

'How could we Essie?' said Mary gently, 'There was no line.'

Kit continued, 'When I was coming back, I saw Mrs Edmunds and her daughter. Harry saw them yesterday. I gather the daughter seems to be somewhat headstrong.'

Mary smiled and raised her eyebrows, 'She's at that age, I suppose. I'm sure Essie and I would've been no different. Well maybe not you, Essie.'

A thought struck her, and she added, 'Why did Mr Miller go to see them? Do you think someone from the Edmunds family would've reason to kill grandpapa?'

'It makes sense to see everyone and check their movements. Only then can we discount their involvement. The particular reason for seeing them is that we found fresh tracks in the snow from their cottage to the Hall. They could only have been made on Christmas morning or late last night. I wanted to check who had made them.'

Esther and Mary nodded but said nothing. Was there a hint of a smile? Kit couldn't tell; it was momentary.

'What's Jane like? I gather she looks after your horses.'

Esther answered, 'She loves the horses; spends all her time with them. Always has. But you're right, she is a bit less friendly now. Not unfriendly, just more distant with us now.' There was a wistfulness on her voice.

'You mean she was friendly in the past?' asked Kit.

'Oh yes,' said Mary. 'She used to spend all her time with us; she was like a little sister for us and Henry. We probably treated her dreadfully, but she was a good sport, and we always had a good laugh. She even joined us in our lessons with the governess. She's actually very bright.'

'Henry? I thought he didn't spend much time here.'

201

Esther chipped in, 'Henry used to spend the summer here when Uncle Robert was still alive. And Christmas, of course. It wasn't until we lost papa and Uncle Robert that things changed. He and Aunt Emily became more withdrawn. We did, too, I suspect.'

Mary continued, 'Jane and Henry were closer in age. They were thick as thieves for a while and then, as Essie says, everything changed. I went away, Esther, too. Jane was left alone. Probably this was a source of resentment. Who knows?'

'I don't think she goes to school anymore,' added Esther.

'Why would she?' responded Mary, 'She would be too advanced for the other children in the village, although I believe Mrs Grout used to visit her. I think she had her eye on Jane as a teacher.'

'Mrs Grout?' laughed Esther, 'Of all the people. I think you're right Mary, Jane would have been a fish out of water at the school. She loves books. Had a free rein in the library – she would spend her time there when she couldn't be with the horses.'

Kit listened intently for the next few minutes as the sisters, virtually ignoring him, discussed Jane. Finally, he asked, 'You say she's distant with you now?'

'Yes, not exactly friendly but not unfriendly either,' replied Esther, 'You're not suggesting she had something to do with Grandpapa's death?'

'No,' said Kit, 'just a loose end, but I think I understand the tracks in the snow better now and why the staff remained quiet on the subject.'

Mary clapped her hands excitedly, 'I think I know. Books. Jane was coming to get books from the library.'

'Of course,' exclaimed Esther, 'Very good Mary, you should be a detective.'

Kit smiled at Mary, 'I think you're right, for the most part.'

This caused Mary to frown at Kit, 'Most part?'

'For another time, Mary. Anyway, I'm not as quick to jump to conclusions as the sleuths of Cavendish Hall. I prefer something the legal profession has designated as being fundamental in criminal cases.'

'What do you mean?' asked Esther.

'He's mocking us Essie, ignore him. Evidence is overrated, sir,' observed Mary.

'I shall remind you of that.'

'Very well Lord Christopher Aston of Clever Clogs,' said Mary, 'If it's evidence you are searching for, have you uncovered anything yet pointing to a motive from a potential killer or, at the very least, person who likes writing threatening Christmas cards?'

Kit sat down on one of the seats and shook his head ruefully. 'Harry and I have spoken to everyone. Some questions remain unanswered but for the most part I can see no obvious motive for either the threatening cards or anything else, so far.'

'You haven't questioned everyone,' pointed out Mary.

Kit looked at Mary and Esther questioningly, 'Who have I missed?'

'Your man, Mr Miller,' answered Mary. Before Kit could speak, she handed him the photograph of the battalion. 'Tell me what you see in this picture.'

Kit looked at it for a moment and said, 'Your uncle is in the centre and Strangerson is sitting at the end.'

'Look at the soldier with the cocked hat,' said Mary looking at Kit.

The reaction of Kit was immediate. 'Good Lord, it's Harry.' Then he looked at the date of the photograph. It read, August 1914.

'Seems a bit funny. Harry said he hadn't joined until at least a year later.' He looked again at the soldier with the cocked hat. There could be no question, it looked like Harry. Even the pose seemed to be very much in the cocky spirit of

Harry. Why would he mislead Kit on his joining up date? The confusion on Kit's face was evident and finally Mary put him at ease.

'It's not your Mr Miller. Look again.'

She was right. It looked like Harry, but it was a different man. Kit took a moment to reflect on Mary's words. Harry had never mentioned family and Kit had avoided bringing the topic up. There were many reasons why Harry might be wary of revealing too much about his family background. From the very start of their working relationship, even friendship thought Kit, Harry had been open about a past which existed on the edge of the law. It was possible his family had also been involved in criminal activity.

Looking up at Mary he said finally, 'Strange, Harry never mentioned a brother to me. In fact, we never really talked much about his family. I always sensed he was a little reluctant to do so. Looking at the face, it seems very like him but, yes, I can see it isn't. How did you uncover this?'

Mary explained, 'You put it in my head when you asked if we'd moved the picture. So, I thought to check it in more detail. This man was the first person I saw, the one with the cocked hat. I'm certain grandpapa saw it too.'

'I'm sure he did, Mary. Harry even remarked on how strangely Lord Cavendish had looked at him. However, it seems odd to me. How could your grandfather possibly have any recollection of an individual soldier? Contact with someone of his rank would have been infrequent to say the least.'

'I know, that's why we checked into this with a friend at the War Office,' said Mary. Kit looked up with surprise at her as she said this. Noting his reaction gave Mary a warm glow of pride. She wanted him to appreciate her intelligence but at the same time she hated the fact that his approval made her happy. For another time she thought. Continuing with her explanation she said, 'We rang Charlie Chadderton this morning, he's an old family friend.'

'Chubby Chadderton!' exclaimed Kit, 'My word, I can't believe you know old Chubby. Actually, I shouldn't really be surprised. Typical Chubby. He seems to know everyone. Particularly if they're young and pretty.'

Mary smiled and curtsied, 'Thank you for the compliment your lordship. Is he really nicknamed Chubby? He's not fat.'

'Exactly.' replied Kit

Mary shook her head, 'Men! I can't believe you're all allowed the vote and we aren't'

Esther laughed also and then tears welled up in her eyes. She took Mary's hand, and the sisters were silent for a few moments. Then Mary continued, 'We asked Charlie about our uncle's battalion and gave him Mr Miller's name. He confirmed Harry had joined in fifteen, but he also mentioned a brother who joined in fourteen.'

'This is all very well but how do you construe a motive from this?'

There was a slight hesitation from Mary. Esther glanced up at Mary and said, 'His brother was executed by firing squad. By our troops.'

'Good Lord. No wonder he never said anything. Did Chubby say why?'

Mary chipped in, 'No this part has been redacted. We don't know why he was executed but this isn't material to any motive relating to grandpapa. However, we know Uncle Robert was in charge of the firing squad. As well as this, Charlie also found out that when his request for a reprieve was denied, it was grandpapa who headed the review tribunal. My grandfather effectively condemned Harry's brother to death,' Mary looked sadly at Kit then added, 'I think he has a very strong motive indeed.'

-

At this same moment, Miller arrived back in the kitchen. All of the staff were there including a rather portly red-faced moustachioed man who was happily tucking into one of Elsie's pies. Beside him was a younger man in police uniform. Miller had too much experience with the police not to recognize a Detective Inspector when he saw one. He calmly walked in and breezily introduced himself, 'Afternoon sir. The name's Harry Miller. I'm his lordship's man.'

Stott had not arrived at his present state of corpulence by allowing possible criminals to interrupt his repast. He spent fully another minute polishing every last crumb of the delicious pie before he deigned to look up at Miller. He nodded and then motioned for Miller to take a seat.

The ever-mischievous Miller smiled and said, 'Good to meet you too.' He winked at Elsie who smiled, as did the young policeman, noted Miller. No doubt, the overweight officer of the law was as sympathetic to his subordinates as he was to suspects. Whatever had taken place with Lord Cavendish, Miller had complete confidence the man before him would not be the one to pull back the curtain of doubt to allow the light of truth to shine. Thankfully Stott decided not to have dessert. Standing up he finally addressed the staff.

'Good afternoon. My name is Inspector Stott,' he paused for dramatic effect then continued, 'and this is Constable Coltrane.' It was difficult not to detect the disdain in Stott's voice for his colleague.

'We will be making some preliminary investigations. However, it must be repeated, there's nothing to suggest that anyone has done anything wrong. I would like you to cooperate fully with Constable Coltrane who will be taking statements from each of you.'

The speech finished, Stott turned to Miller, 'Now, you there, show me where Lord Christopher Aston can be found. Perhaps he's with the two ladies.' Looking at Agnes, he said,

'And can you get Lady Emily? I will see all in the drawing room.'

Miller led Stott out of the kitchen and back up the stairs to the drawing room. Bright was reading a newspaper brought from the village by, the recently returned, Strangerson. He, too, was sitting in the drawing room. Strangerson stood up and proffered his hand, 'Hello old boy, the name's Strangerson.'

It was immediately clear to Stott that Strangerson was a gentleman In Stott's experience, one could intimidate the lower orders with impunity. However, attempting a similar approach with one's betters was fraught with danger. His preferred approach was to pitch himself within a spectrum beginning with deference and going as far as unctuous toadying when the occasion demanded. He shook Strangerson's hand enthusiastically.

'Stott. Inspector Stott. I'm here to look into the matter of the Lord Cavendish's passing.'

'Capital!' said Strangerson, 'I'm sure you're just the man to get to the bottom of this.'

'I've had some modest success,' admitted Stott but could not elaborate further as Lady Emily stalked into the room accompanied by Henry. Forty years of detection, if not at the highest levels, were more than enough for Stott to recognize the manifest superiority of Lady Emily's status. Stott recalibrated his levels of his sycophancy to their highest level. He bowed to the new entrant.

'Who might you be?' asked Lady Emily with a hauteur she always reserved for public officials.

'Inspector Stott at your service, Lady Emily. This,' indicating Coltrane with undisguised dismay, 'is Constable Coltrane.'

Lady Emily nodded and then said, 'You asked for us, I understand.' Stott noted how she did not condescend to add a friendly 'is there any way we can help'? In fact, Stott found Lady Emily an altogether splendid example of the English upper class, a system of social organization he not only believed in but had spent his life upholding.

'I did request that you join us. I won't detain you long.' This declaration was finished off with another bow, the effect of which amused Bright immensely, appalled Henry deeply and, happily, won over Lady Emily to the stout detective.

-

Esther looked sympathetically at Kit, 'I'm so sorry Kit. We're really not accusing Mr Miller of anything.'

'Yet,' added Mary looking at Kit directly. After a few moments silence, they agreed it would be best to re-join others and wait for the police to arrive.

'How do we get out of here?' asked Kit.

'Do you find the idea of being trapped in a secret room with two defenceless young sisters so very frightful?' smiled Mary.

'Mary!' exclaimed Esther chuckling, 'I really don't know where you get these ideas.'

'I agree,' said Kit, 'The idea of you both being defenceless is a complete calumny. I wouldn't stand for it Esther.'

'You're both as bad as one another,' pronounced Esther laughing as they left the secret room and returned to the library. Kit put the picture back on the wall and stood back from it. He heard Esther saying, 'I can hear voices in the drawing room. It sounds like the police have arrived.' However, Kit was not paying attention. Instead, he walked closer to the picture again and looked more closely.

'Kit are you coming?' asked Mary at the door.

It took a few moments for Kit to answer and then he said, 'Yes. Forgive me.'

'What is it Kit? What have you seen?'

'I'd like to get hold of Chubby. I have a few questions for him,' replied Kit, avoiding answering Mary's question directly, which caused her to frown. She brushed past Kit and went to the picture herself to look at it again. Seeing the others had left the room, she put the picture down, with some frustration, and followed them.

Chapter 24

The arrival of Kit and the two sisters into the drawing room interrupted the growing admiration between Lady Emily and Stott. It was rare for her to encounter such a commendable combination of gallantry and veneration. She was particularly pleased by the fact that his admiration stemmed not from a knowledge or appreciation of her qualities so much as her position in society. She had felt for many years such deference was being lost in the uninterrupted march of progress.

Stott excused himself from Lady Emily and took on an increased solemnity of manner as he was presented to the sisters and Kit. His presence was a stark reminder to them of what had happened, and both were visibly upset. To Stott's credit, his manner with the two sisters was gentle and less servile than hitherto. He confined his meeting with them to expressing condolence for their loss and requesting, with a surprising degree of delicacy, their permission to transfer the late Lord to a hospital. It was unnecessary to add this would be for a post-mortem, but he felt relieved by Lady Mary's acknowledgement that the surprising nature of the death would require early confirmation of cause.

Following this dialogue, the sisters retired to their grandfather's room to wait the moment when he would be moved. Stott then turned to Kit and bowed slightly.

'I'm sorry to meet you in such tragic circumstances. May I have a few moments with you in private?'

'By all means, let's go to the dining room.'

Stott had heard of Lord Kit Aston and meeting the man in person, he was every bit as impressive in real life. Aston confirmed everything Stott believed about the superiority of the Englishman and specifically, the English nobility. His height, his noble bearing, the steadiness of his blue eyes, the manifest intelligence and unquestionable courage bespoke generations, if not centuries, of breeding.

This was the kind of man he could look up to. Literally. It was immensely gratifying to Stott how much his lordship looked the part. The exploits of Aston during the War were well documented. If the rumours were true, just as many of his exploits were not. In other circumstances Stott would love to have heard more about what the newspapers called, 'The French Diplomat Affair'. Perhaps if the demise of Lord Cavendish was not brought about by murder, he might broach the subject at a later date.

'I hope I've not upset the ladies with my request,' opened Stott, with sincerity.

'On the contrary Inspector Stott, I must commend your tact. It's clear that an inquest is necessary. The key to this will be a post-mortem. I'm guessing you're familiar with the threatening notes Lord Cavendish received over the last few years.'

'I am, sir. Horrible business. I did the original investigation into the matter but, alas, we were unable to uncover anything.'

'But your presence may have dissuaded this madman from undertaking any violence towards Lord Cavendish. In this respect you did well.'

211

'I am aware from the newspapers and also internal correspondence that you, sir, have experience in investigative matters. I gather also, from the staff and guests, you've made some preliminary inquiries. Would you be able to acquaint me with all you've learned? I'm keen not to take statements from the guests quite yet until we have understood more from the coroner.'

'I quite understand, Inspector.'

For the next half hour, Kit related most of what he'd discovered over the last few days including the missing cards threatening Lord Cavendish. This news dismayed Stott, but he managed to keep control of his reaction. If the cards had not been mislaid then it meant someone had deliberately taken them to avoid them being seen by the police.

The only things Kit held back in his report related to the battalion photograph and the tracks to and from the Edmunds' cottage. The former point might throw an unfavourable light on Miller. This would be a distraction as there was no question in Kit's mind that Miller was unconnected to the notes. A similar consideration informed his reluctance to discuss the tracks in the snow. Kit was fairly certain the tracks were not material anyway, but he needed to confirm this separately.

The questions Stott asked confirmed Kit's impression that the detective was not interested in pursuing an investigation. Furthermore, he did not appear to mind Kit starting an investigation on his own initiative. This was welcome news for Kit. The pliability of the Inspector meant he could pursue matters uncontested. Kit trusted his instincts. He felt sure there was a case here, but its nature was frustratingly just out of his reach.

Having finished his report to Stott, and before returning to the others, Kit asked the Inspector about the original investigation into the threatening Christmas cards. Stott related that the Metropolitan police had been involved when it became apparent, they had come from London. The investigation petered out when no attempt was made on Cavendish's life.

The two men returned to the drawing room. Coltrane was diligently capturing details from Strangerson and Bright on their movements over the two days. He brightened up considerably when Kit nodded to him and said, 'Well done Constable.' Stott looked unimpressed. This lack of enthusiasm turned to outright displeasure with Coltrane's next comment.

'Sir, do you think it would be an idea to conduct a search of the rooms?'

'What are we looking for?' asked Stott.

'Evidence sir?'

'Such as?'

'Poison?' offered Coltrane hesitantly.

'Capital idea,' said Strangerson, clapping the young Constable on the back.

'Indeed, very good Coltrane. Capital. We'll make a detective of you yet,' said Stott trying to make the best of an increasingly bad situation.

'Good idea constable,' said Kit nodding. 'I suggest you start with the guest rooms before going downstairs. It would be counter-productive to the peace of the household if the staff felt they were under suspicion.'

Strangerson stepped forward, eager to help. 'Please feel free to start with my room, Inspector. I've nothing to hide.'

'Very good, Mr Strangerson, we shall do as you suggest. Thank you,' said Stott. He motioned for Coltrane to commence the search.

-

The rest of the afternoon was taken up with a search of the guest rooms. Towards late afternoon an ambulance arrived to remove the body of Cavendish to Lincoln County Hospital, overseen by Bright and Inspector Stott.

This was an emotional moment for the family and the staff. Even Lady Emily, noted Kit, shed a tear. Henry

213

remained inexpressive, but Kit saw the young man's hands gripping one another; the knuckles were white. He was to be the next Lord Cavendish, a title he did not appear to want. Yet his becoming the new Lord Cavendish would be a source of pride for his mother. Quite simply the young man was in an impossible position and Kit suspected there was more to this than simply a desire to work in commerce. As soon as the body of Lord Cavendish had been placed in the ambulance, Henry spun around and stalked back to the house. Kit saw his hand go up to his eyes.

The sight of their grandfather being removed from the Hall was too much for the sisters. Both Kit and Bright comforted the sisters, however, they realized no words could provide adequate consolation.

With the departure of the ambulance, Bright announced he would have to return to Dr Stevens. This was natural as Bright had stayed for two nights and there was nothing to stop him returning to continue his locum duties. The roads were now passable. His reluctance to leave was evident as was the genuine sorrow on the part of the sisters at this news. For Kit, it prompted mixed feelings. The mutual regard between himself and Bright was plain but there was no avoiding the fact that there was rivalry in the air. Once more, Kit recoiled at thought of being jealous and tried to dismiss it from his mind.

One moment encapsulated for Kit the suspicion that Bright was also in a similar state of mind. As Bright bid the sisters and Kit adieu he said in passing, 'All yours.' Kit immediately understood this was probably as much a reference to the sisters as the murder case.

It was clear Mary had picked up on the remark also and understood its import. Although she said nothing, Kit detected anger in her eyes. This made him feel both cheerful and guilty at feeling so cheered up. It acted as a reminder to him of her independent character. She would naturally resent any implied ownership particularly from two males in the herd.

214

Following the departure of the late Lord Cavendish, the sisters and Lady Emily retired to their rooms. Stott, along with Kit, drew Curtis and Miss Buchan aside to tell them about the need to conduct a general search of the staff quarters. Both readily agreed; Coltrane was dispatched to start the search.

Following their discussion with Curtis and Miss Buchan, Kit took Sam for his afternoon constitutional. As he returned from the walk with the little dog, he saw Henry outside also. He called out to Henry, who stopped and looked at Kit with some irritation.

'I'm glad I caught you Henry. I won't keep you, but I wanted to mention a couple of things.'

'Go on.'

Henry had not yet developed the art of disguising his annoyance well. The abruptness of his response confirmed to Kit his suspicions were well founded and that he could proceed with confidence.

'First of all, condolences once more for your loss. I know relations were strained over the last few years, but I think one day you will feel a grief that perhaps you do not feel now.' Kit could see the look of scepticism on the young man's face as he continued, 'I understand you used to spend the summer here with the girls. I'm fairly sure those were happier times. I know so much has happened since then.'

Henry gave a snort. 'And now I'm Lord of the Manor,' he said with some derision.

'Yes, but it doesn't mean you've no say in how you live your life. I'm not just talking about working in business, Henry.'

This clearly cut through to Henry, frowning he asked, 'How do you mean?'

'I know who you're going to see.' Kit could see anger on Henry's face, and he added, 'Before you accuse the staff here of revealing secrets, I can assure you they told me nothing.

215

They respected your privacy. You may want to bear it in mind when this is all yours.' He gestured to the Hall.

'How did you find out?' The tone had softened. It was more accepting. The look in his eyes was different, too. They met Kit's for the first time. Kit studied him for a moment. Something was changing in the boy. Love ennobles, hatred corrodes. How often had Kit seen this in his young life?

'I wasn't sure until I saw your reaction, it was instinct,' admitted Kit.

Henry looked away. Tears formed in his eyes. He fought them back successfully. He turned towards Kit. Once more he looked directly at him. His voice had another timbre. It was as if he was a different person.

'I love her. I've loved her since we were children. I don't want this damn title. My mother will just use this as a reason to stop me being with her. I will be expected to marry someone of my rank,' he said scathingly. 'A stable girl? It will never do. I can already hear her saying this.'

His eyes blazed with a fire that surprised Kit. This was a young man in love; a young man who would now have to grow up rapidly. To do so would require a courage that he'd hereto kept well hidden behind a façade of indifference.

'I realize it's none of my business, Henry. The only reason for mentioning it at all was it came up when Harry and I were collating people's movements prior to your grandfather's death. I would recommend three things, if you are prepared to listen.'

Henry nodded but said nothing.

'Firstly, you should tell your mother. This is the responsible thing to do. It will show her that you're growing up and ready to take control of your destiny. Secondly, I gather from the girls, Jane is very bright. You should encourage her to finish her education. This will benefit her whatever happens in the future. It's in her best interests,' said Kit with emphasis.

Henry's eyes remained fixed on Kit but there was understanding there now. Kit continued, 'Finally, you must respect that Jane is at a vulnerable age. I think you can understand what I'm saying.'

The anger flashed again. 'I wouldn't dream of doing anything to compromise Jane,' snapped Henry.

Kit nodded but added nothing more other than to bid him farewell. Looking down at the little dog, he was aware Sam had been unusually silent during the exchange.

'Was I too hard on him?' Sam yelped in reply which Kit took to mean, "Perfectly judged old boy".

They returned to the Hall, which was in uproar. Curtis was in a state of agitation when he saw Kit enter the Hall. He came running over and said, 'Lord Aston, thank God you're back.'

'What's wrong?' asked Kit, seeing how disconcerted Curtis was.

'It's your man, Mr Miller, sir. He's been arrested by Inspector Stott.'

This news shocked Kit to his core. Regaining his composure, he inquired calmly, 'Where is Inspector Stott?'

'Follow me sir.'

They went to the staff quarters and went to Miller's room. Inside a dejected-looking Miller was sat with Stott, Coltrane, and Mary Cavendish. Miller looked up at Kit and shook his head. He, too, seemed to be in a state of disbelief.

'Inspector,' asked Kit in an even voice, 'What is the meaning of this?'

Stott pointed to some cards sitting on the table beside the framed picture of Robert Cavendish's battalion. 'We found these in your manservant's coat pocket.'

Kit looked down at the cards. He didn't need to read what they said. He already knew.

Happy Christmas, I've killed you.

Chapter 25

It was just after five o'clock. Kit was alone in the library making a phone call. 'Thank you. If you could let Mr Chadderton know that Kit Aston called and ask him to be available for a phone call tomorrow morning at nine o'clock, I would greatly appreciate it. Yes, if you could leave a note on his desk, thank you.'

Kit angrily replaced the earpiece of the telephone. 'Damn, damn and damn again' he uttered between clenched teeth. Rubbing his eyes, he looked out the window. Harry was in deep trouble. If it turned out Lord Cavendish had been murdered, the combination of the threatening cards and the motive uncovered by Mary could be enough to send him to the gallows.

As angry as he felt, he knew it was a waste of precious resource. He needed to be focused on proving the innocence of his friend. The anger would not go away, however. The look of regret on Mary's face did not diminish the enormous disappointment he felt and the emptiness in the pit of his stomach. Of course, it was inconceivable she should withhold anything material from the police. After all, he conceded, it was her grandfather who was potentially the victim of a murder. She had done what was right, yet he could not excuse her for this.

If her findings proved enough to hang Harry, Kit knew he would never be able to forgive her. Tears of rage welled up in his eyes for the man who had risked his life to cross No Man's Land to save him. The tears were not just for Harry, though. He felt a stab of guilt at the thought, no matter how fleeting, that this situation was coming between him and a person who was now uppermost in his mind.

Outside the library window, it was evening. The rain was falling steadily, tapping persistently at the window. The snow lay in patches on the grass and the sky was funeral black. Perhaps it was the sound of the rain and the wind, but Kit felt a chill. He tried desperately to concentrate his mind on a plan of action. Unfortunately, his options were in short supply.

There was no question, in Kit's mind: Harry was innocent. He had not sent threatening cards to Cavendish nor was he a murderer. However, Kit recognized that even if the latter proved untrue, there would still be a case to answer on the former. A clever prosecutor could make it appear that the death of Cavendish by natural causes only forestalled an attempted murder. Undoubtedly this could sway any objective judge and might make sentencing harsher.

Another thought added to Kit's overall mood of dejection. The morning after the death of Cavendish, he had found Harry alone in the library. It was possible Harry had come to the library to retrieve the threatening notes. Just for a moment, doubt crept into Kit's mind. This intensified as he remembered Miller telling him he'd actually seen Cavendish on Christmas night when he came unexpectedly to the kitchen to retrieve his room keys. Harry was the last person to see him alive aside from the potential murderer. This added to Kit's sense of gloom.

Hearing a commotion in the hallway, Kit went to investigate. Mary, Harry and the two policemen were standing by the Christmas tree. It pained Kit to see Harry wearing handcuffs. He could not bring himself to look at Mary, but he

219

could sense she had been crying. Stott looked at Kit apologetically and said, 'I'm sorry, sir, I must follow our procedures. I hope you'll understand.'

'I do Inspector Stott. It goes without question that I vouch for this man. He saved my life.'

'So, I understand, sir. I will make sure he is treated well, sir. You have my word.' The gravity of the situation was apparent to Stott, and, for the first time, he no longer seemed quite so comical a figure.

Kit looked at Miller and said, 'I'll get you out of this, Harry. Count on it.'

Miller smiled, 'I'm not worried sir, we've come through tighter spots than this.'

Stott looked at Miller. He was oddly impressed by the little man and was inclined to believe him innocent. However, for this to be true, it would imply a potential murderer remained loose in the Hall. This did not bear thinking about. Sadly, he concluded, it would be better if Miller did prove to be the author of the notes. There was some good news for Miller, however. No poison had been found. Furthermore, it was always possible, even probable, that Cavendish's death would prove to have been by natural causes.

The police left with Miller. Mary and Kit remained in the hallway looking on. Kit closed the door as they departed. Turning around he looked for the first time at Mary. She wanted to say something, but no words came. She looked down, fighting back tears. There was nothing Kit could think to say to comfort her. It seemed like an eternity to Mary and then she heard Kit say, 'Mary, I understand. You had to tell them what you'd found out.'

She looked up at him. Desolation was etched across her face. Kit felt his throat tighten. The cavity of his chest seemed to shrink; breathing became shallow and difficult. Finally, he managed to say, 'I need to think. If you'll excuse me, please.'

As he went past her up the stairs, she managed to say faintly, 'I'm so sorry, Kit.'

'I know,' he replied resignedly before continuing up the stairs.

Henry knocked on the door of his mother's room. He heard his mother answer then he walked in without answering her. Lady Emily was having her hair arranged by Agnes. Looking up she saw who it was and turned to Agnes saying, 'Thank you Agnes, I don't think there's anything else.'

Agnes set the comb down on the dresser and, with barely a glance at Henry, left the room. Henry sat on the bed and thought about what he would say to his mother. As ever, she pre-empted him and asked him what had happened. With some relief Henry updated her on what he had heard. It didn't matter to him that he suspected his mother knew all this from Agnes. The thing was to talk. As he spoke, he became shamefully aware how little they talked now. This was not entirely his fault, he knew.

Conversation with his mother tended to be asymmetrical and directed, invariably, towards his instruction. This was understandable given his future role as Lord Cavendish, but the yearning he had once felt to be "normal" had given way to indifference. At some point following his father's death he had simply stopped listening or caring what his mother said. He was content to go along with what suited him and ignore the rest. He always accepted future tests of their relationship would come in the form of his choice of further education and Jane. However, these matters always seemed to be far away. Now they were upon him. He realized, with a growing uneasiness, that he was incapable of answering the questions they posed.

Emily was as aware of the distance between them as she was uncertain of how to make it better. She was confident she knew best. But this was a message Henry neither understood

221

nor wanted to hear. Henry's clear preference to participate in the family business and the relationship with a stable girl seemed perverse to her. She could not fathom the appeal of either when the only road he could take was to be the next Lord Cavendish, with all of the highly desirable duties and responsibilities associated with such a position.

The death of Cavendish had upset her more than she realized. It brought home to her that Henry would inherit the title long before he was ready to do so. The responsibilities accompanying the title were significant, but they also brought rank and distinction. Without understanding either of these points, Henry would detach himself from the one thing Emily had craved for him since the early death of John Cavendish.

More unexpectedly, she appreciated Cavendish had felt sadness at the family breach and was keen to rebuild bridges. There had been a time, long before the death of the brothers, when they had been friendlier, if not friends. When Robert had strayed, he had supported her and done his utmost to save the marriage. Yes, it had once been better. Now he was gone, she felt his loss in a way she could not measure, never mind articulate. For the first time she truly felt a sense of aloneness. Even at the height of the family breach following Robert's death, she had never conceived of what her world would look like in the absence of Lord Cavendish. He seemed immutable. His presence both maddened and reassured her. Now his absence was scrambling the sense of certainty she used to cloak both her life and Henry's.

Over a lifetime Emily had developed an ability to confront emotional challenges with a stoicism bordering on brazen disregard. However, this self-defence was proving unequal to addressing the void she felt as she looked at her son now. She broke down and wept inconsolably.

Henry saw his mother's face seemingly crumble. His reaction was immediate. He rushed over and held her for what seemed like the first time ever. As the sobs wracked her thin

222

body, Henry became conscious of something he had never before noticed: how frail she had become.

Chapter 26

28th December 1919: Piccadilly, London.

Charles 'Chubby' Chadderton awoke from a deep slumber. With some dismay he rapidly became aware of three things. Firstly, he had a headache of life-altering proportions. Secondly, as he fumbled for his spectacles, he realized this was not his own bed. Finally, he became conscious there was a young woman beside him who, at first glance, was of unknown provenance, temperament, and dimension. Upon locating his spectacles, he was able to confirm the woman was indeed, unknown. Deeper inspection suggested she was not as young as first supposed.

This presented a conundrum. It was far from the first time in Chubby's relatively young life such a situation had arisen. Over the years he had developed a well-practiced routine for dealing with such unwelcome circumstances caused by excessive consumption of alcohol. Being of a pragmatic streak, his solution was either flight, when the lady in question was in a state of happy unconsciousness, or, when not completely insensible, an expensive breakfast with promises rarely kept.

Judging the former to be the best option he quietly attempted to extricate himself from the bed. This was not an easy operation. Despite his moniker, Chubby was, in fact, very tall and quite thin. Consequently, he tended to move in ill-coordinated sections. Sadly, for Chubby, on this occasion the lady he had spent the night with was not such a heavy sleeper as he had hoped. She opened one eye and looked at Chubby. Chubby returned her look with what he hoped was a winning smile. In reality, given the state of his pounding temple, he accepted that it might appear as more of a grimace.

'Good morning.' he said in as cheerful a voice as he could muster.

The lady shut her eyes and groaned. She waved her hand in the direction of the door and said in a voice muffled by the bedclothes, 'Quick, my husband might come back.'

There were few words in the English language more likely to galvanize Chubby than the word 'husband'. With almost Olympian speed he was dressed, out of the apartment and loping along Piccadilly, past Green Park tube station, towards Whitehall.

A small clock overhead told him it was nearly quarter to nine. Just enough time for a spot of breakfast he thought. It might settle the stomach. Just as this happy thought struck him, he remembered something about needing to speak to Kit Aston at nine o'clock. It all came back to him now. His secretary had left a written message on his desk which he had picked up as he left to go to his club. Thought of the club made him groan as he began to recall the events of the previous evening. It was always the same. 'Spunky' Stevens would suggest an aperitif with some chums and before you knew it, this would turn into several bottles of cheerfulness and the rest would be history. If only he could remember.

As Kit was being so specific about time, there must be a good reason. Despite the ability of his long legs to devour distance, he realized his chances of reaching the office by nine o'clock, in his current delicate state, were remote. Fortunately, he was able to hail a taxi and it took him to the door of the War Office. Chubby had worked there since nineteen fifteen after being invalided out of the army. His naturally cheerful disposition meant that the loss of his left hand following a foolhardy charge on a heavily defended German position was accepted without complaint. In fact, he actually considered himself somewhat blessed as he was, in fact, right-handed. His golf handicap had suffered, however.

Arriving at the door of his offices, he bounded out of the cab and up the stairwell and through the front door with a nod to the doorman. The phone was ringing as he burst through the door. It was nine o'clock. Grabbing the telephone, he said, 'Kit?'

On the other end of the line Kit spoke, 'Hello Chubby old fellow, thanks for taking my call.'

'My pleasure,' said Chubby breathing heavily into the phone. It occurred to him he was somewhat out of condition. The same thought seemed to strike Kit.

'You sound like you had to make a sprint for the tape, Chubby.'

'It was a close shave,' agreed Chubby. At this point, a combination of the excesses of the previous evening and the exertions of the morning combined to distressing effect on Chubby and he began to throw up prodigiously into his wastepaper basket.

Hearing the commotion on the other end of the line, Kit inquired, 'Are you all right, old man?'

'Never better, the window is open, some seagulls outside,' answered Chubby.

'Were they out on the lash last night also?' responded Kit sardonically.

'You know me. Sociable to the last.'

'All too well, Chubby, all too well. I've had a few headaches to prove it.'

Kit went on to explain the nature of his call and what was required from Chubby. Upon hearing the news about Miller, he was surprised, 'Anything to help - stout fellow that Miller - carried you halfway across France, if I remember.'

'It felt like it at the time. One more thing, have you any files on Liam or William Devlin, Eric Strangerson and also Dr Richard Bright? I'd like to know more about them.'

'Shouldn't be a problem, Kit, but it may be early afternoon before I have anything for you. I'll make it a priority and look into this personally. Something is nagging at me about the Cavendish's also. I'm sure it'll come back to me. I'll take a look at their files.'

'I appreciate it, Chubby.' Kit was interrupted as Chubby offered up another sacrifice to Bacchus. When Chubby returned to the phone Kit asked him, 'What on earth were you doing last night?'

Always appreciative of an audience, Chubby gave an uncensored, albeit slightly exaggerated, description of the previous evening at Sheldon's with their mutual friend Spunky through to the romantic finale.

'How did you manage to win this young lady's heart?' asked Kit after he had finished laughing.

'Usual line about my wife not understanding me.'

'Bounder.' chuckled Kit, 'You're not even married. How could you stoop to such naked deception?'

'All to easily old chap. We're not all born looking like a Greek God and you've a title as well, you scoundrel, as if you didn't have enough going for you,' laughed Chubby. 'How about the girls Kit? Desperately sorry for them, losing their grandad and all that. Don't break their hearts, old boy. I like them. They're good girls, both of them.'

'It's my heart you should be worried about Chubby. I'm out of my depth here.'

The conversation finished soon after. Chubby went to the window to let in some fresh air. Just as he did so, his secretary, Miss Brooks looked in. She recoiled at the smell in the office and exited immediately.

Chubby popped his head out the door to apologize.

'Must've taken something that disagreed with me.'

'The third bottle of champagne perhaps?' said Miss Brooks cynically.

'It was the Gin Rickey, I believe, but no matter. Actually, while I have you here, Miss Brooks, I need you to find some files for me, if you don't mind.'

Chubby proceeded to list out what he needed before finishing, 'You'll find my rotting corpse in here.'

'Very good sir. Shall I bring you a gun to speed things up a little?'

'Capital idea Miss Brooks. Full bore if you can. That should do the trick, I think.'

Another day had begun in the life of Mr Charles 'Chubby' Chadderton.

Chapter 27

28th December 1919: Cavendish Hall

Lord Cavendish's room was silent save for the persistent pulse of the ticking clock. Esther and Mary sat by the window gazing out at the leaden sky and the wisps of morning fog. More grass could be seen peeking through the remaining snow. The sisters had come here separately. Both felt the need to be in the presence of their grandfather.

After a few minutes when neither had spoken, Mary turned to Esther, her eyes red-rimmed from the tears.

'You're not angry?'

Esther reached over and held her hand. She looked at her sister, normally so strong and independent. There was a sense of vulnerability in Mary she had not seen before. Overnight, Mary seemed to have become smaller and, for the first time in recent memory, she felt protective towards her.

'Don't be silly,' said Esther, 'If I'm angry at anything, it's that you didn't tell me before now.'

Wiping her eye with the heel of her hand, Mary shook her head, 'I thought…' She left the sentence unfinished.

Esther began to giggle which made Mary frown questioningly. When the fit of giggles subsided, she explained in answer to the unasked question, 'This is terrible, I can't believe I'm going to say this.' Esther took a deep breath, 'I'm not interested in him. Part of the reason is his name.'

'Name?' said Mary mystified.

'Yes, the name. I just didn't think Esther Aston sounded right.' Esther laughed at herself but there was a hesitation, too. It was absurd and at any other time both would have been in fits of giggles for the afternoon.

Mary smiled tearfully and said in a school-mistressy voice, 'Esther Cavendish! That's possibly the most ridiculous thing I've ever heard. I don't believe you.'

Esther grinned and nodded in agreement. Then the silence returned for a few minutes. Finally, Esther looked at her sister and said, 'You have to tell him.'

'He hates me.'

'Now you're the one who is being ridiculous, Mary.'

'I could see it in his eyes, Essie. He'll never forgive me. If anything happens to Harry, he'll never speak to me again. I mean it, Essie. I don't think he'll trust me after this.'

Esther shook her head in disagreement, 'It's not true; he's not like that. You did the right thing, and he knows it.'

Mary looked doubtful but did not respond. They sat in silence once more. Esther took out a cigarette from a silver case. Motioning to Mary to take one, her sister shook her head and continued to gaze out of the window.

A man appeared in the grounds accompanied by a little terrier. Esther grew excited, 'Mary look! It's Kit!'

Mary looked back at her sister and shrugged despondently, 'So?'

'What are you waiting for?' exclaimed Esther excitedly. 'Go!' She rose from her seat and began to lift Mary from the chair. 'I mean it, Mary, go!'

Mary looked at Esther and could see a level of intensity in her older sister's eyes she had not seen before. Normally Mary was the one to give the orders. She felt confused.

'Quickly for goodness sake.' Esther was almost shouting in desperation at her and pulling her to the door.

-

It felt good to be outside. The air was moist but had lost some of the biting chill from the previous days. Kit strode away from the Hall. Sam trotted happily alongside him. Rather than fetching out towards the usual spot near the wood, he went in the other direction which led towards a brook. It had been covered by the snow for most of the last few days.

The previous night he'd has trouble sleeping. Partly it was anger and frustration but also, for the first time ever, he had wanted to see the dream again. The more he wanted it, the less able he was to sleep. In the end he'd given up and read. His stared ahead unblinking, letting the profound sorrow he felt for Harry wash over him. His head felt heavy; the cold gripped his muscles, fatiguing him quickly as he walked with Sam. Taking the lead off the little terrier, he bent down and picked up a stick.

'Fetch boy,' he said, throwing it as far as he could. The little terrier tore off in pursuit but then, on reaching it, lost interest. Kit slowly caught him up and they continued walking.

So much depended on Chubby now. He realized a continued stay in the house would be impossible while he was waiting for something that could help Harry. He also considered the possibility of leaving Cavendish Hall and going down to London to help. There was nothing more to be done at the Hall except wait and this was proving excruciating. Another part of him did not want to leave.

The ground underfoot was still a little hard thanks to an overnight frost. Behind him he could hear the crunching sound of footsteps, running towards him. Sam began to bark excitedly. He turned around.

It was Mary.

She fell into step beside him but said nothing. Kit had nodded to her but he, too, remained silent. They walked alongside one another for a few minutes. The only sound was Sam's breathing and the rattle of his lead. Finally, Sam indicated, with a light yelp, a lift was needed. Kit stopped but Mary put a hand on his arm and said, 'Let me.'

The little dog seemed eminently pleased with this arrangement and rewarded Mary by licking her face. They both laughed at this, Kit shaking his head, 'Shameless little beggar.'

They continued walking towards the brook. Mary asked Kit, 'You spoke with Charlie?'

'Yes, half an hour ago. He's going to do some checking for me.' He stopped and looked at her, 'If he finds nothing then I might go down to London myself.'

'What are you hoping to find?' asked Mary.

Kit shrugged his shoulders, 'If it's all right with you, I'd rather not say just now. Sorry.'

'I understand.'

They continued their journey towards the brook. Mary let Sam down onto the ground and he ran into the water, splashing and barking happily. They both looked at the little dog in silence. Eventually Mary looked up at Kit, 'Can we talk about Harry?'

Kit looked at Mary and nodded. He could see her fighting to control the tears but couldn't think of anything comforting to say. The thought of how she had provided the police with evidence of a motive that could see Harry hanged reverberated in his head. He felt hollow.

'I would give anything to prove Harry innocent. I know how much he means to you.'

'Do you?'

'Yes, Kit. I know. I know what he did. I know you owe him your life.'

Kit stared ahead and a voice inside his head said, "*Don't worry, we'll have you back soon.*" He sat down on a fallen tree trunk to rest his leg. It was beginning to hurt. The cold weather did not help.

Mary sat beside him and watched Sam frolic in the water chasing birds. Kit leant down to rub his leg. 'Are you alright, Kit?' asked Mary very concerned.

Kit shook his head, 'It's my leg. Feeling it a bit in this weather.'

'I'm sorry.'

Eventually Kit reached a decision and said to Mary, 'I'm sorry Mary, but do you mind if I do something rather awful?' Sweat was beading his forehead despite the cold. His leg was agony.

'Of course, Kit,' said Mary putting both her hands on his wrist.

Kit reached down and rolled up his trouser leg. Slowly he removed the prosthetic limb that made up the bottom part of his leg from the knee down. He set it down on the ground and looked back up at Mary to see her reaction. There was something in her eyes. Sympathy? No, something else.

'You knew?'

Mary looked at him, tears brimming once more and nodded yes.

Kit continued, 'I wasn't sure who knew. It was not something the War Office wanted to make public, at least not yet. So, I've never publicly admitted to it. Close friends knew of course and the brass. Did your grandfather tell you?'

'No.' This was barely a whisper.

This surprised Kit. He was curious and asked her, 'How did you hear?'

Mary narrowed her eyes and smiled, 'Wouldn't you like to know.'

All at once the air around Kit seemed to evaporate, his mind began to swirl, and his breathing became shallower. His

233

heartbeat faster, and he felt light-headed. Mary could see he was pale and looked at him with alarm.

'Kit, is something wrong? You're very pale.'

A light breeze had arisen and the sound of it echoed in his ears. After a few moments Kit managed to say falteringly, 'I'm fine, Mary. Really.' Looking at Sam playing in the water, he slowly regained his composure. Turning to Mary again, he looked at her for what seemed like the first time. Finally, he whispered, 'What did you just say?'

'You heard,' came the faint reply.

Chapter 28

8th December 1917: British Casualty Clearing Station, Grévillers, France

The soldier awoke.

He opened his eyes, but his vision was blurred although he could sense the movement around him. It was the smell he noticed first. A foul combination of rotting flesh, antiseptic medicines, and soap. The noise was no more welcoming. Groans and screams. The anguish from the wounded men around him was palpable.

Slowly his eyes became accustomed to the light. His sight remained hazy, and he felt as if he were dreaming, such was his sense of unreality and displacement. Movement was difficult. He could feel a throbbing pain in his leg. Looking left and right, he could make out that he was in a hospital. There were beds either side of him and in front. People were moving around; men and women floated past dressed in white medical clothing, stained red.

After a few minutes his head cleared enough for it to dawn on him: he was alive. One other thought formed like a scream in his head. He tried to look but his courage kept failing him. Slowly he remembered the events which had brought him here, but still he dared not look at the extent of his injury. The pain was agonizing.

Above he could make out what seemed like canvas. He was in a tent, probably a Casualty Clearing Station but he had no idea where. This was a short-term deposit for the wounded before they were moved to hospitals further away from the front line.

The soldier lay awake for a few minutes. Around him he was conscious of the constant activity as doctors, nurses, orderlies moved around the beds. Stretchers bearing more wounded arrived frequently and some men were taken away. Lifeless. In front, he could see one nurse mopping the floor, moving deliberately in the nominal corridor between the two rows of beds. As she passed the soldier's bed she stopped and looked at him. Her face was indistinct even when she moved closer.

The touch of her hand on his forehead made him start. Her hand felt soft, slightly warm. She was saying something to him, but he could not make it out. His ears were ringing. Shaking his head, he tried to speak and could not. His mouth felt like it was full of cotton wool. What was wrong with him? She put her mouth up to his ear and finally he was able to make out what she was saying.

'Try not to move. You might start bleeding again. The bandages won't hold,' said the nurse.

The soldier nodded. She left him for a few minutes and then a doctor came over with the nurse. They consulted for minute in low voices. Following this the doctor put his mouth near to the soldier's ear.

'Do you understand me?'

The soldier was confused at this question, he was injured: he hadn't become an idiot overnight. Still unable to speak clearly, he merely nodded yes.

'Are you a British soldier?' continued the doctor.

If the last question had confused him, this made him angry. He nodded his head more vigorously. As he did so, it occurred to him why they were asking these questions. The doctor was saying something else.

'I'm sorry but you have been seriously injured. We will move you in the next day to a field hospital. Please try not to move.' The soldier nodded in response to the voice in his ear felt like he was in a different room.

The nurse put a glass to his mouth, and he felt water trickling down his throat. She was well practiced at this, and he was able to drink without choking. The doctor seemed to nod to her and left. In the meantime, she mopped his forehead with a rag. He felt feverish and soon the pain became unbearable. Slowly he slipped out of consciousness.

-

The trench was barely yards away. It looked like they were going to make it. The man carrying him was panting heavily from the weight and the effort. Then he heard the explosion and the man carrying him collapsed to the ground. He collapsed on top of the man. Ahead he saw the British trench. It was so close. He could see some men climbing out of the trench. They were coming towards him. The first man was an officer. All of a sudden, his head became a grotesque, bloody mask as a bullet exited from his cheek.

-

The soldier woke from the dream and groaned. He couldn't see anything. For a few minutes he lay staring at the ceiling of the tent. As his eyes grew more accustomed to the light, it became apparent he was still in the same place. A figure came towards him. It was a nurse, but he could not make out if it was the same one. She put her hand on his forehead. He recognized her touch.

A glass was put to his lips, and he drank thirstily, coughing a little because of his desire to consume so quickly. The nurse wiped his mouth and the soldier managed to say, 'Thank you.'

For the first time he felt his voice seemed stronger and the nurse heard him. She stood up and left him for a few minutes before returning with a doctor. The soldier felt his pulse being taken and then was aware of the consultation happening about him. The pain in his leg was throbbing but not as intense as previously. He looked up and said falteringly, 'Anything I should know?'

The doctor left, and the nurse sat down beside him and mopped his head. When she had finished, she set the rag down on a small bedside table. The soldier moved his arm and little and felt for the nurse's hand. Finding it he took hold of her hand and weakly shook it.

'Pleased to meet you,' he said faintly.

Although it was difficult to focus on her face, he could see she was smiling. Her hand felt so soft he was reluctant to let go, so he continued to hold it. The nurse did not stop him.

'The other soldier? What happened to him?' he asked after a few moments.

The nurse put her mouth to his ear and said, 'He's alive. He wasn't badly hurt. Scratches really.'

A tear rolled down the side of the soldier's cheek and he fought hard to contain his emotion. The nurse used the rag to mop his cheek with her free hand.

'My eyes. I can't see very well; did something happen to them?' he asked after a few moments.

'We weren't sure if you had suffered any ocular lesions due to exposure to gas. We gave you some eye drops as a precaution. The morphine will also be affecting your vision; we've had to give you frequent doses,' she replied into his ear. 'We don't think your eyes have been affected, but your vision might be impaired for a day or two.'

'And my leg? It's not good, is it?'

The nurse was silent. He looked up and could make out her free hand rubbing her eyes. Finally, she replied in his ear, 'No, I'm sorry. There was nothing they could do.'

'I understand,' he whispered. 'I'm sorry to put everyone to such trouble.'

The nurse continued to hold his hand. They were both silent for a while. The soldier contemplated what his life would be like now. The pain was relentless, however the morphine was doing its job and making things bearable. Strangely, he felt he could wiggle his toes.

'You are very kind to stay with me like this,' said the soldier finally.

'I don't mind. I'll have to go soon, though. Sorry.'

For the next few minutes, she gave mopped his brow and gave him some water. After this she inspected the wound but decided to leave it. Replacing the blanket over his leg she told him that she would return.

He stayed awake for another hour but eventually gave way to sleep.

-

He awoke to the sound of screaming in the next bed. A doctor, a nurse and an orderly were all holding down a young soldier. All of them were covered in blood.

238

Another day. He was still alive. A good sign and then he felt the pain in his leg. It was brighter inside the tent, yet he had no idea what time it was. His vision was still blurred, and he was unable to focus on the people walking up and down the corridor between the beds. The smell was still bad, but he had become accustomed to it.

The soldier in the next bed to him had stopped screaming. He was whimpering now. Glancing over to him he could see how, in all probability, he had lost both legs. Poor devil, he thought. The doctor and the nurse left him and came over.

'I see you're awake. We shall be moving you later today. Unfortunately, we're running short of beds, and it looks like you're well enough to travel,' said the doctor.

The soldier smiled grimly and said, 'I'll just pack my things then.' The doctor was already moving on as another soldier was crying out in anguish. The nurse remained behind, however and sat down beside him.

'We'll make you ready for the ambulance,' said the nurse. The soldier recognized her voice. His hearing was still affected by the ringing from the bombs; however, he could tell a little bit more about her from the way she spoke. It was clear she came from a wealthy background.

'You don't sound like a nurse,' said the soldier.

'Well, I'm not allowed to be a doctor for some reason, so I'm a nurse. Would I sound more credible if I were your doctor?'

'I believe you would,' laughed the soldier before breaking into a coughing. 'I've heard voices like yours elsewhere. Feels like a lifetime ago.' He squinted at her but still could not get a clear picture of how she looked. The nursing cap covered her head, so it was not possible to see the colour of her hair.

The nurse did not reply to this but instead put some water to his lips and said she would bring some food. Putting her hand to his forehead she said, 'Your fever is well down now. You're definitely fit to go. Are you feeling a lot of pain?'

He was in great pain. His leg was in agony and all he wanted to do was scream. He replied, 'Only my heart. Must I leave you?' He smiled despite the pain, and it was apparent she was smiling also.

'I'm sorry nurse, I don't think I ever caught your name.'

There was a hesitation then the nurse replied, 'Tanner. Nurse Tanner.'

'You seem unsure,' said the soldier.

The nurse laughed at this but said nothing. Finally, the soldier persisted a bit more. 'Am I allowed to know your first name?'

She seemed reluctant but finally relented and said, 'It's Mary.'

'Mary Tanner,' said the soldier, 'I shall remember you. I just wish I could see you better.'

'Indeed, but this brings us to an interesting subject,' replied the nurse.

'Really?'

'Yes, what exactly is your name? You were carrying three sets of identity cards. One Russian, one German and one British. On the one hand you could be a Mr Alex Chekov, on the other Herr Klaus Adler or, finally, Simon Page.'

'Yes, I can see how this might appear a little strange,' admitted the soldier.

'You could say that. We weren't sure if you were British.'

'I am.'

'I know,' laughed the nurse, 'This much is apparent.'

'Can you do me a great favour, Mary? Can you get in contact with Major Roger Ratcliff? Please tell him that you have Simon Page in your care.'

'Simon Page. Is this really your name?' asked the nurse, sceptically.

The soldier smiled and said, 'Wouldn't you like to know?'

Chapter 29

28th December 1919: Lincoln County Police Station

Harry Miller lay on his bunk in the police cell. He was bored. It was now around ten and breakfast had been two hours ago; he was hungry again. The cell was small, barely six feet wide and ten feet long. He knew this because he had measured it earlier. It was empty except for the bed, a slop bucket, and a wash hand basin. The window was too dirty to allow light in and too high up for Miller to look out.

Apart from a pre-bedtime walk, he had not been able to leave the cell since his arrival. In the absence of anything better to do, he fell to the floor and did some press-ups. This is how Inspector Stott found him.

'Jolly good idea. I wish I'd the energy for this sort of thing,' said Stott as he entered.

Miller leapt to his feet and nodded. Despite his pre-army career taking him onto the wrong side of the law, his experience with the police and detention had been minimal. It seemed to Miller that Stott was not a bad lot. In fact, he suspected that Stott doubted Miller's involvement in any murder but was unable to admit as such.

'Any news, sir?' asked Miller politely.

'No, still waiting for the coroner's report, Miller,' said Stott glumly before adding, 'Nothing from his lordship either.'

Miller looked disconsolate. He had no doubt he would be cleared but was feeling frustrated by the incarceration. Stott could see he was vexed.

'We need to conduct a formal interview now, Miller. If you'll come with me.'

Stott led Miller out into the corridor, and they walked to an adjacent room, which was as densely furnished as the cell he had left. It consisted of one table and two chairs. The inspector and an unnamed police officer joined him in the room. Miller sat down opposite Stott and the interview began.

The initial questions dealt with Miller's whereabouts over the previous three days, who he had been with, when and what he had been doing. Miller answered the questions truthfully. This included acknowledging he had possibly been the last person to see Cavendish alive on Christmas night. He also admitted to being in the library alone following the death of Cavendish.

Stott appreciated the little manservant's honesty. He also noted how Aston had not mentioned either of these things. It added to an overall impression that either the man before him had committed no crime or else he was playing a dangerously disingenuous game. However, the latest disclosure, if Cavendish had been murdered, would potentially tighten the noose around his neck. Unusually for Stott, he felt sad about this.

The thought of Kit prompted a different tack in the questions and Miller recounted how they had first met in No Man's Land and his subsequent employment. These questions confirmed to Stott the reason for Lord Aston's intense loyalty to Miller as well as the possibility that Kit would not necessarily be a trustworthy witness. It disappointed Stott to think anything bad of a man whom he esteemed but he also took it as a very English sort of loyalty. On reflection, this recommended Kit even more to him. They turned next to the subject of Lord Cavendish. Stott looked at Miller and asked, 'When did you first meet Lord Cavendish?'

'Never met him until we arrived Christmas Eve?' responded Miller.

'But you were aware of his connection with your brother's execution?' continued Stott.

'I had no idea. The first I heard about my brother was a fortnight after he was dead.'

Stott seemed genuinely surprised by this. 'Really, weren't you told anything?'

'No, I was at the front. Communications were patchy,' Miller shrugged. 'I sent a letter to the War Office last year to find out more about what had happened. They weren't very forthcoming. I'm sure you can check all this Inspector Stott. I still don't know why they executed Dan. There's absolutely no way I would've been able to obtain information on who conducted the tribunal, who ordered the execution and who did the shooting.'

'Then how did the Cavendish sisters acquire this information if it's not available?'

Miller gave Stott a look that suggested he was being naïve. 'I don't have the same set of friends, sir.'

Stott nodded but said nothing. It was certainly true it would have been difficult for Miller to obtain this information. He concluded that it was improbable Miller could have found out from loose talk or private inquiries about the circumstances of his brother's death without his master. This presented the extraordinary prospect of Kit Aston being an accomplice. Stott was certainly not the man to waste time on such a line of inquiry.

'So, you do not know why your brother was executed,' confirmed Stott.

Miller pondered for a moment and then replied, 'I know a few blokes who were executed for desertion. Poor devils. But Dan, I don't know. Wasn't the type to scare easily.'

243

He remained silent for a minute thinking through his answer and then added, 'Dan was not what you'd call a natural order taker. He had problems with authority. I think the only reason he joined up was to avoid the nick. I can see him causing a bit of trouble for the brass. You'd meet a few blokes like Dan. Mouth off a bit about the War; refuse to obey orders. Things like that. Truth is I don't know, but this has always seemed the most probable explanation.'

'I see,' said Stott scribbling on his notebook. 'Why did the Christmas cards with the threatening messages end up in your pocket?'

Miller slumped a little.

'Someone planted them.'

'Who? Why?' said Stott, getting to the point.

'Well obviously the man who killed Lord Cavendish. He wanted to avert suspicion. It's not like it wasn't easy to plant 'em. My coat was hung up in a cloakroom. Anyone could've done it. The thing is, why would I leave them in my pocket after Lord Cavendish was found dead? It doesn't make sense. I mightn't have a university degree but I'm not a total idiot either.'

In fact, Stott agreed with Miller on this. If Miller had murdered Cavendish or unless he was playing a double bluff, it was madness to keep the Christmas cards. However, if Miller was telling the truth then he was right to say anyone could have planted the cards. This was becoming more involved, thought Stott. By now he hoped the coroner's report would show Cavendish had died of natural causes. Life would be easier for him. When all was said and done, this was all that mattered.

There was a knock on the door.

'Yes, who is it?' shouted Stott.

-

Doctor Noel Farrell turned seventy on Christmas Day. Sitting at his desk, he regarded the finished report with distaste. Looking up at the calendar on the wall his eyes fell on a date circled in red ink: the last day of December. This brightened him up, for a moment anyway. He returned to his usual mood of sour dislike of everything and everyone.

He hated Christmas, he hated his name, and he hated the fact that every day this combination would be a reminder of the astonishing lack of imagination on the part of his parents. Some of his colleagues would have described the worthy Doctor as crotchety. If being mean-spirited, cantankerous, and rude was what they meant, then they were underselling him considerably.

In all probability, this was going to be his last ever post-mortem. Retirement beckoned on the last day of 1919 for the coroner. The only people looking forward to his imminent retirement more than he was, were his colleagues in the hospital, the police, and many upright members of the legal profession, all of whose misfortune it was to have had dealings with him over the years.

One final check of the report on Lord Arthur Cavendish was made and then he placed his report in an envelope and scribbled a note on the front. With some effort, he stood up from his desk walked to the door. Outside was a police constable he had not seen before. He shoved the envelope into the outstretched hand of the young man, turned and slammed the door before the policeman could say thanks.

Three more days and then he would be free. No more dead bodies before then, he prayed. He turned around in his chair and lifted a book from the bookcase behind him. Opening it he began to read.

-

Constable Coltrane exited Lincoln Hospital and walked over to his bicycle without any apparent urgency. Although wintry, the sun was shining. It was quite a pleasant day really, he thought. Then he remembered he had forgotten his gloves. It might only be a few minutes back to the police station, but

245

he was worried about frostbite. He had read all about the Antarctic explorers and what they had faced. Best to be quick.

One final check of his satchel, everything was in order. The coroner's report was still there. Unfortunately, it was inside a sealed envelope, so he could not get an advance viewing of the old scroat's findings. Hopping on his bike, he made his way out of the hospital as quickly as he could.

The journey back to the station took less than five minutes. It was a very cold Coltrane who made his way through the station entrance, past assorted civilians, and some rough looking young men.

'Where is Inspector Stott?'

'Interview room,' came the reply from a colleague. Coltrane turned and made his way towards the room. Along the way he lifted a colleague's cup of tea from his desk and drained it.

'Oi!' shouted his colleague laughing at the impudence of the new recruit. Coltrane laughed and waved the report in the air. His colleague guessed its probable contents and raised his eyebrows questioningly.

Coltrane shrugged and whispered, 'Sealed.'

'Pity,' came the reply.

Coltrane walked to the door of the interview room and knocked. He heard Stott asking who it was. Coltrane announced himself and did not wait for a reply. He entered brandishing the report.

'The coroner's report?' asked Stott, looking at Coltrane with ill-disguised disdain.

'Yes sir,' replied Coltrane.

'Well give it here,' said Stott grabbing it from the young constable. He opened up and read the contents quickly in silence. Miller looked at him expectantly. His heart was thumping. He had not felt such anguish since that night two years ago in No Man's Land. Resisting the urge to rip the report from the policeman's hands he waited patiently for news. Stott did not keep him waiting long.

Chapter 30

28th December 1919: Cavendish Hall

Henry and Lady Emily came down the stairs together. Curtis immediately went towards them and bowed slightly saying, 'May I help you with anything?'

Henry replied, 'Can you round up the staff Curtis? In the kitchen. Don't forget the Edmonds family. Can you also ask Lady Esther and Mary to join us in the drawing room?' A moment later he added, 'Please.'

'Yes sir,' responded Curtis and headed towards the kitchen. Something in the tone of voice from Henry perturbed him. Gone was the disdain. The lack of interest was also missing. In its place was a note of authority he'd not heard before. This did not augur well, thought Curtis.

Arriving in the kitchen he said, 'Quick, Lady Emily and Lord Henry are going to come down. They clearly want to make an announcement.' Looking at Devlin, he said, 'Can you get the Edmunds family here immediately?'

Devlin went to get his coat. Curtis turned to Elsie, 'Tidy the kitchen a little, it sounds important. Polly, can you find Lady Esther and Lady Mary and ask them to join master Henry and Lady Emily in the drawing room? I'll find some seats from the storeroom.'

248

'What about us?' asked Agnes, who was sitting with Godfrey.

'I should stay if I were you,' replied Curtis before disappearing into another room. He came back a few minutes with a couple of additional chairs.

'I think we should all stand but the ladies can sit, what do you think Miss Buchan?'

'Good idea, Mr Curtis. Should we have any food?'

'No, I think Lord Henry means business,' said Curtis grimly.

'Why, what did he say?' asked Elsie.

'It's not what he said, it's how he said it.'

This bemused Elsie and Miss Buchan, but both remained silent. They all stood waiting for someone to say something. No one did. The atmosphere was gloomy and remained so for the next few minutes while they waited.

The silence was broken by the arrival of the Edmunds family. All three trooped into the kitchen followed by Devlin.

'What's happening?' asked Edmunds to Curtis. His tone was, as ever, brusque.

Curtis stiffened a little but replied, 'We were requested to assemble by Lord Henry.' He could not resist glancing at Jane Edmunds, but her face revealed nothing. Edmunds merely nodded in response.

Much to everyone's surprise, the back door opened and into the kitchen walked two people they had not expected.

-

The walk back was made mostly in silence. Even Sam was unusually quiet as if sensing the anxiety in Kit and Mary. From time to time they would glance at each another. Neither could think of anything to say. Both were thinking of Harry. Until news came through on the coroner's results any other discussion was impossible. Instead, both were in a limbo that left them feeling hollow.

It was still freezing, and Kit was glad to be back in the Hall. The break had helped rest his leg, but the walk back had made it sore again. When he returned to London, he resolved to find a better prosthetic limb.

Arriving at the back of Cavendish Hall they saw the Edmunds family along with Devlin trooping the sludge. They all entered via the back door leading to the kitchen. Kit turned to Mary to inquire what was happening, but she shrugged, clearly no wiser than he.

'Shall we go and see?' he asked.

She nodded, and they changed direction. A minute later they walked into the kitchen. Everyone turned around and looked at them.

'Hello everyone, are we missing something?' said Mary brightly.

Curtis was the first to react, 'Lady Mary. We weren't expecting you like this.' Turning to Miss Buchan he said, 'Perhaps you should go up to the dining room and tell Lady Emily.'

Miss Buchan rose from her seat and headed out of the kitchen as Curtis explained to the new arrivals, 'We were asked to assemble by Lord Henry. He and Lady Emily are coming down to make an announcement, I believe.'

Mary nodded to Curtis and looked up at Kit, 'News to me,' she said taking a seat at the kitchen table.

'Intriguing,' said Kit.

A few minutes later Miss Buchan and Polly returned accompanied by Lady Emily, Esther, and Henry. Esther smiled when she saw Mary. It was difficult for her to tell Mary's mood from her face, but she hoped all would be well with them.

Esther and Lady Emily joined Mary at the table. Henry was standing in the centre facing everyone. He looked at Kit and made a half smile and then faced his audience and began to speak in a tone that surprised everyone by its authority.

'Thank you everyone for coming together like this, at such short notice.' Turning to Mary he said, 'My apologies Mary for not speaking to you before now, but you'd already gone out for a walk.'

Mary nodded and smiled to him, still mildly shocked by the young man before her whom she barely recognized. Then she realized she did know him but that had been a long time ago. An image of the boy before the teenager came into her mind. She found herself relaxing a little.

'My reason for calling you together was to address, briefly, the future. I'm sure this is something uppermost in many of your minds and probably a cause for some concern.'

It was clear from the reaction of the staff, as he looked at them, he was accurate in this assessment. Kit glanced around at the audience. He suspected they were as impressed as he was.

'This may surprise you, but I'm as saddened by the passing of grandpapa as all of you. You'll have probably guessed by now, this is not something I wanted. But I, like all of you, will now have to adjust to a future without him.' He paused and there was a genuine emotion in his voice few would have believed him capable not one day previously, 'We will all miss him greatly.'

Esther made little attempt to hide the tears in her eyes as she saw her cousin speak. Lady Emily also looked emotional but maintained her composure.

'I wish to reassure each and every one of you that you are welcome here at Cavendish Hall; now and in the future. I do not wish to make any changes that will affect you. You're as much a part of this house as we are. We value you and hope you will stay.'

Looking deliberately at Jane he continued, 'I realize also that many of you knew a certain secret that regrettably I'd kept from my mother.' Henry glanced at his mother who looked up at him admonishingly but not angrily. This was greeted with smiles from the staff, none broader than Elsie.

'You respected our privacy in this matter. Jane and I will always be grateful for this. There's nothing else I wish to say for the moment, other than to thank you for your service here on behalf of Esther, Mary, my mother, and myself.'

He finished this announcement with a nod and then taking his mother's hand, led her to the door. Kit, Mary, and Esther also took this as their cue to leave and followed them away from the kitchen.

Upstairs in the hallway Kit went over to Henry and took him to one side. 'Henry, I may be presumptuous here, but I think your father and grandfather would have been very proud of you today.'

'Thank you, Lord Christopher,' replied Henry a little stiffly.

'Kit,' came the reply and he shook Henry's hand. The young man seemed to relax a little. A half smile crossed his face. Something had changed in him. It was as if a mask had slipped to reveal the real man underneath.

Esther and Mary went upstairs together soon followed by Henry. Lady Emily did not accompany them, and Kit noticed she went back downstairs to the staff quarters instead.

Kit saw Devlin at the foot of the stairs. He went over to him and exchanged a few brief words before heading into the library and making straight for the phone.

'What news, Chubby?' said Kit into the receiver. After a minute, listening he replied, 'I see. Listen can you do one more thing for me? This may seem strange and its certainly not very legal.'

-

Curtis sat in his room gazing at the picture on the wall. He felt relieved. His worst fears had not been realized. In fact, the Henry who had spoken to them today seemed unrecognizable from the morose and surly young man they had grown used to over the last few years. However, like Mary he remembered a

252

spirited young boy. A sadness swept over him immediately as he thought of his wife. However, for the first time since Lord Cavendish's passing, he felt optimistic about the future.

His reflective mood was interrupted by a knock on the door. 'Come in,' he shouted. Lady Emily entered his room nearly causing Curtis to fall off his seat. He stood immediately and reached for his jacket. She shook her head and motioned for him to sit down. All of a sudden, his worries returned, he looked up at Lady Emily nervously.

'Lady Emily, how can I help? Is there something you need?'

'No, I wanted to talk to you.'

Unusually for Lady Emily, she seemed nervous to Curtis and, for once, unsure of herself. She walked hesitantly over to the desk and looked at the picture on the wall. After a few moments she looked at Curtis, who had remained standing, and said, 'We never really spoke about what happened.'

Curtis nodded and looked at the picture also. The sense of sadness lay heavy with him as he looked at the picture on the wall of his wife. He forgot the worry he'd felt regarding his future at Cavendish Hall.

She continued looking at the picture and asked, 'Do you hear from her?'

'Yes, every Christmas,' responded Curtis, 'She sends me a card.'

'Where is she now?

'Near Lancaster. Lord Gresham's estate. She's still a governess,' replied Curtis. Then in a faraway voice he added, 'I never reply.'

Lady Emily seemed surprised by this and looked at Curtis, 'You never forgave her?'

Curtis fought back tears said almost in a whisper, 'I didn't know how to.'

He looked at Lady Emily. She realized it was not that he was an unforgiving person; he genuinely seemed at a loss as to

253

how to absolve her. Nothing in his life had prepared him for the pain of betrayal by someone he lived for. In that moment, Lady Emily understood how much hurt had been caused by her husband's adultery and she felt ashamed. Looking at Curtis, Lady Emily wanted to say something to comfort him. With some dismay, she realized that she didn't know how either. A life of unswerving certainty had not prepared her for the space between sympathy and disdain, right and wrong, fidelity and betrayal. Like him, she was lost in an emotional desert.

Finally, she said, almost to herself, 'I forgave. At least he thought I forgave. There isn't much choice if you're a woman. A part of you expects him to stray. You hope it won't happen. You hope when you have a family this will protect you,' she laughed bitterly, 'How naïve.'

Curtis nodded, and she looked at him. His face showed gratitude, so much so she had to look away before the remorse overcame her. Turning back to the picture she said, 'I hope it's not too late,' then looking back at Curtis added, 'I'm glad we talked.'

'I also, Lady Emily.'

She took her leave. Curtis watched her leave the room before sitting down. He looked up at the picture. Without looking away he opened a drawer in his desk and took out a small sheet of paper. Taking a pen out of his pocket he began to write.

Chapter 31

Chubby Chadderton put the phone down following his call with Kit. The documents he he'd requested were sitting on his desk. However, some pieces of the jigsaw were missing. He walked to the door and peeked out.

'Miss Brooks, can you get me Spunky?'

'Pardon me?' said a confused Miss Brooks.

'Can you get me Spunky?' repeated Chubby somewhat chagrined.

Miss Brooks was beginning to look alarmed.

'Spunky Stevens, Miss Brooks. At the S.I.S,' said Cubby with exaggerated patience.

'Oh, I'm sorry sir. Immediately.'

Chubby closed the door and shook his head. 'I don't know what gets into her sometimes.' He returned to the desk and sat down to await the call from his yesterday evening's drinking partner. The phone rang. Chubby picked it up immediately.

'Hullo, is that you, old chap? Yes, I'm better now but let's not go into last night. Another time. Look I need to see you pronto. Kit needs our help. Let's meet at the Savoy, I'll fill you in.'

-

Fifteen minutes later in the Savoy Grill, Chubby was seated with a strong coffee to hand. He thought it prudent to set the tone with Spunky otherwise matters could get out of hand, as they so often did, when they were together.

A few minutes later Aldric 'Spunky' Stevens arrived in the Grill. Dressed in a blue blazer and grey cavalry twill trousers, he was tall, with dark hair and a pencil slim moustache. He would have seemed nondescript were it not for the presence of an eye patch which gave him a faintly piratical look. An otherwise dashing appearance was offset by the monocle in his good eye.

With a cheery wave he said, 'Hullo Chubby.' By the time he'd reached Chubby all the diners were looking his way. This was not what Chubby had in mind when he'd suggested meeting away from their respective offices. For a supposedly secret service type, Spunky was one of the least secretive individuals Chubby had ever met.

'C'mon, tell teacher what happened last night,' said Spunky after warmly shaking Chubby's hand.

Chubby laughed, 'Well she was an interesting filly, I have to say.'

'Really, sounds like you had a good gallop.'

'Definitely a stayer once she was out of the stalls,' replied Chubby conspiratorially.

'How did she handle?'

'Jumped all the fences, no refusals. For one awkward moment I thought the game was up when her husband was supposed to be on his way back.'

'You exited stage left pronto, I'll bet' continued Spunky.

'Did I ever? Anyway, I can't understand what sort of woollen-headed blighter would let a filly like that loose in the paddock.'

Turning to more serious matters, Chubby gave his friend a brief synopsis on the latest happenings at Cavendish Hall and also what he had uncovered. He finished by saying, 'So you see, Kit needs us to help him get his man off the hook.'

'This is the same chap who carried him across Europe?' asked Spunky.

'One and, Spunky, one and,' responded Chubby.

'Well, anything I can do, old boy just say the word. Now, what do you need?'

'Ah, now we get to the crux of the issue. I need your help on something which is a trifle unconventional'

'By which you mean illegal,' suggested Spunky.

'Highly, old boy. Highly.'

Chubby then related what was required. Through all this Spunky nodded, noting the urgency of the task.

'Soon as old boy, soon as. Man's life depends on it,' finished Chubby.

'You'll know one way or another within the hour.'

'Excellent, I knew I could count on you.'

Spunky took a piece of notepaper from Chubby containing a scribbled address and went to make a phone call. He returned a few minutes later.

'All sorted. I've asked them to come here with the intelligence. Now, let's get something stronger to drink.' He raised his finger to attract the attention of a waiter.

Chubby's heart sank, he'd barely recovered from the previous hangover. Well, this one's for Kit, he thought despairingly. A large gin was placed in front of him.

Chapter 32

28th December 1919: Cavendish Hall

Esther and Mary were back in their grandfather's room. Mary had related all that had passed between her and Kit. When she'd finished Esther summed up what they were both thinking, 'Let's hope Harry is innocent.' Mary remained glum, however.

'I'm not sure it'll guarantee I'm forgiven.'

'Don't be such a sour puss, Mary. Firstly, it's not like you and secondly, I think you should trust Kit. Present company excepted, he's the smartest person I've met. Well, Henry too, I suppose. Anyway, you take my point.'

Mary laughed at this.

'Granted that's not saying a great deal,' acknowledged Esther, 'I'm sure he'll think of something to help Harry.'

'I know, but you do realize what this would mean?'

'No?'

'If Harry didn't send those vile Christmas cards, who did? This person is still free. Who knows what they'll do now grandpapa is?' she couldn't finish the sentence and her eyes filled with tears.

Esther held Mary's hand. Both looked out the window. Outside they could see Henry walking with Jane towards the

Edmunds cottage. Esther looked at her sister, 'I'm happy for him. I can't believe someone could change so quickly. He seems more like the old Henry.'

Mary smiled as she looked out the window. 'I know. Kit guessed what was happening between them. I can't believe he kept it such a secret. In fact, I can't believe Curtis and all of them knew and said nothing.'

'Yes, I was a bit surprised they kept quiet about Henry and Jane. Pleased also, I think.'

'I know what you mean. Gosh when I saw Jane earlier in the kitchen, I was struck by how beautiful she is. I mean, I was aware but hadn't thought of it like that. Then when I saw Henry and her, my goodness, where have the years gone?'

Esther laughed and then her eyes also began to sting with the tears that came from the memory of children in a library with Governess Curtis.

'Are you thinking of the library; all of us together?' asked Mary.

Esther couldn't speak but just nodded.

Mary continued, 'It was such a happy time. I wonder where she is now. Curtis never speaks of her. Of course, I don't feel it's something I have a right to ask about.'

They silently watched the two young adults walk all the way to the cottage, reflecting on a world always changing, moving this way and that like light rain caught in a breeze. As they gazed out of the window, there was a knock on the door.

'Yes?' responded Esther.

The door opened. It was Miss Buchan. 'I'm sorry to bother you but Dr Bright has just arrived. I took him to the drawing room.'

'Thank you, Miss Buchan, we'll be down presently.'

Miss Buchan withdrew. The sisters looked at one another. Both broke into grins.

'Don't just sit there, you ninny, what are you waiting for?'

-

259

In the garage, Strangerson and Devlin were drinking tea and smoking. When both had drained their cups, they climbed into the Austin.

'Jolly kind of you to invite me for a spin,' said Strangerson.

'You're welcome Mr Strangerson, I'd a feeling you fancied the idea of putting her through her paces. You've definitely driven before?' asked Devlin with an apprehension he could not hide.

'Yes of course, many times. Just not one of these chaps,' said Strangerson patting the bonnet appreciatively.

Devlin gave some brief instructions on how to start and get going. A few minutes later they were driving out of the garage. The car sped along, Strangerson making sure not to go too fast. This settled Devlin down. His appraisal of Strangerson was of a man who enjoyed speed. In this he was not far wrong and by the time they reached the empty road Strangerson decided to let the Austin show him what she was capable of.

-

Kit sat alone in the library. He tried to read a book but put it down impatiently. Still feeling restless, he walked over to the window to get a better view of the driveway. Finally, he saw what he had been waiting for. Devlin and Strangerson were driving in the Cavendish car away from the Hall towards the village.

After they reached the open road, he looked back at the photograph on the wall. It had been there in front of him, and Cavendish, all this time; if he had only known. Another glance out of the window and he saw Devlin and Strangerson moving out of sight. He walked away from the desk and left the library to go upstairs. There were voices in the drawing room, but he did not stay to find out who was there.

-

Richard Bright sat in the drawing room. He felt unaccountably nervous. Just like a schoolboy, he supposed. This agitation had not left him since he had departed

260

Cavendish Hall the previous day. Unable to sit still, he rose and went to the window. There was a slight drizzle making water droplets on the window. They trickled down the length of the window, distorting his view. Cavendish Hall had that effect on you, he realized.

He looked in the mirror. The old tweed suit was showing its age. It was time to invest in a new suit. This would be one of his first priorities when he finally returned to London. He heard a gentle knock at the door.

'Come in.'

The door opened, and Esther glided in. Bright gave a small sigh of relief. They looked at one another before Esther smiled and said, 'Is this a professional call, or do you have other reasons for visiting?'

Bright frowned, 'Are you always so flirtatious with men you barely know?'

'Yes. I daresay you'll become used to it,' replied Esther before adding, 'Alternatively you could find something to cure me.'

'I have something in mind, Esther,' replied Bright with exaggerated care, 'Are you sure you want to undergo the treatment? It's long term with some interesting side effects.'

'Will you attend to it personally?' asked Esther.

Bright nodded.

Esther walked forward towards him smiling, 'Well Doctor, it looks like I'm in your hands now.'

-

Strangerson was having an absolute ball driving the Austin. Once they reached the open roads, he put the car through its paces reaching sixty miles per hour on an empty stretch of road. Devlin was relaxed about Strangerson driving at speed when the road was wide and empty but his instructions to slow down at corners were ignored or greeted with laughter. Strangerson was having too much fun.

261

After twenty minutes driving at speed through the Lincolnshire countryside, a thoroughly contented Strangerson and a terrified Devlin returned to the safety of Cavendish Hall.

Climbing out of the car, Strangerson passed judgment on the Austin as being the absolute pip. Devlin had been around Englishmen long enough to able to understand that this represented a high watermark of praise. He was relieved to be back in one piece, and even more relieved to learn Strangerson did not own a car. The man was a maniac behind the wheel and capable of creating carnage in a populous place like London.

Devlin walked through the kitchen without a word to anyone and made his way upstairs. At the top of the stairs, he met Kit. They nodded to one another, and Kit put several pound notes into his hand. Devlin returned downstairs richer but with several years less on his life, he reflected ruefully.

-

Just after lunch, Inspector Stott arrived with Miller and Constable Coltrane. Kit met them at the door. He immediately led all of them into the library. Under Stott's arm was an envelope and Kit looked at it, then Stott, with something close to hunger in his eyes. Stott handed him the report.

Kit read the report in silence. When he had finished, he said, 'Constable, if you and Harry want to go downstairs and have some lunch, we'll wait here. Harry, can you ask Elsie to send some sandwiches up for Inspector Stott, please? I'm sure he's famished.' Stott nodded: he had a very agreeable recollection of the food at Cavendish Hall and was already looking forward to what Elsie could provide.

After Harry and Coltrane had left, Kit updated Stott on what he had learned as well as what other information he was waiting to receive. A few minutes later Elsie appeared with a tray of sandwiches for the voracious Inspector. Stott listened intently while he ate. Kit outlined his plan for the afternoon and what Stott's role would be.

The sandwiches were polished off with remarkable alacrity by Stott. On Kit's instruction the Inspector made some phone calls to the Metropolitan Police in London. Almost as soon as he had made these calls, the phone rang. At the other end of the line was a well-oiled Chubby.

'Chubby,' exclaimed Kit, 'What news?'

Chubby was still at the Savoy, and a long lunch with Spunky was taking its toll. 'I have to say, old boy,' said Chubby, 'I hope you close this case soon, I'm not sure my liver can handle it.'

'Still with Spunky then?'

Chubby glanced over at the gentleman in question who raised his glass in response. 'Yes,' replied Chubby, 'He sends his regards.'

'Have you anything to report?' asked Kit

'You were right, Kit. All present and correct.'

'I thought so. I'm with Inspector Stott. He's the one, if you remember, holding Harry. At my request he made some calls to the Metropolitan Police. I imagine they'll soon be at the scene.'

'Not a problem, I gather Spunky's team has been and gone, so to speak,' added Chubby.

Kit breathed a sigh of relief, 'I'm glad to hear it. Last thing we need is for them to meet up with our friends from the police. Pass on my thanks to Spunky. I owe him.'

'Will do old boy. Case closed, then?'

'Almost. I'll let you know what happens. Take it easy on the gin. Spunky isn't always the best influence in these matters.'

'This is true but suffer I shall for such a noble cause. Pass on my thoughts to Esther and Mary.'

'I shall, bye Chubby and thanks again.' Kit hung up. The Inspector looked at Kit shrewdly.

'I suspect I don't need to know all the details of your call.'

263

Kit laughed and regarded the stout policeman with a smile. 'I think not.' Then getting up from the desk, he walked towards the door and said, 'Time to assemble everyone.'

Chapter 33

Kit walked into the corridor just as Bright, and Esther were leaving the drawing room. They were holding hands. Both were startled when they saw Kit. A broad grin broke out on Kit's face, and he said, 'I'm glad to see one or both of you have seen sense.'

Esther looked up at Bright and smiled, 'I'm not a mind reader.'

Bright laughed, 'That is something men have never been very good at. Especially me.' Then looked serious for a moment, 'After what we all went through, I decided that I'd never sit back or be a bystander on my own life. You don't know what the future may hold.'

Kit nodded at this. He understood all too well a promise forged in the suffering of the last few years. Then he smiled, replying, 'All the same, you're certainly a fast worker.'

'I'm the fast worker,' corrected Esther with a smile, 'You must excuse us though. Mary is rather curious to know what happened.'

'Of course,' responded Kit, 'But can you all join us in the library afterwards?'

Bright looked at Kit and said, 'Have there been some developments?'

'Yes, but I'll wait until everyone is together if you don't mind. Anyway, please don't let me slow you down.'

The couple took their leave and went up the stairs. Kit watched them go and he felt immense relief as well as happiness. Esther was one of the most beautiful women he had ever met and yet he had realized soon she was not the one for him. Unquestionably, he had been dazzled both by her beauty as well as a grace that disguised her playfulness, a delight in the ridiculous which surfaced most when she was with her sister.

And then there was Mary.

She had seemed to be trying to push him and Esther together. Even Lord Cavendish often looked at him when he was standing with Esther. Something in his manner suggested the old boy had a romantic streak in him. It was the arrival of Richard Bright which crystalized where his feelings lay. Until then he had been caught in a quandary, not just in choosing between the two sisters but also a feeling of insecurity that either would be interested in a cripple like him. This uncertainty extended to the seeming inseparability of the sisters. Thankfully this problem was going to be resolved. But would the events of the last few days forever throw a shadow between himself and Mary?

He had found his discomposure difficult to overcome since the arrest of Harry. It stemmed not just from his fears for Harry but also in Mary's role in bringing it about. Now he hoped this uneasiness would end. Seeing Polly come out of the dining room, Kit asked her to have Curtis assemble the staff, for the second time this morning and bring them to the library. He went upstairs to ask the guests to join him there, too.

-

Half an hour elapsed before all of the staff and guests were gathered together. Kit was standing by the desk alongside Stott. All of the ladies sat at the front with Miller, Constable Coltrane standing at the back beside Bright and Strangerson. The staff were arrayed along the back wall along with Henry

266

who was with Jane. The change in Henry, in such a short space of time, had astonished all. Kit had no doubt that Henry and Jane would make a beautiful couple despite the mismatch in social rank.

The final person to arrive was Reverend Simmons and he made his way to stand with the other male guests. Kit nodded a greeting to him and then began to speak.

'I want to talk to you about the recent events, specifically, the sad loss of Lord Cavendish and the arrest of my manservant Harry Miller. You'll no doubt have seen that Harry is back with us along with Inspector Stott and Constable Coltrane.'

Stott looked on at Kit but remained silent.

Kit continued, 'A few days ago, following Lord Cavendish's passing, I asked you to assemble. At that time, I alerted you to the probability of a police investigation. For a number of reasons, I was not at liberty to explain why beyond acknowledging the unexpected nature of his death would be grounds for some kind of inquiry. With Inspector Stott's permission I can now tell you the reason we interviewed you. Over the last few years Lord Cavendish received Christmas cards threatening his life. This meant we could not rule out the possibility of foul play being a cause of death.'

This announcement caused a stir amongst the staff.

'After the death of Lord Cavendish, these Christmas cards went missing from the library and were subsequently found in the coat of Harry Miller.'

There was further stir from the staff and even Reverend Simmons glanced at Harry with surprise.

'I have reason to believe the Christmas cards were planted there by another person and that Harry is innocent of having sent them. I will return to this in a moment, but I will ask Inspector Stott to update you on the results of the coroner's report.'

Kit stood back and let Stott take centre stage. In his hand, he held the envelope containing the report.

'Thank you, your lordship,' said Stott before looking directly at the Cavendish sisters and Lady Emily, who were sitting beside one another.

'I'm sorry to have to discuss so distressing a subject in this public forum, but Lord Christopher and I agreed it was entirely necessary.'

The three ladies nodded, and Esther took Mary's hand as they waited for Stott to continue.

'I can confirm that the coroner, Dr Farrell, is firm of the belief that Lord Cavendish died of natural causes.'

Stott paused to let this news to permeate. Mary and Esther hugged one another, and both fought to control their tears. Kit looked down at Mary. She turned around and held his gaze. She wasn't sure what he was thinking but her hopes began to rise.

'Further confirmation of this view comes from Lord Cavendish's physician in Harley Street. We understand Lord Cavendish had recently made several visits to him and that he was under medication for a weak heart. This was clearly not a murder, and therefore Harry Miller has no charge to answer. I'll hand back to his lordship because this is not quite the end of the matter.'

Stott stepped back allowing everyone to see Kit, who had perched himself on Lord Cavendish's desk. He was holding the photograph of the army battalion in his hand.

'The key to this affair has been sitting in the library all along. It's why we're all here today. The murderer tried to frame Harry because of an extraordinary coincidence.'

Bright spoke up at this point, 'Murderer, Kit? I thought the Inspector had just confirmed no murder took place.'

Kit looked directly at Bright, 'Oh there was a murder all right, Richard. In fact, had Lord Cavendish not passed away when he did, it might've been two.'

268

From where he was standing, Kit could see the confusion on most of the faces in the room.

'With Harry's permission I will explain why the murderer framed him.' Kit held up the photograph of the battalion and pointed to Miller's brother.

'Clearly not everyone will be able see this but the soldier I am pointing to is Harry's brother, Daniel. He fought in the same regiment as Robert Cavendish. Sadly, he died for reasons that remain unclear, but I will say it was a military execution. Robert and Lord Cavendish each had a role in the execution. Robert headed up the firing squad that executed Daniel and Lord Cavendish headed the tribunal which turned down his request for clemency. This would, in theory, have constituted a clear motive for Harry to murder Lord Cavendish or, at the very least, threaten to do so. But Harry did not. Harry had no idea of the connection with the Cavendish family.'

Bright put a hand on Harry's shoulder as he listened to Kit talk about the death of his brother. The tension in the room was palpable.

Kit continued, 'Harry's not the only person in this room who had a brother in this battalion; a brother, I might add, who was executed.' Kit paused and waited for someone to speak.

Finally, a voice said, 'Very clever Aston, but none of this proves anything.'

All heads turned around to the speaker. It was Eric Strangerson.

'I think you should hear the rest of my story, Strangerson.'

'Dragging it out a bit old boy, aren't you? You detective-types really are frustrated actors, you love being the centre of attention.'

Gone was the buffoon. Instead Strangerson's tone was of the cold killer that had dispatched so many German soldiers in No Man's Land.

269

'Proof? Oh, I think you should stick around for the rest,' returned Kit, drawling sarcastically, 'Old boy.'

'Well, I can tell you that I fully intend catching the five o'clock train to London, so if you don't mind, I'll be going,' responded Strangerson.

Stott nodded his head and Coltrane put a hand on the shoulder of Strangerson. 'If you don't mind Mr Strangerson, I think you should wait for his lordship to finish,' said the young Constable. Stott raised his eyebrows. Perhaps there was hope for the young pup yet.

'Thank you, Constable,' said Kit. 'As you may have gathered, our friend Strangerson also had a brother in the battalion.'

Out of the corner of his eye, Kit could see the sisters look at one another. He asked them where they thought Eric Strangerson was sitting.

'Front row, far right,' replied Esther.

'Correct. But did you notice the man with the cocked hat at all, sitting at the opposite end of the row? You correctly identified him as Harry's brother. However, you failed to look at the very last man in the row. His head is turned slightly away.' Kit handed Esther the picture.

'Oh, my goodness,' said Esther, showing it to Mary.

'Indeed. At first, I thought Strangerson had pulled the old trick of running around the back to the other side so that he could appear twice in the same photograph. But I checked just in case. It turns out this man was, in fact, Joseph Strangerson. Sadly, he was also executed by a British firing squad on the same day as Harry's brother.'

Strangerson broke in, 'Thank you for bringing up my poor brother's death. I don't see how this is relevant. You've just confirmed Lord Cavendish died of natural causes.'

'True,' acknowledged Kit. 'However, you'll at least concede that it provides a motive for sending the threatening Christmas cards.'

270

Strangerson shrugged. 'Maybe, but you've no proof I sent them never mind planting them in your man's coat.'

'But Kit,' interjected Bright, 'Why do you keep referring to a murderer?'

'Because a murder did take place, let me explain.'

Kit surveyed the room. The silence was almost oppressive.

'We have to go back to Cambrai in France, just before Christmas 1917. I was returning from a mission which had taken me behind enemy lines. When I say returning, I mean I was crossing over No Man's land in the middle of the night from the German side, hoping to God no one would see me. I nearly succeeded but not quite. Not sure if it was a mine or a bomb, but before I knew it, I was lying in a crater and pretty badly injured. I couldn't move; my arm was trapped on barbed wire, and I kept losing consciousness.'

The audience was rapt. Mary seemed to be fighting back tears. Kit continued, 'I would've been done for had it not been for an extraordinary man.'

Everyone turned to look at Harry who smiled and held out his hands to indicate it was all in a day's work.

'Harry was a sentry on this particular night. He spotted me almost by accident. He was asked by the commanding officer if he would go out and see if I was alive. Incredibly, and luckily for me, he agreed. This meant crawling out into No Man's Land. Let me add, he could've been shot at any point on his journey. His courage still astonishes me. Anyway, before I knew it, I was being dragged and carried back to our front line. I owe this man my life. It seems the very least I can do is make sure he is not falsely accused of something that it's certainly not in his character to do.'

Mary turned around to Miller and looked at him in gratitude. From this, Miller understood life could soon change for Kit and him. He smiled and shrugged to her. The attention was becoming too much; he hoped Kit would move on. The tension was unbearable.

271

'The commanding officer that night was,' Kit's voice faltered for the first time, he looked down at Lady Emily, 'Robert Cavendish.' She looked back at him. Tears were brimming in her eyes as she realized what Kit would say next.

'As Harry carried me, a bomb landed near us, and we fell just short of the trench. Robert was the first man out of the trench to drag me in. I have no words to describe his bravery, Emily. There are none. He risked his life for me by climbing over the top to help drag me in.'

Kit paused for a moment to compose himself.

'He was shot as he attempted to help me into the trench.'

Kit also felt tears sting his eyes, 'I'm sorry Emily, Henry, I was partly the cause of Robert's death.' Mary put her arm around Lady Emily who could no longer hide the fact that she was crying. Moments later Henry had joined them. He knelt down and held his mother tightly.

'For the last two years the assumption was a German sniper killed Robert. It wasn't.' Looking directly at Strangerson, Kit pointed to him and said, 'It was you, Strangerson. You murdered Robert Cavendish.'

Chapter 34

'How dare you!' roared Strangerson. 'I've had enough of this slander, Aston.' Strangerson shrugged off Coltrane and started forward towards Kit. However, a combination of Miller, Bright and Simmons restrained him as Kit looked on coolly.

'I haven't finished with you yet,' snarled Kit with evident dislike.

'All lies, you can't prove any of this,' said Strangerson.

'Can't I? What if I told you there were two witnesses to the murder of Robert Cavendish? Would this convince you?'

This stopped Strangerson in his tracks. He was clearly astonished by the new revelation.

'I saw the shot which killed him. I've seen it virtually every night since then,' confessed Kit. 'I've seen enough men die to know that the direction of the bullet could only have from behind. It couldn't have been a German.'

'Preposterous, you're making it up.'

'Really? Then how do you explain a letter the War Office received earlier this year? A German commander wrote claiming to have witnessed a British army sniper murder a British officer. The date and the time tallies exactly with the death of Robert and, crucially, he described you perfectly. Not only that, according to this officer, your partner Teddy Masters saw what happened. It was the night he was killed by a sniper. He probably took a bullet meant for you.'

Strangerson looked dismissive, 'Are you really going to take the word of a dirty Boche ahead of a British officer? Fritz was after me for half the War. I killed so many of their men. They couldn't kill me so now they want to smear me, and you're falling for it.'

'You're forgetting one thing Strangerson. The Christmas cards,' pointed out Kit.

'Back to those, are we? So? Why would I send one to Lord Cavendish?'

'Because he headed up the tribunal that did not reprieve your brother. And you didn't just send them to Lord Cavendish. Robert Cavendish led the firing squad. Two Cavendish men, both connected to the execution of your brother. You didn't just send them to Lord Cavendish; you sent one to Robert, too.'

Lady Emily who had been watching with growing astonishment gasped, 'Robert said nothing to me about a threatening Christmas card.'

'It was found among his belongings. The ministry kept it back for fear of distressing you further, Emily,' explained Kit. 'The truth was the army didn't believe the message in the card. They thought it a German trick, perhaps to unsettle Robert.'

Kit looked back at Strangerson and said, 'The note inside the card was typed. The police are in your Bayswater flat as I speak, Strangerson. What do you think the chances are they'll find a typewriter? I'd say they were very strong, wouldn't you? Oh yes, there's a bottle of a foul-smelling liquid underneath the mattress in your bedroom. My guess is that it contains a poison. Probably a curare or some such thing you picked up on your travels. I think you intended to use this on Lord Cavendish, possibly in small doses, certainly enough to make him ill and give you time to exit before the cumulative impact of the poison wrought its deadly impact. As I recall you offered to pour him a drink on a number of occasions. Sadly, for you

274

he declined. If fate hadn't given you such a helping hand, I suspect you would've become quite desperate.'

Strangerson looked defeated. His shoulders slumped; his body seemed to go limp. Then, without warning he sprang to life and threw off Bright and Miller. He reached into his pocket and pulled out a gun. Pointing the weapon at Kit, Strangerson's composure returned.

'Well, I suppose congratulations are in order, Aston. You've assembled a fairly effective case which could put a noose around my neck. However, I'm not sure I want this to happen quite yet.'

He looked down at the sisters. It was clear to Kit he intended taking a hostage. Strangerson continued talking, 'Yes, it was a useful drive I had with Devlin. Familiarised myself with the car and the area, too, just in case things went a bit sticky. I think it's time to say toodle pip, though. Unfortunately, I'll have to take one of the lovely ladies with me as security. Don't worry, I shan't harm them. My business with the Cavendish family was strictly with the males. Now, who shall I choose?'

'Take me,' said Mary.

'No!' shouted Esther but Mary was already on her feet and moving towards Strangerson.

'Let the lady through, gentlemen,' said Strangerson, while gesturing to Miller, Bright and Simmons to stand aside. He walked slowly backwards towards the door holding the gun at Mary. Kit looked on, impotent with rage. His mind raced furiously about how to rescue the situation. He was angry at himself for not anticipating that Strangerson might have a gun. If anything happened, he knew he'd would never forgive himself.

The room seemed to part for Strangerson as he led Mary towards the door. The killer of countless German soldiers looked like he was on an afternoon stroll. 'Thank you, gentlemen,' said Strangerson, smiling malevolently at the men he was passing. They reached the door of the library. A strange silence descended on the room. The only sound came from the grandfather clock ticking solemnly. Without looking at Curtis, Strangerson ordered him to open the door.'

Curtis did as he was told. Strangerson's right hand gripped Mary's elbow. His left pointed the gun at the men to his left. The door opened. First there was a bark and then the sound of claws on the parquet floor. Moments later, Sam came running in. Caught by surprise, Strangerson looked down. This was his mistake.

Cometh the hour, cometh the butler. Curtis, saw his opportunity. He chopped down on Strangerson's arm. The gun stayed in his hand but pointed downwards. Strangerson leased off one shot that flew harmlessly into the floor. Sam liked nothing better than a good fight. The sound of gun fire was like a starter's pistol for the temperamental Jack Russell. He leapt up immediately and bit Strangerson's hand.

Strangerson screamed out an oath and let go of the gun. Seconds later, a single punch dispatched Strangerson into a state of unconsciousness. Reverend Simmons stood over him, holding his hand and said, 'I'll never know how bareknuckle fighters did it.'

Kit was by Mary in seconds. She seemed much more in control than he. Bending down he retrieved the gun and patted the little dog, 'Good boy. Extra biscuits for you tonight.'

Mary bent down and picked up Sam who started to lick her face, 'My hero.' she said laughing in relief.

Simmons looked at Kit but tilted his head towards Strangerson, 'I think he could be out for a while.'

'I wouldn't be surprised. You certainly caught him. I'm not sure Sam Langford would've survived a punch like that. I can't thank you enough,' said Kit, putting his arm around Mary. She looked at him doing this but did not seem to object.

'I'm sure I'll think of something,' replied Simmons looking at Mary then Kit, a smile on his weathered features.

276

The prone Strangerson was dragged onto a seat by Coltrane and Miller. Bright came over to examine him. It looked as if his nose was broken, and both his eyes were starting to swell. Coltrane checked his pockets for other weapons. There was only a wallet and a cigarette case. Glancing at Stott about what to do with these items, he received a shake of the head, so he returned both items into Strangerson's pocket.

Stott came over and shook the uninjured hand of Simmons, 'If you ever decide to have a change of career, Reverend, I'll happily have you in my team. You too, Mr Curtis.'

Kit smiled and looked at the butler affectionately, 'I think that the Cavendish family owes you a great debt. It was remarkably quick thinking.'

A glowing Curtis bowed slightly but for once decided to let his actions speak for themselves. The glow turned a very bright red seconds later when Mary kissed him gently on the forehead and smiled. Moments later Esther embraced him also saying, 'Thank you Curtis. Thank you so much.'

Strangerson slowly began to regain consciousness. Through his half-closed eyes he saw Lady Emily looking at him. He looked up at her but was too groggy to think of anything to say. She turned away to look at Reverend Simmons and nodded to him before moving out the door of the library.

The library cleared as Stott, Coltrane and Bright took Strangerson to the drawing room to give him time to recover. Coltrane put handcuffs on his wrists which allowed Bright the opportunity to examine him before he was taken away.

'Looks like a broken nose, Inspector,' noted Bright.

'No more than he deserved,' replied Stott.

'Indeed,' agreed Bright. 'After you leave, I'll call the County Hospital and maybe they can have someone meet you at the police station to fix it. I'm afraid I can't do much here.'

Under the calm direction of Curtis who, in the eyes of his colleagues, had gained in stature over the last half hour, the staff returned to their duties and normal routine.

For Curtis, the sooner life returned to its traditional rhythm at Cavendish Hall, the better it would be. He was a man wedded to tradition. Any deviation from this was unwelcome. Although he recognized life would have to change following the passing of Lord Cavendish, he saw his role as ensuring that the running of the house would continue in the same ordered way it had for generations.

He had never been the most self-aware of individuals, but for the first time Curtis became conscious of how his colleagues were looking at him. It dawned on him how much their respect meant something. This was as surprising as it was humbling. As he looked at the hum of activity in the kitchen, he felt a sense of pride. Spying Elsie attempting to lift a box of supplies he walked over, 'Let me help you with this.'

-

Half an hour later, Strangerson had recovered his senses but was still in pain from the force of the blow delivered by Simmons. Cold packs had been applied to his eyes to control the swelling and Doctor Bright finally declared the "blighter" was ready to be moved to Lincoln and a police prison cell. Bright and Coltrane helped Strangerson to his feet. As he was still unsteady, they assisted him from the drawing room into the hallway.

'Bring the car around Coltrane,' ordered Stott, who took over holding the prisoner.

Only Kit and Mary remained in the library. They stood by the window and looked at one another. Then they both spoke at the same time.

'Kit.'

'Mary.'

'Or should I say Nurse Tanner,' said Kit with a smile.

278

Mary shot him a look and narrowed her eyes. 'You may,' she replied before adding, how would you like to be addressed? Mr Chekov or should I say Herr Adler or Mr Page?'

Kit laughed guiltily and held his hands up.

'Touché. I had my reasons. I'm sure you did, too. From now on, and for the rest of our lives, I think it should simply be Kit or,' he thought for a moment, 'my love.'

Mary pretended to ponder the matter before a smile erupted across her face, 'I think that's acceptable.'

'I'm sorry it had to be this way,' said Kit thinking about Lord Cavendish. 'I'd like to have known him better.'

Mary turned away to look out of the window but mainly to hide the tears stinging her eyes. She nodded but did not say anything.

Kit took hold of Mary's hand, 'Mary, there's something I must say.'

She looked up at him. Kit opened his mouth to speak when there was a knock at the door.

'Kit, Mary, we're taking Strangerson away now.' It was Bright.

Mary smiled and put her hand on Kit's arm, 'I've waited two years for this, I think I can manage a few more minutes.'

THE END

I hope you will consider leaving a review. **They really do make a difference. Thank you.**

A Note from the Author

I have made every effort to ensure historical authenticity within the context of a piece of fiction. Similarly, every effort has been made to ensure that the book has been edited and carefully proofread. Given that the US Constitution contained around 65 punctuation errors until 1847, I hope you will forgive any errors of grammar, spelling and continuity. Regarding spelling, please note I have followed the convention of using English, as opposed to US, spellings. This means, in practice, the use of 's' rather than a 'z', for example in words such as 'realised'.

About the Author

Jack Murray was born in Northern Ireland but has spent over half his life living just outside London, except for some periods spent in Australia, Monte Carlo, and the US.

An artist, as well as a writer, Jack's work features in collections around the world and he has exhibited in Britain, Ireland, and Monte Carlo.

There are now six books in the Kit Aston series. The latest, The Medium Murders, was released in May 2020. The next Kit Aston will hopefully be published before the end of 2021.

Jack has just finished work on a World War II trilogy. The three books look at the war from both the British and the German side. Jack has just signed with Lume Books who will now publish the war trilogy. This means that although they were available on Amazon formerly, they have now been taken down in readiness for publication with Lume in summer 2022.

A spin off series from the Kit Aston novels was published in 2020 featuring Aunt Agatha as a young woman solving mysterious murders.

Jack is working on a new detective series featuring the grandson of Chief Inspector Jellicoe.

Visit Jack's Facebook page: fb.me/jackmurraypublishing

Or you can contact Jack: jackmurray99@hotmail.com

Visit Jack's Facebook page: fb.me/jackmurraypublishing

Or you can contact Jack: m.me/jackmurraypublishing.

Acknowledgements

It is not possible to write a book on your own. There is a contribution from so many people either directly or indirectly over many years. Listing them all would be an impossible task.

Special mention therefore should be made to my wife and family who have been patient and put up with my occasional grumpiness when working on this project.

My brother also helped in proofreading and made supportive comments that helped me tremendously.

My late father and mother both loved books. They encouraged a love of reading in me also. In particular, they liked detective books, so I must tip my hat to the two greatest writers of this genre, Sir Arthur, and Dame Agatha.

Finally, my thanks to the teachers who taught and nurtured a love of writing.

TASTER FOR SECOND KIT ASTON MYSTERY – THE CHESS BOARD MURDERS

Prologue

Petrograd, Russia: 30th December 1916

Oswald Rayner gazed at the semi-conscious man lying at his feet. Calmly, he removed a Webley Service revolver from his overcoat pocket, aimed at the man's head and fired one shot. The bullet entered the forehead, ending the life of Grigori Rasputin.

Prince Felix Yusupov looked on. He betrayed little emotion at what he'd just witnessed. Instead, he merely nodded to Rayner. Kneeling, Rayner gazed without pity at the dead man. He lifted Rasputin's lifeless arm, pulled back the sleeve of his coat and checked for a pulse. The former adviser to the Tsarina had proved a little more durable than Yusupov had anticipated. Rayner was keen to make sure he really was dead. Satisfied his mission was accomplished, he rose and pocketed his revolver. A half-smile appeared on his face.

'Look on the bright side, Grigori Yefimovich, it would've been an awful hangover,' said Rayner, eyeing the corpse.

Yusupov rolled his eyes and said sardonically, 'Good to see such respect for the dead Oswald.' His English was perfect.

Rayner smiled and replied in Russian, *'I'm sure you gave the poison respectfully Felix.'*

This made Yusupov grin. The smile turned to laughter when Rayner added, *'And the bullet was delivered with such affection.'*

'I think, Oswald, you should take your leave. I'm not sure how much it would be appreciated if His Majesty's Government were found taking an active role in the politics of Mother Russia.'

'Perish the thought old chap,' replied Rayner wryly, before adding, *'Are you certain you don't want some help in moving our friend, here, into the river?'*

'We can manage, Oswald. Time to make an exit,' said Yusupov with one eye on the street. He seemed on edge again and could not hide his nerves.

'Hopefully not pursued by a Russian bear,' smiled Rayner.

The two old friends embraced. Then Rayner walked away from his companion and the lifeless body of Rasputin without looking back.

Yusupov regarded the dead body again before turning to the car parked some way behind him. He signalled for help and then lit a cigarette. The cigarette helped settle him. It had been a traumatic night.

Killing someone in cold blood was a new experience for him. He hoped one he would never have to repeat. This was not because he felt that a moral line had been crossed. Far from it, the rightness of his action was clear to him. Rasputin was a malign influence on his country; a danger who was better off dead. His distress stemmed from Rasputin's ungentlemanly refusal to die at the first time of asking. This necessitated more violent measures. His hand went to his neck as he remembered how the poisoned man had come back to life suddenly and attempted to strangle him. He shuddered involuntarily. It was over. Or so he expected.

One unwelcome thought lingered like the last guest at a party. If this was an example of the Russian peasantry given a glimpse of real power, what would the rest of the country be like? Were the millions of illiterates, uneducated animals living and dying in filth, as strong as this man? What would happen when they decided enough was enough? This was too depressing to contemplate. He fought to empty his mind from such thinking. However, this would be a temporary respite. The fear would never go away. For him, his friends and for people of his class, the future was more uncertain than he could ever remember.

His associates walked up to him, and they set to work moving the body towards the River Nevka.

-

The journey back to his apartment took Rayner twenty minutes. His chief concern was ensuring he wasn't followed. There was no reason his presence should have aroused suspicion, yet the worry remained. Rayner had to be careful. Russia was an ally against Germany albeit an unreliable one. He was a British agent operating within its borders. Close friends, like Yusupov, were aware of his role, but it was not something that Britain wanted other members of the Russian elite to know. Rayner intended keeping it that way.

Arriving back at his apartment, he found three men already there. All three looked up as he entered. If he was surprised to see them, Rayner kept it to himself. They looked at Rayner expectantly.

'How is our mad monk?' asked the seated man. He was the oldest of the three. His hair greying at the sides; he wouldn't see sixty again. The ruddy complexion suggested someone who was seconds away from exploding, even when he was relaxed.

Rayner nodded confirmation. 'Yes Ratcliff, we're free of that particular problem.' He took off his hat and coat. Underneath he wore several layers of clothing. It was very cold outside and only marginally warmer inside.

The other seated man spoke, 'Any complications?' His dark hair was brushed off his forehead. A trim moustache made him seem older than his thirty-five years.

286

'Sadly, yes. I had to apply the coup de grace, so to speak,' admitted Rayner.

The two men looked at one another. This was not good news. The idea of the British secret service being implicated in the murder of a Russian citizen had the potential to create many problems for Britain, not the least of which was the exit of Russia from the War.

'Nobody saw me, if that's what you're worried about, and we all know Felix can be trusted.'

The second man spoke again, 'Felix might talk. If not now, then sometime in the future. We have to think beyond the here and the now.'

'True, but he and I go back a long way. I trust him, Cornell.'

Cornell nodded but remained grim. Ratcliff looked down into his empty cup. This was unforeseen. The silence was heavy in the air; Rayner expected Ratcliff to explode any moment. He was not known for his self-control. Finally, he looked up. He was angry but, thankfully, in control.

'That damned fool Yusupov. Why couldn't he do what he said he would do. How difficult can it be?' Ratcliff thumped the table. 'Colin's right, this could come back to haunt us.'

'What are you suggesting, Ratcliff?' said Rayner.

Ratcliff glared up at Rayner, 'Don't worry, I'm not suggesting we add to our body count. One execution is quite enough for the moment.'

Finally, the third man spoke. He was the youngest of the three. His fair-haired flopped down from his forehead and he brushed it back.

'You do see that Yusupov only has to mention this to one other person, and we have a big problem. We wouldn't like it if Russia started killing people in England; even people we don't like.'

He was standing by the window smoking a cigarette. His tone was nonchalant, but the message was clear and unarguable. Rayner poured himself a drink and sat down. Their main problem had been dealt with, but it risked creating another in *its place. Which was worse? Embarrassment for Britain or seeing Russia pull out of the War because of the increasing influence of Rasputin on policy? Rayner was clear on this answer. Before he could speak, Ratcliff, almost reading his mind, responded to the younger man.*

'*I think "C" won't be happy at the way it was done, but he won't shed any tears for Rasputin. Hundreds of thousands of lives have been saved by his death.*'

The young man nodded coolly and removed the cigarette that hung magically on his lower lip. He mouthed the words, "cock up" to Ratcliff. Fire burned in the older man's eyes for a moment and then he shook his head. It wasn't worth it. Not tonight.

Ratcliff turned to Rayner, "Might be best if you went to Stockholm for a while.'

Rayner nodded in agreement. This made sense. He was also relieved that Ratcliff had seen sense. Cornell seemed to calm down too. The tension slowly left the room. Seen through the lens of the lives that would be saved by the death of Rasputin, it seemed pointless to worry about how it had come about.

Cornell refilled his own cup with vodka and Ratcliff's. They clinked cups. The young man, noticeably, did not join the celebration. Instead, he returned to gazing at the street below. He liked staying by the window, endlessly fascinated by the people scampering around in the cold.

'*Will you tell Hoare?*' *asked Ratcliff.*

Rayner laughed at this. Soon he was joined in the laughter by the other two men. Samuel Hoare was in overall charge of the British Secret Service mission in Russia, but he had not been privy to this operation or any run by this little group.

'*Only that our chap is dead. It's too late now to tell him what we knew, never mind our involvement. Remember, this came directly from "C". We shouldn't worry.*'

Rayner glanced at Ratcliff. He had a faraway look in his eyes. Cornell noticed this also but remained silent. It was late. Britain had saved Russia from itself. The mad monk was dead.

What could possibly go wrong?

Printed in Great Britain
by Amazon